To My Favorite
Librarian on staff

Keep it

Steampunk Rules:
Miracle Run

By
Jerry Battiste

Acknowledgements:

For everyone who told me to write a book.
Here you go.

PREFACE

The universe in which we live is infinite. So too is the number of universes which surround us, perhaps even share this same space with us. A universe of universes, each infinite in size and reach, full of diversity beyond imagining.

There are similarities among this infinite list of universes; places, names and events may seem familiar, but do not be fooled. Each is a unique individual with sometimes small differences and sometimes much larger differences from those you know, depending on decisions made and actions taken, both voluntary and involuntary. Sometimes the drifting of a single feather is enough to change the wind.

You may recognize some of the names in this story, some of the places, even the very world in which it takes place. But you have never known these people and you have never been to these places, for this universe exists outside your own.

Together we can glimpse their world, but that is all. Yet it is in these glimpses that we are afforded a chance to know a world which might have been. To understand how a different choice made at a different moment in time might have created a different world for us all.

What shall we learn of their world through the telling of this story? What shall we know of our own lives through the knowing of these other lives? What shall we know of our future through the viewing of their past? What difference will it make, or will it make any difference at all?

What you know might fill a book, or even a set of books, but what there is to know fills the universe.

Steampunk Rules

Chapter 1: The Professor

When the old bronze bell down by the dockside rang out the little boy, dressed in a tattered tweed coat that was too big for him and shoes that had long since served their purpose, ran through the streets in response.

His name was Jeremiah Maddy. At just 13 years old Maddy was a fully emancipated youth. That meant he lived on his own, took care of himself. He worked for himself, a sort of self-made kid. His name was Jeremiah but on the streets of Trenton, New Jersey, everyone knew him as the "Little Wizard." He got the nickname during the Orphan Uprising, when as a nine-year-old he earned a reputation for being able to get messages from the orphanages into and out of the city seemingly by magic. When the uprising was over Maddy sought emancipation like hundreds of other orphans, and without parents to contest his right to personal liberty he was freed immediately. Free to starve, or go without shelter or suffer the indignity of turning to the state for a handout like so many of the others. At first that is exactly what Jeremiah did. It was hard, finding his way without the steady income, meager as it was, that he had earned at the sweatshop. But he persevered, and eventually he thrived. These days he made a decent living as a pseudo-assistant to Professor Harold Nettles, the local inventor and quasi-hermit who lived in an old red brick warehouse on the shore of the Delaware River. The professor was a quiet man, hardly ever came out of his improvised laboratory. If he did it was just to conduct an outside experiment—something weather related usually.

When Professor Nettles needed food, or a piece of equipment; something from one of the local shops or a package from the docks, he didn't go himself. Professor Nettles just rang the large bronze bell on the roof of his laboratory and Jeremiah came running from wherever he was. When he wasn't running errands for the professor he had several part-time jobs; doing everything from washing laundry, to mowing lawns to fetching groceries.

He took the stairs to the laboratory two at a time. At the top he banged heartily on the heavy iron door knocker before letting himself in.

"Professor, sir! I'm here, sir!" he shouted.

The laboratory buzzed with electricity and a faint smell of chemicals mixed with heavy steam wafted through the air. Every table was covered with assorted mechanical parts; some had gas burners boiling unknown mixtures in glass beakers, while still others were covered with what looked to Jeremiah to be miles of multicolored wires.

There was no reply to his call, so he wandered deeper into the room. He stepped gingerly around the dimly lit and cluttered laboratory, careful not to jostle the tables or upset the experiments he saw bubbling and smoking away. In the corner two tall metal wires produced a glowing bar of blue electricity between them, starting at the bottom where they were closer together and moving farther up and further away from each other like a set of skinny rabbit ears. It crackled and hissed with each passing arc.

"Did you have something you needed done professor, sir?" he called again. Still no answer.

The laboratory was a large, dimly lit room and he had been there often enough to know the professor was prone to falling asleep while waiting for an experiment to complete, or just getting so caught up in some dusty old tome of his that he was completely unaware anyone had come by at all.

"Look, professor, I've got other things to do you know," he called again. But that was stretching the truth. He only needed to eat and for that he needed to get some money, and he knew doing whatever Professor Nettles needed done would likely earn him at least a couple bits. "Can't hang around here all day."

At the back of the laboratory was a large table, and atop the table was a jumbled white sheet. Jeremiah approached the table for a closer look. He'd seen some awful things in his short life and what he saw before him he recognized. It appeared that beneath the sheet was a body. The sheet didn't stir so he assumed it was not a living body. He wondered briefly if it was the professor. He stepped a little closer to the table and reached out to the sheet. He carefully lifted one corner of the sheet and tilted his head down slightly and slowly to get a glimpse of what was beneath it.

"Professor?" he said quietly. He gasped at what he saw.

"There you are, boy," came a sudden voice from the shadows and a hand on his shoulder. He jumped despite himself, dropping the sheet, twisting out from under the hand and starting away.

"Professor, there you are, I've been looking for you," he said more bravely than he felt at that particular moment. "I got your message that you be needin' something."

"Yes, yes, right indeed, boy. Take this." The professor grabbed his hand and shoved a half crumpled envelope into it. "See that it gets into the post right straight away. Don't delay. Now go."

Jeremiah looked at the envelope. It was marked, addressed to one Percival Lowell, Flagstaff, Arizona.

"Another thing. After you deliver the letter to the post office do not return here. Go directly to the butcher shop on the far east side of the city—not the one on the corner here as I don't like the way he cuts his meat. No, go to Barley's. Yes, I insist you go directly to Barley's and tell him 'Professor Nettles wants his usual cut of meat'."

Jeremiah had been running errands and picking up groceries for the professor for more than a year and not once had the old man ever mentioned a visit to Barley's butchery on the far east side. But he only gave it a moments thought. If the professor wanted him to go somewhere far away at the moment, that was fine with him.

"Oh, and here you go, boy, take this for your trouble." And with that the professor shoved a coin in his other hand.

Jeremiah, still shaken by what he saw beneath the white sheet, thanked him, immediately shoved the coin in his pocket and began backing away. Clutching the envelope tightly he dashed back out of the laboratory, through the heavy iron door and back down the steps, three at a time, to the post office around the block.

As the iron door clanged closed behind him the professor chuckled softly to himself. "You didn't even look at that coin, boy."

Then he turned back to the sheet shrouded slab.

"It's time," he said aloud. "Come."

The thing under the sheet, as if roused from a deep slumber rose up before him to a sitting position. With only a slight "tick-tick, whirrrr."

"Good boy. Good," the professor cooed.

Then he leaned down to the nearest laboratory table and carefully blew out the flame on the gas burner. The invisible gas, heavier than air, slipped silently across the laboratory table and down one side to the floor. Tendrils of gas curled through the lab like long witches fingers, touching desks and chair legs; slipping silently, inexorably, around the room. Filling every corner, seeping into every tiny crack in the floor. It was expanding as it went, pumping in through the valve on the laboratory table.

By the time the gas crept across the room and was ignited by a random spark from one the other experiments it exploded with enough force to blow the roof off the old two story laboratory, and shatter windows in half of downtown Trenton.

Jeremiah had already dropped the professor's letter into a post box and was nearly to Barley's when he first heard the boom, then felt the shock wave. As small as he was and as big a blast it was, he lost his footing and fell face first into the sidewalk. He rolled onto his back and saw the column of smoke rising into the air. He knew at once it was the professor's lab.

Chapter 2: The Man In The Courtyard

Looking out the window across the courtyard Miracle Lowell found herself lost in a daydream. Rather than sitting in a stuffy classroom, listening to her professor drone on and on about the probability of multiple dimensions she was lost in the cool tree lined and shaded garden down in the courtyard below. A single wispy red curl dangled down in front of her eyes, and she reached up a slender finger and twirled it absently. There was a young man down there, outside the window; a handsome young man, reading the newspaper. He wore a rather large top hat and slick button down coat with fashionable leather boots. There was a gold glint at his waist where his pocket watch chain caught the late morning autumn sun. As she looked down at him he suddenly glanced up at her and smiled. It was warm and inviting and at that precise moment she wished she were down below in the cool garden, sitting on the bench beside the handsome young man rather than stuck in the stuffy, hot classroom above. She was shaken from this reverie by the booming voice of her professor now just inches away, speaking directly at her.

"Miss Lowell, can you please tell the class who it was that first postulated the theory of multidimensional physical states?"

His breath reeked of bourbon, but Professor Yeardly was an expert in the field of theoretical physics and had a reputation for being unflinching when it came to discipline in his classroom. He didn't punish his students for inattention, he failed them. Immediately. She hesitated only a moment before replying.

"It is a commonly held belief that Einstein first spoke of multidimensional physics as it pertained to his theory of Special Relativity..."

"Ah-ha!" said her professor as he turned to address the class. "And yet..."

Miracle cut him off mid-sentence.

"Of course this is entirely untrue as special relativity refers only to our ability to recognize measurements from a distance and note movement. Instead it was noted physicist Hertz Brodbeck who first theorized that multiple dimensions not only exist, but co-exist on altered planes of reality. In essence, according to the Hertz Theory, there are an infinite number of physical states, dimensions if you will, which occupy the same space and occur simultaneously, differentiated by the altered harmonic resonance of particles which comprise their universe. This accounts for the increased weight, energy and gravity of the universe in which we exist, which we can detect but find no physical cause for."

Professor Yeardly smiled.

"In fact, in his autobiography, Einstein himself wrote that he is much more interested in 'proving the existence of God than in proving yet another fact about the world outside Heaven.'"

"Quite right Miss Lowell." He sighed and turned again, half addressing her, half to the class. "So you see, as you sit here, gazing out the window, in another dimension you might not exist at all. Your father, noted astronomer Percival Lowell though he may be, might never have married your mother; might instead have married someone altogether different, and then bore no off-spring who could deplete his well-earned financial resources by taking a class at university which she has no need for."

Miracle shifted in her seat; sat up just a tad bit straighter; embarrassed.

Someone behind her whispered "and ruin the bell curve for everyone else in class." There was a murmured chuckle and Miracle turned a darker shade of crimson.

"Enough. Class, you are to re-read the chapter on Einstein's theory of general relativity and special relativity, read the next chapter on the Hertz Theory and write a comparative analysis detailing exactly how each differs and why. For tomorrow, if you please."

Everyone in the class except Miracle let out a great sigh of exasperation .

"Class dismissed."

Miracle stood and gathered her belongings.

Professor Yeardly stood smiling at his desk as dismayed students hurried passed him, afraid he might assign them yet another nearly impossible task on a whim.

"Miss Lowell, if you please," he called as she headed for the door. Miracle approached with confidence and waited patiently. She had heard the stories about Professor Yeardly and had specifically requested his class. His was considered the toughest class to pass at Princeton University and Miracle had every intention of getting an A. Just for the fun of it.

Professor Yeardly waited until the last student had slipped silently from his classroom before addressing her directly.

"Miss Lowell, why have you taken my class when it is clear to me I can offer you nothing which you haven't already learned from your father?"

She was taken slightly aback, but not staggered.

"Professor Yeardly I resent the insinuation that I am incapable of having any thoughts of my own or that I am unable to learn what is available to learn without the careful instruction of my father. Furthermore, were your lectures more current then perhaps you would not find yourself bested in thought or practicality by a nineteen-year-old young lady."

Professor Yeardly chuckled.

"Miss Lowell you are every bit as rambunctious and opinionated as your father."

She started a retort, but he held up a hand to silence her.

"Which is exactly why I want you in this class. But while you may find the subject matter unenlightening thus far, many of your fellow students are struggling to comprehend even the simplest theorems I present to them. I would respectfully request you at least attempt to set a better example for them by engaging more—or at least paying attention when I am speaking."

Miracle was silent. She was suddenly aware of her position as a thought leader, a position she both cherished and abhorred.

Embarrassed yet again, she blushed, feeling the heat rising to her cheeks.

"I understand professor, and I heartily apologize. I should do better—I WILL do better in the future."

"Good." he said. Then he abruptly walked behind his desk, sat down, and began shuffling through his papers.

Miracle remained standing.

"That's all Miss Lowell."

She turned and walked away. Professor Yeardly glanced after her, smiling, but only to himself.

The hallway was mostly empty as Miracle stepped through the

doorway, her boots clacking away on the hardwood floors. She was lost in thought as Digby Ross slipped silently behind her and put his hands up to cover her eyes.

"Guess who?"

"Digby, I'm not in the mood for games," she said, pulling his hands away without breaking her stride. He fell in step beside her.

"Oh, c'mon Miracle, what's gotten into you?"

She huffed. "Yeardly just gave me a proper dressing down for failing to pay attention in class. Is it my fault I find his material boring; his lectures abominable? If he were more topical, more interesting-"

"He wouldn't be Professor Yeardly, now would he?" Digby said. "You knew he had a reputation before you signed up for his class."

"Of course I did, but I thought I could breeze right through. I know the material. That's not the problem. But the man drones on and on so, I find myself fighting the urge to fall fast asleep every day." Digby laughed.

"It's hardly funny, Mr. Ross."

"Oh, "Mister Ross" now is it? I feel like you're speaking to my father."

"Would that I were speaking to your father instead of you. At least he might adequately understand the struggle of bearing the teachings of someone so..."

The pair came to an abrupt stop as a young man stepped suddenly before them.

"Miss Lowell?" he asked, tipping his tall hat down and bowing slightly. "Please allow me to introduce myself. I am Mr. Crosby, Detective Mark Crosby if you will, of the Trenton Police Department. I wonder if I might have a moment of your time."

Miracle recognized the young man as the one who had smiled up at her from the bench in the garden during Professor Yeardly's lecture. He was even more handsome close-up than he had been from a distance. She felt the blood rushing up the back of her neck and hoped she could maintain her composure for the moment.

Digby immediately stuck out his hand. "I'm Digby Ross, detective. Might I be of assistance?" Digby was both jealous of his precious time with Miracle being stolen away by this usurper, and curious as to what was amiss with his friend.

Crosby smiled and shook the proffered hand. "No, I'm afraid not. Only Miss Lowell is needed at the moment." He smiled at Miracle.

"Might I have a word and a moment then? If it's not too inconvenient a time."

"Of course not detective," she faltered. "I mean, of course you may, of course it is not too inconvenient a time at all. Come, it is stifling hot in this building at the moment. I would like to get some air in the garden and you may walk with me there. Talk even, if you'd like."

Her slight verbal mis-steps were enough to send the blood rushing to her cheeks, but Miracle tried to ignore it and simply started walking again. She hated her involuntary blushing, but was forced to accept it as a minor defect in her otherwise perfect physiology.

"Digby, I'll meet you in Professor Stewart's class," she called over her shoulder as they walked away.

Detective Crosby fell in step beside her, saying nothing. Down the wide wooden staircase, through the long hall and out the main doors into the garden.

There were a handful of students, mostly men and but some young women as well, wandering through the shaded garden. Most were in a hurry, likely late for their next class. Those who were not were either engaged in conversation or lost in a textbook.

Crosby had been silent since the initial introduction and remained so as they now walked in the garden.

"You had some questions for me, detective?" Miracle said.

"Oh, yes, right," now it was his turn to stammer. "It's about your father, Miss Lowell. Have you any idea where we might find him? It is of the utmost importance that we speak with him regarding an urgent matter."

"To what sort of urgent matter do you refer, detective?"

"Well, I'm afraid it's official police business, Miss Lowell. You understand of course."

"Of course. But I'm afraid that unless you tell me what "urgent business" you feel might be worth me divulging my father's whereabouts, I simply cannot say."

Crosby stopped mid-stride.

"You understand that you would be interfering in official police business. That this might cause you to become suspect yourself!"

"'Suspect' now? So, a crime has been committed?"

Crosby stammered.

"I said no such thing. It's just, I-"

"Detective Crosby, you said yourself that if I did not tell you what you want to know I might become, how did you put it? Yes, 'suspect yourself.' What else am I to infer except that a crime must have been committed. You see, were there not a crime, then there would be no suspects. So, I ask again: what police matter is it that you wish to speak with my father about?"

Crosby hesitated. Now it was his turn to blush, and small beads of sweat began to form on his temples.

"Fine. If you must know, it is concerning a missing persons case. And that's all I can tell you."

"Who?"

"What?"

"Who—who is the missing person?"

"I'm afraid I cannot tell you that Miss Lowell. This is a very high profile case and it requires the utmost confidence from all involved. I'm afraid I've told you too much already." He pulled a brilliant white hanky from his vest pocket and dabbed it at his temples.

"Well, if you've already told me too much, why not just tell me everything?" She smiled at him, her biggest, brightest, most winning smile. And like all the men she had met so far, Crosby was simply no match for it.

"Miss Lowell, if you please," he was practically pleading now.

"Detective Crosby, what harm could it do for you to tell me who might be missing and how? After all, I know something of my father's friends and if this person is among those he counts as friends then perhaps I can help solve the case straight away."

Crosby considered this a moment.

"Are you familiar with Professor Harold Nettles? He was a school mate of your fathers and served with him for a time at the embassy in Korea."

"Professor Nettles? You must mean Uncle Harry. Oh! Has something happened to him?"

"Well, that is exactly what we are trying to ascertain. Professor Nettles' laboratory in Trenton suffered a major explosion yesterday and-"

"Oh my!" Miracle impulsively put her hand to her mouth.

"--and we have so far been unable to determine if Professor Nettles was inside at the time or not. We're hoping your father might have some information about what the professor has been working on. We understand the two of them have remained close, so perhaps he can help shed some light on exactly what transpired and why."

Miracle slowly brought her hand down from her mouth. Clearly Crosby had told her everything he knew, which was not very much at all. The least she could do was provide him the same courtesy.

"Although I find this news very troubling I'm afraid I cannot help you," she said. "You see, I have no idea where my father is at the moment and even if I did I wouldn't tell you- Mr. Crosby."

Crosby's eyes crossed as his fury rose.

"Miss Lowell, you are flirting dangerously close to disaster," he said through clenched teeth. "I am an officer of the law and you-"

She cut him off.

"You are no such thing, Mister Crosby. First of all, you are much too young to have earned a detectives rank. Secondly, you dress in much too fine attire for the wages earned by a police detective in Trenton."

He came up short. His eyes quickly scanned the area around them and he moved in closer.

"Why don't you just tell me what you know about your father Miss Lowell and we can avoid any unnecessary unpleasantness," he grinned wickedly. His hands rose to her shoulders and gripped lightly, but with enough force to make his point.

"Unhand me right now Mr. Crosby or I shall scream bloody murder!"

He grinned maliciously. "In the time it takes anyone to come you'll be lying in a heap and I'll-"

He never finished his sentence.

From halfway across the garden Digby Ross came sprinting and threw himself head-on into Crosby's side, knocking the man flat.

"Digby!" Miracle called out.

Of course his technique was flawed because by the time Digby had risen to his feet Crosby had jumped up and sprinted away.

"What the devil was that about?" Miracle asked.

"Me?" Digby said, quite indignantly. "I was rescuing you, thank-you-very-much!"

"If I needed rescuing, which I did not, I would have simply called out."

Digby was dusting off his trousers.

"Oh yes? To whom? The garden is empty except for you two love birds."

Miracle glanced around. Digby was right. What people there had been in the garden when she and Crosby first walked out were long since gone. She had been so caught up in his deception that she had failed to notice. Had she screamed it would indeed have been unlikely that anyone would have heard her.

However, she thought, that didn't excuse the fact that Digby had obviously been following her, attempting to eavesdrop on her conversation with 'detective' Crosby no doubt.

"Digby, what are you doing here? Were you following me?"

He blushed without embarrassment.

"Of course I was Miracle. It would not have been gentlemanly of me to allow my young lady friend to walk off into a secluded garden with a young man she just met."

Miracle had to admit inwardly that he had a point. Outwardly, however, she would do no such thing.

"I can take care of myself, Digby," she said. "Now come along, we'll be late for Professor Stewart's lecture on clockwork engineering."

And she turned and walked off.

Digby was flexing his right shoulder and adjusting his twisted neck as she turned her back on him and strode away.

"Oh yes, 'come along' Digby old boy," he said quietly. And so he did.

Chapter 3: Digby Ross

"So you mean you don't know this 'Professor Nettles at all?" Digby Ross whispered quietly. In the background Professor Stewart was lecturing the classroom about the miniature tools required for the delicate work of building automatic clocks. His voice boomed across the lecture hall, although the subject matter was rather dull.

"That's right," Miracle whispered back.

"And your father? You actually do know where he is, right?"

"Of course. Father writes me regularly from his new observatory in Arizona. Says the weather is quite nice there this time of year."

Digby was confused and not afraid to let his friend know just how confused he was.

"Then why on earth didn't you just tell this Crosby fellow what you knew and be done with it?"

Miracle flashed him a smile. Her cheeks pink and flushed with the glow of knowing that once again she had her friend at a disadvantage.

"Crosby was a crook, Digby, I could tell the first moment I laid eyes on him in the courtyard."

"Then why did you walk away with him? Alone! In the garden!"

Digby's voice rose above a whisper, catching Professor Stewart's attention.

"Digby Ross," he called.

"Um, Sir?" Digby squirmed in his seat. He and Miracle were sitting at the back of the lecture hall, quite a ways from where the professor stood, up a long set of stairs. Professor Stewart put one foot on the first step and called again.

"Digby Ross I dare say what you have to say must be awfully important. How about if I come up there and you come down here and tell the class what you know about the process involved in making and using miniature tools?"

Digby squirmed again. "Um, no, sorry, sir. Please, carry on. I apologize for my rudeness."

Professor Stewart stepped down. "Quite right. Now, as I was saying...."

Miracle jabbed an elbow into Digby's side.

"Keep your voice down before we both get tossed out on our ears. Professor Stewart promised us a special show today and I'm dying to see it. Whatever it may be. Now shush!"

Her words were sharp, but she flashed him a grin and winked. Digby settled down, though he had many more questions on his mind. Including the ones she had already left unanswered. As he stewed on his list of unanswered questions he glanced at his friend. Friend. Miracle Lowell was indeed his friend, yet even he had to admit that at times she pushed his buttons and drove his blood pressure much higher than he was comfortable with.

Looking at her now, still slightly winded from his quick tumble with the strange 'Mr. Crosby', Digby was smart enough to see her both as his dear friend from childhood and the stunningly attractive and intelligent young woman she now was. Her flowing red hair tumbled across her bare shoulder, standing out brilliantly against her flawless ivory skin. Her green eyes were fixed on the stage where Professor Stewart continued to drone on and on; her thick black lashes slowly flicking open and closed. Her purple corseted dress made her relatively modest bosom heave with each breath. Despite his best efforts – always despite his best efforts - Digby found himself hypnotized by her subtle movements; a flash of her smile, a gentle flick of her wrist, and her ability to retain her wit and charm regardless of the obstacles she faced.

So lost in the artistry of his friend's beauty Digby Ross never once noticed Professor Stewart slowly moving up the stairs in his direction until he was just a few inches away.

"Mr. Ross will now demonstrate," came Professor Stewart's booming voice, catching Digby totally unaware; shaking him from his reverie.

"Professor-uh, yes," Digby squirmed. "Um, demonstrate what, exactly?"

There was a raucous laughter from the crowd in the lecture hall, but one glance from Professor Stewart was enough to silence them instantly.

Miracle Lowell sat stock still, daring not a sideways glance at her friend.

"Demonstrate the proper use of the tools I have just described to re-assemble the automatic clock I have spread out on the table below."

Professor Stewart smiled down at him benevolently, yet not wholly without malice. The malice of one who knows, facing one who still has much to know.

"Yes, right, the automatic clock. On the table. And the tools you just spoke of," he glanced down at the table below and saw a jumble of parts spread out haphazardly across it. To one side sat a table with instruments so small he could hardly make them out and a small brass-framed magnifying glass mounted on a moveable arm.

Digby took a slight breath and rose from his seat. He stood a full head taller than professor Stewart but felt small in comparison. All eyes in that lecture hall were on Digby Ross and he could feel their gazes piercing his flesh, straight into his heart.

"I'll get to that right away Professor," he said, pulling his linen vest down taut across his stomach, and pushing a long brown forelock of hair from his eyes. "Right away."

He walked somewhat slowly but steadily, down the long stairs to the stage. He looked at the myriad parts strewn across the table, then at the miniature set of tools on the polished chrome side table. There was a small stool just behind the table and Digby moved around to position himself there. He sat down and reached out to the polished chrome table to position it within easy reach.

One glance at the table told him there were more parts on the table than were needed to build a simple automatic clock. No doubt a surprise Professor Stewart intended to throw off whomever he had determined to be the most vulnerable. In this case Digby, through his own ineptitude and careless inattention, had become just what the professor needed.

"Right," Digby said to no one in particular. "Building an automatic clock. Let's begin."

Just as he picked up the first piece the bright glare of light from a mechanical television located just above his field of vision at the back of the lecture hall flashed on. Digby was slightly surprised, but not much. The professor often used it so students throughout the hall could easily see when there was a live demonstration. The light was hot and Digby immediately felt beads of perspiration begin to form on his forehead.

"You don't mind if we all get a good look at what you are doing, do you Mr. Ross?" Professor Stewart was clearly expecting the worst. No doubt he was also recording this demonstration on film for use as a lesson to future students. The very idea that he might be remembered not for his intellect or ingenuity but for his incompetence alone suddenly cemented Digby's resolve.

He looked up to where Miracle sat. She looked slightly worried, but smiled at him nonetheless. Her lips moved and he thought he could make out the words, "you can do this." She might have been trying to tell him something different, but he told himself that was definitely what she said and he felt better for it.

"Not at all professor," he said confidently. He pulled the little polished chrome table closer and positioned the magnifying glass before his face. "Now class, watch and learn."

Digby Ross was raised on a farm but he was as far from a farm boy as one could be and yet still smell of hay and livestock. As a child he would delight in taking his father's steam driven tractor apart and putting it back together before breakfast. Not one mechanical device in their house did not at one time or another find itself on his small workbench. Sometimes to be fixed and sometimes just because Digby was bored and wanted to know how it worked.

His mother once told him his first words were, "What's that 'ticking' sound?"

Digby Ross knew very little when it came to fine society, charm and certainly when it came to women. But at least he understood mechanical devices. And this automatic clock was simply no match for him.

Suddenly the room before him was empty space. His universe now contained nothing but the pieces of the automatic clock before him. The pieces he needed glowed brightly in his imagination and he snatched them, in order, and the tools required to bend them to his will, effortlessly. His movements were a blur. His single minded nature meant at this very moment the lecture hall itself could erupt in flames and Digby would remain sitting, re-assembling the automatic clock which lay before him.

His initial reluctance was now completely gone and he was fiercely committed to re-assembling this automatic clock, even improving on the design he could sense was embedded in the pieces.

Springs, gears, screws, magnets – a place for everything and everything in its place, he told himself.

He made not a sound as he fashioned the guts of the device. His breathing was calm and he looked quite relaxed, snapping some pieces into place and using the miniature tools to deftly assemble what to the untrained eye just a short while before looked like a pile of spare parts.

Professor Stewart came down from the stairs and moved quietly around behind him as he worked, peering inquisitively over Digby's shoulder. If this bothered Digby in the slightest he gave no sign of it, intent as he was on the task before him.

Time passed as Digby worked. The room was hushed, with only an occasional shuffling foot or muffled cough to break the silence.

As he clicked the cover plate into place, and adjusted the time, Digby Ross couldn't help but smile. He turned it around to face the class and said, rather more proudly than he ought, "And there class, is an automatic clock."

Professor Stewart stepped suddenly to the front of the table, casting a long shadow across Digby's smiling countenance.

"Mr. Ross, hold up the timepiece if you please."

Digby did as instructed, beaming with confidence.

"Turn it around so the class can see all sides."

Again, Digby complied.

"Class, can someone please tell me what Mr. Ross has forgotten?"

Digby stopped, and frowned, momentarily surprised and doubtful.

Hands shot up around the room.

"Miss Mapleton, if you please."

A chestnut haired girl from the middle row left called out: "The key! There's no way to wind it, Professor Stewart."

The hall erupted into laughter and someone from the back called out - "Nice job Digby!"

"Well, Mr. Ross?" Professor Stewart asked, stepping aside and turning toward the gathered students. "What good is a wind-up clock we cannot wind?"

More laughter from the hall and Professor Stewart reveled in his own wit.

Digby Ross seemed beaten. Then suddenly he turned the clock to face him, looking down, and gave it a few quick yet vigorous shakes. It began to tick. Tick-tick-tick-tick-tick.

Digby looked up at Professor Stewart, rose from his seat and the mechanical television light followed him.

"Let me ask you this, professor," he said, voice slightly quavering, but confident. "What good is a mechanical clock you must remember to wind?"

Time in the room stood still. Digby could see Miracle from the corner of his eye. She was leaning forward in her seat with an expectant look on her face.

Suddenly Digby gently tossed the automatic clock to Professor Stewart, who managed to catch it and hold onto it.

"This one is now self-winding."

An eruption of applause broke out in the lecture hall. Self-winding time pieces were certainly not new, but that Digby Ross had managed to assemble one, without instruction, under the hot light of a mechanical television, with his professor looking over his shoulder the entire time and without detailed instructions, was something new. The students liked new and they replied in kind. Rising to their feet with thunderous applause as Professor Stewart continued to examine the clock he held in his hands.

Digby Ross bathed in the adulation of his peers, beaming up at Miracle Lowell who beamed right back.

Chapter 4: The Steam Carriage Man

Outside the lecture hall Digby Ross pushed his way through the crowd of students gathered around him, slapping his back and congratulating him for his demonstration. At least a few told him he did a great job "showing up Old Stewey" - the nickname students had for Professor Stewart. Digby smiled, and said thanks, but kept his eyes on Miracle Lowell who was hurriedly walking down the hall, away from the crowd. Just as he was about to start after her, a girl he had never seen before stepped to block his way.

"Mr. Ross, I was quite impressed with your demonstration," she said. "I just wanted to shake your hand." She held out her hand and Digby took it, feeling her warm soft skin against his, noting her long slender fingers. He had never seen her before. He would have remembered if he had; she wore a floor length, soft yellow dress with long sleeves. Her cuffs and collar were accentuated with a layer of frilly lace and her neck was adorned with a large timepiece. Her lips were bright red and her eyes a deep emerald. Digby found himself lost in her eyes for a moment, clutching her hand.

"Um, yes," he stammered. "Thank you...for, uh...your attention."

She smiled at him and he felt his pulse race as blood flushed his cheeks. He was still clutching her hand and he felt beads of sweat return to his brow.

More hands pounded his back as his peers filed past him. "Way to go Digby!" They called.

"Well, I think I might be keeping you Mr. Ross," she said and withdrew her hand gingerly from his.

"Yes, I, um, must be going," he stammered again.

The girl smiled as she turned abruptly and wandered away through the crowd which had gathered again around him. He was trying to thank all those congratulating him while his eyes did their best to not lose sight of the young lady in the soft yellow dress. She looked back at him once as she was walking away, and smiled.

In the midst of the throng his mind suddenly lurched to thoughts of Miracle walking alone through the campus.

Digby broke free from the crowd and rushed after her.

The site of her walking ahead of him was not at all displeasing to his eye, but he was focused instead on finding out what she had in mind to do next. If there was one thing he knew about his friend Miracle Lowell it was that she definitely had something planned, and he wanted to be in on it. Whatever it was.

"Miracle," he called. "Miracle slow down will you please."

She glanced over her shoulder at him and smiled.

"Have you finished appeasing your fans, Mr. Ross?" she smiled again.

"That's ridiculous. They are only happy with me in as much as I made Old Stewey look like the buffoon that he is."

"Don't be so hard on Professor Stewart, please. He's a lovely man and a very intelligent one. Consider yourself lucky that he chose a task for which your talents were admirably suited. Having said that, however, I must admit you did put on quite a show."

Digby blushed at her praise even as he felt shame at her point. He hadn't anything against Professor Stewart really, he was just caught up in the moment. He wasn't accustomed to being admired by his peers. He pushed the conversation in a different direction.

"So, what's next?" he asked.

Miracle kept walking.

"Where are we going?" he asked.

"I am returning to my room, Mr. Ross, where I shall study for my philosophy text for my exam tomorrow as well as write a comparative analysis between Einstein's theories of general and special relativity and Hertz Theory, also for tomorrow.."

"Philosophy exam? Analysis? We're in the midst of something here. Aren't you the least bit curious as to what might be going on? What about your father? Don't you think you should at least try to reach out to him-find out what might be happening and what he might be involved in?"

They reached the end of the long corridor and proceeded down the stairs. All the while Miracle walked confidently, eyes forward, as Digby trailed alongside her, spouting questions as they went.

"I'll likely send him a telegram at some point, once I've turned this over in my mind thoroughly and analyzed every aspect of what might really be going on."

Digby paused. "So, you do think something is going on then?"

Miracle kept walking, right out the auditorium doors, into the yard. Outside the sun was lower in the sky and the air was beginning to cool. Students were wandering from place to place, most having finished their classes for the day, heading back to their dormitory rooms or the library, to study or to rest.

Miracle turned north toward the young ladies dormitory with Digby following close behind.

"Mr. Ross," she called over her shoulder. "Do you plan to walk me all the way to my room?"

"Indeed I do, Miss Lowell."

"Then you should walk beside me like a gentleman not behind me like a shadow."

Digby hurried up beside her, side by side. "Better?" he asked.

"Much," she said, and smiled.

As they approached the young ladies dormitory both Digby and Miracle noticed a rather smallish, well-dressed livery driver standing awkwardly at the base of the front steps, glancing left and right as if he was looking for someone. Upon seeing Miracle his somewhat gloomy countenance brightened.

"Ah-Miss Lowell? Miss Miracle Lowell?" he asked hesitantly.

Digby puffed out his chest and answered before she had a chance to open her mouth.

"Who wants to know," he said, stepping up and putting himself between his friend and the stranger.

Miracle quickly pushed him aside. "Mr. Ross, if you please!"

Digby yielded to her shove but remained close by, glaring suspiciously at the livery driver. For his part the livery driver seemed none too interested in Digby, with all his attention focused on Miracle.

"Yes, I am Miracle Lowell. How may I help you, Mr.--"

"I am called Callis, Miss Lowell," he smiled and snapped to attention smartly. "I represent a party interested in having a conversation with you. If it wouldn't be too much trouble, that is."

Miracle glanced sideways at Digby, expecting him to erupt in anger, but he was clenching his jaw tightly and seemed to be holding his breath. He knew what his friend would say to the invitation and knew as well that no matter where she went this time he was definitely going with her.

"Of course Mr. Callis," she said.

"Just Callis, Miss."

"As you wish," she said. "Please lead the way Callis."

"And I'm coming too, just so we're clear – Callis," Digby said through gritted teeth.

Callis turned, "Of course, Mr. Ross. I was advised you might be joining us."

"Damn right I'll be joining you," Digby muttered. Miracle cast him a sideways glance of dismay and he buttoned his lips closed, following closely behind his friend.

Callis led the pair down the paved walking path and around the young ladies dormitory to a larger paved pathway which led out to the gates of the university. Parked to one side of the cobblestone roadway was an enormous steam powered carriage with three doors on one side. It was covered in shiny chrome and polished copper, with bright electric lights at the top and huge rubber tires. The sun was lower in the sky now and the car cast a long dark shadow that stretched across the entire cobblestone road. Callis led Miracle and Digby to the rear of the car, opened a door and motioned with one hand that they should climb inside.

Miracle moved without hesitation. Digby paused for a moment to eyeball Callis then slipped in behind his friend.

The inside of the steam carriage was as luxurious as the outside. The seats were cushioned in red velvet. It was roomy and well lit, with what appeared to be mahogany trim throughout and it had the distinct smell of money. Digby knew the smell of money though his family had little of it. And this smell was big money.

Miracle and Digby slid across the seat easily and found themselves face to face with a wrinkled old man with sparkling green eyes and a surprisingly benevolent smile comprised of rather large, bright, white teeth. The pair were seated facing the rear of the car. Behind their heads was a frosted glass partition to separate the driver (likely Callis) and the passenger compartment where they were now seated.

"Miss Lowell," said the old man. "Please forgive my intrusion into your studies. A college education is a valuable resource which will surely serve you well in the future. I apologize again for disturbing you."

"I'm afraid you have me at a disadvantage, Mr-" Miracle said without hesitation.

"Quite right, I must apologize again for my rudeness, Miss Lowell," he said. "Paulson. My name is Charles Paulson and I am here seeking your assistance."

Digby took a breath as if to speak, but Miracle shot him a sideways glance. He held his breath and let it out very slowly so as not to make it obvious he was bursting to say something

"I see," she said, drawing one leg slowly across the other, adjusting her long dress and smiling brightly. "You seem to be doing quite well for yourself already Mr. Paulson. Unless I am mistaken you are the owner of the Paulson Steamworks which supplies most of the homes in the northeastern United States with power, not to mention your holdings in the paper industry; Paulson Mining, Paulson Dirigibles and the Paulson Rubber Company. It seems unlikely I could be of any assistance to you, given the resources you no doubt have at your disposal."

"Quite astute, Miss Lowell. I see my reputation precedes me."

"Not really Mr Paulson. It only takes a quick glance at my surroundings to tell me you are a man of means. This car cost more than an entire four years tuition at university. Why, the imported Honduran mahogany panels I see here are worth more than I paid in tuition this past year. This, plus what I've read of Charles Paulson in the papers, told me you were likely he, although I wasn't certain until you yourself just confirmed it."

"Indeed, I did," he said, raising an eyebrow at the paneling approvingly.

"So tell me, how is it I could possibly help you," she continued.

Paulson sat back, pushing himself further into his cushioned seat.

"You are right, my dear," he said with a sigh. "No point in beating around the bush, as it were, so let me get right to it."

"I wish you would," she said.

"Let me simply ask you, have you spoken to your father recently?"

"My father? No. I haven't heard from him in quite some time. Why? What do you want with my father?"

"I'm afraid it's a rather complex issue and not something I could go into here with any decent amount of elaboration."

"No?"

"No. Definitely not. Suffice to say that I am in desperate need of his counsel with regard to a very delicate matter."

"Exactly what sort of 'delicate matter' are you describing?"

"If only I had the time to explain it all, I'm sure you would agree that your father must be put in touch with me immediately."

"I would?"

"Indeed."

"Then perhaps you should simply tell me an abridged version of why you need to speak with my father."

"Yes, perhaps I should," he said, raising a wrinkled hand to his chin and rubbing it gently.

"You see, there is something that belongs to me which has been stolen and I need your father's help in retrieving it."

"Surely you realize my father is a scientist; an astronomer, not a detective. Perhaps this is a matter best left to the authorities."

"The authorities simply cannot be involved in this matter. It is much too delicate an affair for their clumsy efforts."

"Well, if the authorities cannot be of assistance I don't understand how you think my father can be of any help."

"I believe he has some idea of the whereabouts of the person responsible."

"So you know who is responsible?"

"Indeed I do."

"Who?"

He stopped. "I'm afraid I cannot tell you that for reasons of liability," he said. "In fact, truth be told, I only believe they are the responsible party. But with your father's help I would be able to clear their good name, and likely retrieve my property."

Miracle sat perfectly still. Digby squirmed in his seat, tiny beads of sweat soaking his shirt collar and running down his back. He didn't like confrontation and this was clearly a confrontation. Miracle did not seem likely to budge and Paulson – one of the richest most powerful men in the world – was also unlikely to budge.

The unmovable object meets the unstoppable force, Digby thought to himself.

"There is something else, Miss Lowell," Paulson continued after a moment.

"Of course there is," she said.

"I'm afraid this situation of mine might inadvertently have put your life in danger."

"Indeed?"

"Oh yes, quite right. The people who I believe may have taken my property without permission are also aware that your father has the ability to point a finger at the culprit. In your father's absence, it is common knowledge that his daughter, you, resides here in Princeton and attends this very university."

Paulson relaxed further into his seat and drew in a long breath. He gazed out the window, seemingly at nothing, and spoke again.

"You see Miss Lowell, whether you help me or not, your involvement in this situation is guaranteed regardless. If I was able to make the connection and find you so easily, how difficult do you think it will be for these nefarious people I speak of to find you?"

Miracle sat erect, unflinching. Digby had no idea what to make of the situation now. Was Paulson threatening her in some way? Was he actually trying to help? Digby was a terrible judge of hidden intentions, instead relying on his friend to sort it out and let him know if someone, anyone, needed a good knocking down. Like Crosby.

"I see," she said at last with a slight sigh. "That is indeed regrettable."

"Mmhm," Paulson grunted.

"I do appreciate the warning Mr. Paulson, but I regret that I am still completely unable to help you. You see I can only reach my father in person, and with us being so close to final exams I simply cannot leave at this time. Perhaps if you waited until the end of the semester?"

"Quite impossible, I'm afraid." Paulson said, frowning.

"Well, that's all there is to it then. Come along Digby," she said, motioning for him to exit the car.

"Wait a moment if you please, Miss Lowell," Paulson said. "I certainly understand the importance of a good education these days, especially for a young lady with your natural talents. If you cannot leave your studies, and I'll assume also not tell me where or how your father might be contacted-"

"Absolutely not, he left instructions that he was not to be disturbed for any reason."

"-then perhaps you could simply take a message for me, for when you do see him?"

Paulson reached inside a beast pocket and drew out a small envelope with a wax seal pressed into it.

Miracle looked at the proffered envelope. Digby saw her considering the envelope carefully, lifting one delicate hand to it.

"I cannot promise when I will see him again, and you say the matter is of some urgency. Does it do any good at all me taking this letter now?"

Paulson smiled. "Oh yes," he said. "If nothing else it would give me a sense of reassurance that I had done everything I could to avoid anything untoward happening as a result of this dreadful situation." Miracle sat still for a moment.

"Well, I suppose it couldn't hurt," she said as she gently took the envelope he offered.

"Yes, yes, it couldn't hurt," he said. "And it would do this old heart good to know I had endeavored my utmost to rectify this situation as safely as possible."

"Safely?" Miracle said as she gripped the envelope in her lap.

"Safely—perhaps that's the wrong word," he said, fumbling. "I simply meant that it would do me good to know I had tried my best to rectify the situation without involving the authorities-"

"I thought you said the authorities couldn't be involved in this situation at all?" she asked. Digby knew she had the old man on the ropes now and expected a knockout punch any second.

"Did I? Well, yes, I mean no, no they can't," he stammered. "But eventually my property must be returned to me and I promise I will use whatever means are at my disposal to see that it is returned. Sooner rather than later, I might add."

"Very good then Mr. Paulson," Miracle said with the utmost calm. "If that will be all, we shall be going. Digby?" she motioned for him to exit the car. Digby reached for the handle.

"Miss Lowell," Paulson said through the open window as they stood alongside the car. "I do hope you will keep our conversation private."

"Of course," Miracle said. "I shall treat our encounter as if it never happened."

"I knew I could rely on your discretion," he said, and reached out to take her hand. "Perhaps upon your graduation I might find a place for you at one of my companies. You will consider it, won't you? You can bring your little friend there as well if you'd like." Paulson smiled at Digby with a face full of bright shiny, unusually large teeth. Digby felt as if he was looking into the face of crocodile, only not as friendly as a crocodile.

"Thank you for the kind offer," Miracle said. "Perhaps I will take you up on it."

"I hope you will," Paulson said.

The window went up silently and Digby heard Paulson speaking to Callis, who was presumably in the front seat behind the frosted glass partition, "Move along now please. We're done here." And the car silently moved forward, onto the road and away from the university. Miracle watched the car slip away into the distance. Without a sound she turned back toward the school and started walking. Once again Digby struggled to keep up with her.

"What was that all about?" he asked.

"Mr. Paulson wants to find my father and he believes – much as Mr. Crosby believed – that I could be of some help."

"But that was Charles Paulson, the richest man in the country; one of the richest men outside the Persian Empire. Why doesn't he just hire someone to find your father and be done with it?"

Miracle stopped. "Digby Ross, surely you realize, if my father doesn't want to be found, he won't be. And all the money in the world won't help someone find a man who definitely doesn't want to be found. Hiring someone to find him would alert even more people to whatever the mysterious "missing item" is, something which I have a feeling is not in Mr. Paulson's best interest. And considering my father has promised to devote every waking hour to finally proving the existence of his so-called 'Planet X', he is not likely to make his presence known wherever he might be."

"But you know where he is?"

Miracle sighed, loudly. "Digby Ross, must you make me repeat myself – repeatedly?" She kept walking.

Digby paused a moment, remembering her exact words about the location of her father. Then he remembered the envelope Paulson had given her and scrambled to catch up to her.

"But what about the letter? Will you send it to him?"

Miracle paused a moment allowing Digby to catch up.

"Definitely not," she said, her gaze on an empty space in front of her. "I think Mr. Paulson is definitely not to be trusted. In fact, I expect him to use his powerful influence against us immediately." Then she started walking away again.

"Wait- what?" Digby asked, but she was several steps ahead of him again.

"Paulson? You think he's going to move against us? What the devil for?"

"Because clearly he knows I know where my father is and it irritates him that he cannot manipulate me the way he no doubt manipulates everyone and everything else he encounters."

Digby considered this a moment, and felt assured that his friend was indeed quite right.

"So, what are we to do next?" he asked.

"About what?" she said, as if their day thus far had been just like every other day, instead of being the strangest day either of them had yet experienced.

"About what? About Crosby, about Paulson, about your father."

"Oh, well, for now, I'm going back to my room to study. I have an exam tomorrow morning and I would like to score well."

Digby stopped and stared incredulously as Miracle walked on. She noticed and stopped too, turning to face him.

"There is nothing to do at this moment, Digby, so we might as well continue on with what needs to be done until I determine exactly what our next actions should be."

"So, you understand more about what is going on than I do?"

"Undoubtedly, Digby Ross. Undoubtedly."

Miracle Lowell smiled at her friend and despite his concerns, he found himself smiling right back.

They walked the rest of the way to her dormitory in silence, both lost in their own thoughts of everything that had happened. They parted at Miracle's dormitory, with Digby promising he would be waiting out front first thing in the morning to walk her to class and she insisting that he needn't worry. Digby was adamant however, so Miracle finally agreed, and the pair of friends parted for the evening.

Chapter 5: Midnight At The University

Digby's roommate Franklin Thomby was sitting at the desk in their room, furiously scribbling away in his notebook. He barely acknowledged Digby's presence, just grunting when he entered, too busy trying to master whatever formula or process he was working on.

Digby pulled off his boots and set them by the door. Then he sat down on his bed. "I've had the most exhausting day, Franklin," he said.

"Mmm." Franklin replied.

"Miracle and I, well, Miracle mostly, seem to have inadvertently become involved in some sort of strange mystery that began, in all places, Trenton. What do you make of that?"

"Mmm," was the only response.

Digby considered this and said, "It wouldn't have been too bad if it hadn't been for all those damn flying monkeys. Hundreds of them, streaming out of the sky, dropping exploding pomegranates all over the central quad."

"Mmm," Franklin said.

"I suppose as roommates go I could have done worse," Digby said, this time mostly to himself. He undressed, changed into his pajamas, grabbed his physics book and climbed into bed. He himself had some reading to catch up on. Although Autumn had begun and today had been warm as summer, the mid-winter finals were fast approaching and Digby fully intended to outperform his friend Miracle at all costs—well, all costs short of cheating however. He simply couldn't abide a cheater. He would stand or fall on his own merits.

Across campus Miracle Lowell entered her room and was greeted with a giddy "Hello!" from her roommate, Darling Kinder. After almost a full semester of rooming with her Miracle now fully understood the unfortunate name she bore.

"How was your day today, Miracle?" Darling beamed.

"Fine," Miracle said.

"Anything exciting happen today?" Darling asked.

Miracle wondered briefly if her roommate knew anything of the day she'd had, but then dismissed the idea just as quickly.

"Not particularly," she said.

"It seems something exciting always happens with you, Miracle," Darling said. "You seem to lead such an interesting life-full of excitement! I envy you sometimes, but then I think how much better it is to just watch you live the excitement and know that my life, while not nearly as exciting as yours, is at least stable and safe."

Miracle was sure Darling didn't mean this to come across as an insult, but it sure sounded that way.

"Indeed," was all she said.

Darling sat down on her bed. Miracle began changing her clothes, shifting off her dress and pulling on her riding pants, blouse and boots. Then she started packing a small overnight bag.

"Are you planning a trip," Darling asked.

"No," Miracle said.

"You're packing a bag and putting on riding clothes," Darling said.

"Just being prepared," Miracle said.

"Prepared for what?" Darling asked, tilting her head slightly to the side in the quizzical, childlike way she had.

"Frankly, I don't know," Miracle said. "When I know – if I know - I'll tell you."

Darling clapped her hands and giggled.

"You are doing something exciting, aren't you!"

Miracle frowned.

"I told you, I'm just being prepared."

"And with an exam tomorrow morning, and finals just weeks away—so much excitement!" Darling seemed giddy with vicarious excitement.

"Calm down, Darling," Miracle said as she fastened her bag closed and tucked it under her bed. Then she climbed in and reached up to switch off the light at her nightstand. "Now I'm going to sleep, and I recommend you do the same. Then if something exciting does happen you'll be well rested and better able to endure it."

"Oh Miracle!" Darling said. "This is already so exciting." and she clapped her hands again.

"Darling?" Miracle said, over her shoulder.

"Yes, Miracle?"

"Go to sleep."

"Oh, yes, right," she said. Miracle heard her roommate go to the dresser. She heard drawers opening and closing, then some rustling around in the wardrobe. Finally, she heard Darling climbing into her own bed. Then the light switched off.

"Goodnight, Miracle Lowell," she said, with a smile in her voice.

"Goodnight Darling Kinder," Miracle said.

Silence. Then -

"Miracle?"

Miracle sighed, "Yes, Darling?"

"I'm sleeping with my boots on too!" and she giggled again.

"Fabulous," Miracle said, but she didn't roll over. Her eyes tightly closed she tried desperately to force herself to sleep. It was earlier than she might usually go to sleep, but she had a suspicion that she wouldn't have long in bed tonight and so wanted to make the most of it.

Digby Ross was having a most unusual dream. He was lying in his bed, but not in his room. He could feel himself floating up, out of his room, out of his dormitory; above the town of Princeton he drifted with the clouds. Normally fearful of heights, Digby felt unusually at ease. He peered over the side of his bed, looking down at the patchwork of city blocks below him. As he drifted further and further the quilt of city blocks changed to fields of winter wheat. He saw small farmhouses below him now, rather than the row houses and shops of the town. Cobblestone streets were gone now, and instead gravel roads snaked across the landscape.

Night gave way to daybreak now, and Digby felt the sudden warmth of the rising sun on his face. He shielded his eyes from its bright orange glow.

Digby had never been interested in flying. The sky these days were criss-crossed with dirigibles and bi-planes. Commerce today was global thanks to the many flying machines which filled the air. It seemed everyone, his friend Miracle among them, was learning to fly these machines. But not Digby. No. His feet were made to be planted firmly on the ground.

This dream, however, was different. His heart didn't feel squeezed with iron bands the way it did when he thought about flying above the ground. In fact, his heart felt more free than it ever had before. He could sense it beating wildly in his chest – with excitement, not fear.

This was a good dream, Digby thought to himself. He propped himself up on his pillows and watched the world pass beneath him. Suddenly he heard someone calling his name. In his dream.

"Digby! Digby!" they shouted, from somewhere far away.

He leaned over the side of his bed again and looked down. None of the vertigo he might feel if he were not in a dream, he noted. He peered at the ground far below him.

"Digby! Digby Ross!"

Far, far below him he made out a small figure. They had their arms outstretched and were waving to him.

"Digby Ross!" they shouted again.

"Yes—I'm here!" he called back.

They said something else, but a gust of wind was blowing in his ears. The roaring of the wind was covering their words.

"What? I can't hear you!" he called back.

"I said, GET OUT OF THERE RIGHT NOW!" they shouted back, much louder now.

Digby sat back up in bed. Something didn't seem right now. The solace and peacefulness of his dream was quickly dissipating. The light of the risen sun seemed brighter now and it was no longer providing warmth, but heat. Severe heat. He could feel it baking into his skin, his head was already wet with sweat. The winds now were blowing cold and his bed began to rock and shake and shudder. Gone were the feelings of joy and exhilaration Digby had been feeling, replaced with a sudden urge to wake up.

"Digby! Get out—you must get out!" came the voice again, but he was frozen in place. Fear had begun to tighten that iron band around his heart. Fear of heights. Fear of flying. Fear of whatever was going on, because he suddenly realized that something was not right with this dream.

"Digby Ross—you absolutely must get out of there right this instant!" came the voice again. "Don't make me come up there!"

Digby realized slowly, as if pulling his feet free from a puddle of glue, that he was still asleep, but he needed to be awake. He tried forcing himself to awaken, fearful of what might be waiting for him in the conscious world, but more fearful still of the dream he was having; rocking, flying bed, burning sun and extreme height.

"Digby Ross—are you still asleep?" came the voice again. It seemed so far away, yet, it was spot on. He was asleep. Sound asleep. In his bed. While his dormitory was burning all around him.

Digby Ross slowly opened his eyes. He felt the heat still, but now saw it was coming from the beams and wood scattered around the room, all engulfed in flames. He rubbed his eyes, bleary from soot and the haze of still being half-asleep. He felt a cold breeze blowing in his face and it refreshed him.

He looked around and in the moonlight and orange glow of the fire burning before him, he understood the rocking of his bed and cold wind. His bed was tilting precariously halfway out of his room, presumably where the window had once been, now shattered into a million pieces on the ground three stories below. His head hurt and when he reached a hand up to feel it , it felt damp. And hot.

Digby sat up quickly, but felt the bed tilt further out the window, so he laid back down again just as quickly. His head throbbed.

"Digby! You must get up and get out of there, right now!"

Digby was awake now and fully aware that the voice was that of his friend, Miracle Lowell. She must be on the ground below, outside his building. He tried to move again, but felt the iron bands tighten around his heart as he considered the ground below—directly beneath his bed, which, unlike a bi-plane or a dirigible, did not have wings or an engine, and was definitely not intended for flight.

From his position laying on his bed he could see into his decimated room. The fire was quite intense now. One large burning beam was resting right atop Franklin's bed. He could barely make out the form of his former roommate beneath it – quite dead by now.

Digby knew his only chance was to escape this room, but he also knew any escape began with him getting out of his bed. And that seemed all but impossible at the moment.

Like a snake he began to slither down beneath his covers, closer to the foot of his bed, closer to the fire and devastation which had once been his dormitory room. He tried his best ot ignore the pounding in his head.

Suddenly there was a loud roar and Digby felt the head of his bed rising up, tilting him toward his room. Within a half-second the bed was on top of him as he was thrust back inside his room.

"That's slightly better," Digby said to himself.

Beneath the bed Digby was protected from the flames. The force of whatever had flipped his bed also seemed to have partially snuffed out the fire which had been raging around him. Back on solid ground – or at least with the security of the floor beneath him, Digby took advantage of the minutes calm and squirmed from under his upturned bed. The wood was still hot, if not actively on fire, and he felt it burning him through his pajamas,

Slithering out from under his bed he had only a second to look around his room. There was only rubble and debris now. Broken chairs and tables. His dead roommate. Some burning books and blankets.

Then he spied his boots, by what remained of their door, sitting almost exactly where he had left them. He grabbed his boots, pulled them on, and quickly exited the room.

The rest of this floor of his dormitory was a shambles. He heard some yelling from below him. Above him he could see the dark winter sky and the faint glow of the moonlight where it slipped between clouds of black smoke coming from the burning building around him.

He turned toward the stairs, but they were completely gone, laying in a pile of burning lumber on the floor beneath him.

Digby went back to his room. The fire was beginning to grow again. He scanned the room, looking for something, anything he might use to escape.

Another roar, this time further away. Digby could see it was the physics building, across the campus, exploding into a ball of fire. The shock wave was strong, but he was ready for it, so he didn't fall. His building shook with the force, and the rushing air which came in through the broken wall where his window had once been again momentarily snuffed the flames of room.

Digby took advantage of this to look around again.

The beam which had crushed Franklin was mostly a glowing red ember now.

An idea suddenly came to him. He dashed for his roommates bed. "Sorry Franklin," he said, as he tore what remained of the man's covers from him. They were partially burned, but manageable. He strung them together.

His room was three stories above the ground, approximately thirty feet. He had no idea how many feet of improvised rope he could make from some tattered bedsheets and blankets, but he surmised it wouldn't be enough to reach all the way.

The room continued to burn and he heard at least two more explosions come from somewhere, most likely other buildings on campus.

He rushed on, quite aware that whatever was happening had so far allowed him a few extra moments of life, unlike his friend Franklin. He intended to use them.

"Digby!" came Miracle's voice from outside and below. "Are you coming or not?!"

"Coming Miracle!" he shouted back, though he wasn't sure she could hear him. "I'm definitely bloody well not staying here."

He hurriedly grabbed the covers from his own upside down bed and began fastening them to his existing bed sheet rope. When it was done he had no idea how much length it had, he just began tying one end of it around his waist anyway, rolling as much of it around him as he could, much like winding a yo-yo. The other end he tied in a knot around the post of his small bed. It seemed secure, he thought, but secure or not, it would have to do.

"Digby!" came Miracles voice again.

He felt a rumble beneath his feet and expected the building to collapse around him at any moment.

"Miracle!" he shouted back. "Get back—here I come!"

Without looking he ran toward the broken wall and jumped, rolling sideways as he went so his makeshift rope would unroll him downwards.

As he rolled and turned he could catch glimpses of the campus around him. It seemed everywhere was destruction. Buildings were burning; students and administrators were rushing around. The campus fire department was nowhere to be seen and he thought that odd, but he was rushing toward the ground at breakneck speed. The fire department wouldn't be able to save me now anyway, he thought.

The bed sheet rope ended, and he felt it grab his middle tight, knocking his breath away.

He was still quite a ways from the ground. He grabbed at the knot and began tugging it free. His weight was holding the knot tight, and his fingers fumbled to free it.

"Digby!" came Miracle's voice once again.

Just then his fingers worked their way into the knot and pulled it free. He dropped suddenly, but grabbed an end of the rope with one hand, holding tight. He was swinging now, feet still several feet from the ground. Despite his better judgment at falling any distance, he shut his eyes, forced himself to let go the rope and dropped. He landed with a thud, and fell flat on his back.

"Digby!"

He opened his eyes and took a breath. Miracle was crouched down beside him. "Digby, are you alright?"

He took a few deep breaths and didn't feel as if anything had been broken. His hands and face felt singed, but otherwise he seemed to be in one piece.

Miracle lifted him into a sitting position. In the moonlight and orange glow of the burning dorm he noticed immediately she was fully dressed.

"I'm afraid you have me at a severe fashion disadvantage," he cracked.

She smiled at him.

"I believe in being prepared," she said. "Slept in my clothes I'm afraid."

"Wait—so you knew this was going to happen? And you didn't tell me?"

Miracle frowned. "Now is definitely not the time," she said, pulling him to his feet. Except for the boots he managed to grab he was still just wearing his pajamas

"Quite right, I suppose," he said. "Where to?"

Miracle looked around, pulling him a little distance from his burning dormitory.

"Well, by the looks of things I'd say the girls dormitory is only the building left undamaged," she said. "Let's go there first and get you cleaned up."

She started pulling him in that direction. People were running in all directions, some screaming, some silently wandering, shuffling, definitely in shock.

"Shouldn't we be trying to help here," Digby asked.

"The best thing we can do for these people is to get as far away from them as possible," Miracle said.

Digby shook his head. "This has something to do with us, doesn't it," he said. "Something to do with you."

Miracle stopped and turned toward him.

"I'm afraid so, Digby," she said with a frown. "Someone wanted me involved in whatever is going on, and now they've done it. I'm involved alright, but I don't think they'll like the end result. Come along, Digby, we must hurry."

With Digby in tow Miracle Lowell pulled and pushed their way across the quad to the girl's dormitory. As she had said, although just about every other building on campus was in flames, the girls dormitory remained untouched. People were taking refuge inside and around the outside of the building. It was crowded, and Miracle and Digby had to carefully weave their way through and amongst the wounded and the workers.

Inside and up the stairs they went. When they reached Miracle's door she stopped, and knocked three times in succession, then twice more, slowly.

Digby heard furniture being moved and the door being unlatched. It opened slowly, and a small blonde head peered around the corner of it at them.

"Miracle! I've been worried, come in, come in."

Miracle strode into the room, dragging Digby with her.

"Darling Kinder, Digby Ross – I believe you've met before," Miracle said.

"Good evening Miss Kinder," Digby said, standing as upright as he could. "Please excuse my attire."

Darling Kinder blushed. "Of course, Mr. Ross. Pleasure to see you again."

"Perhaps different circumstances would make it a 'pleasure' Darling," Miracle cracked.

Darling blushed a deeper red. "Oh, you're so right, Miracle. Thoughtless of me, really. Please, excuse my poor choice of words, Mr. Ross."

"Think nothing of it, Miss Kinder."

"Please, call me Darling."

Now it was Digby's turn to blush. "Oh, Darling. Yes. And you may call me Digby, of course."

Miracle looked at her two friends.

"If you are both quite done..." she trailed off.

Digby shuffled his feet.

"Indeed," he said.

Darling turned away so as not to blush further. "Yes, Miracle."

"Good," Miracle said. "Now, I just need my bag, a few pieces of equipment, some writing utensils and we can be off."

Darling came to life.

"How exciting this all is!" she said.

"Yes," Miracle said. "Except for all the death and destruction it is simply marvelous, isn't it?"

Darling either ignored the comment or didn't hear it. Digby winced at the thought of the dead and injured friends he had passed in the quad. His roommate, Franklin, among them.

"Where are we going now?" Darling asked, innocently.

"We?" Miracle turned toward her. "WE—Mr. Ross and I – have business to attend to. YOU – are staying here of course."

Darling's face fell.

"Surely you don't mean to leave me behind, do you?"

Miracle stood silent a moment.

"Darling, why on Earth would you even want to come along?" she asked.

Darling looked down for a moment and Digby thought she might begin to cry. But when she lifted her face again her eyes were alight. Not with fear, or shame or concern, but something much closer to anger. And when she spoke, she confirmed it.

"It's so easy for you, Miracle, isn't it? To just decide what is best for everyone else, as if you are the wisest sage among us all, your poor, unintelligent friends."

Miracle stood silent.

"Did it ever occur to you that I might enjoy some excitement in my life for a change? That while your father encourages you to seek out adventure and rise to every challenge, mine might do just the opposite. Your father's goals for you include doing something extraordinary. My fathers goal for me is to graduate with a degree which will make me more likely to marry a man above my status. When I first met you I knew exactly what I wanted to be. You. And if I couldn't be you then perhaps I could merely be near enough to you that some of that adventurous life you always seemed to be living might rub off on my own dull and dreary existence. That maybe, just maybe, one day something would happen and I would be thrust out into the world, instead of staying behind, waiting for some man to come sweep me off my feet." She glanced at Digby, but he was lost in a world of his own.

Miracle looked exasperated listening to Darling talk as she went about stuffing a small duffel bag with assorted bits and pieces. She grabbed a short coat for herself, and a long, fur lined coat which she handed to Digby.

Digby took the coat and slipped it over his shoulders. He felt, and looked, ridiculous, but he resigned himself to it. He leaned back against the wall of their room. He raised a hand to his face, felt the singed hair on his face and the bump on his head. The back of head felt damp and sticky. When he took his hand away and looked at it he could see traces of blood. He must have hit the ground harder than he thought.

He definitely didn't feel well at the moment, although, who would. The university was blowing up and burning around them. Many of his friends and classmates were dead or dying. His best friend, though alive and well, was dragging him off on some adventure he may or may not want to be a part of, although he did not seem to have any say in the matter. And now this young lady, Darling Kinder, was practically begging not to be left behind, while he, Digby Ross, could think of nothing better at the moment than finding a nice warm (and safe) bed to lie down in.

"Darling," Miracle said suddenly. She had her bag and was reaching for the handle of the door as she addressed her roommate. "As much as I'd like to bring you with us there are two problems: First, it's dangerous, and I simply cannot be responsible for your life in addition to Digby's. And second, I can't think of a single good reason, nor have you mentioned one, for bringing you with us."

Darling's face, momentarily fallen, suddenly brightened. She spun around and grabbed her Nehru jacket off the rack.

"Let's go then," she said with a smile.

"But-" Miracle was incredulous, but before she finished her sentence Darling continued.

"You're going somewhere, but in reality you're going nowhere fast because I know you don't have any way of getting anywhere and I can't imagine you'll be able to find a hire cab at this time of night, in the midst of this conflagration."

Miracle looked frustrated. "And your point?"

Darling smiled brightly. "Father insisted I keep my own private handsome cab at the university in case I needed it. 'It's not proper,' he said, for a young lady to rely on a young man who has not yet met her father.'"

Miracle smiled in spite of herself.

"Point taken," she said. "Let's be off. Come along Digby."

Digby forced himself off the wall.

"Right-O, Miracle," he said, with none of Darling's enthusiasm or his friends determination.

He paused a moment, holding the door, waiting for Darling to gather a few things and stuff them hurriedly into an already stuffed bag she dragged from under her bed.

"Thank you, Mr. Ross," she said as she passed, smiling.

"Digby, please," he said quietly. "Just Digby."

The three made their way downstairs which was now crowded beyond capacity. There were injured people laying everywhere. Other students were caring for them, while some were bringing news of the devastation.

"Heard it was a chain reaction gas explosion," said one young man, talking with a young lady who was busy wrapping his burned hands in bandages. "It started in the gentleman's dorm and spread from there."

Miracle, Digby and Darling didn't stop as they moved through the front room of the dorm and out the door.

Once outside Darling took the lead. "This way," she said, and moved quickly through the darkness, silhouetted against the orange glow of the still burning buildings. Miracle matched her step for step, but Digby, still a bit dazed and uncomfortable in his friends fur lined coat, a pair of boots and his now sooty pajamas

They crossed the quad, making their way to the stables where Darling kept her handsome cab. It was a stunningly handsome, handsome cab. Totally enclosed, except for where the driver sat, there was room for the three of them to ride inside comfortably. It had chrome fenders and giant wheels with four large springs each to provide a cushioned ride. The sides were polished white and the top was a shining black leather.

It must be at least decades old, Digby thought, but it's still in fabulous condition.

While Darling hitched up the horses, Miracle tossed both bags into the back of the cab, grabbed a nearby lantern, lit it and attached it to the front. She opened the door and motioned for Digby to climb inside.

"Feeling a little useless here, Miracle," he grumbled.

"Shut up and get in," she said. "Darling, almost ready?"

Darling was just finishing hitching the second of the two horses to the cab. With the horses hitched she turned to Miracle with the brightest, widest smile. "I've been ready for so long – you have no idea!" Then she swung herself up to the drivers position.

Miracle climbed inside, next to Digby, their bags on the seat across from them.

"Alright Darling, let's go," she called.

"Um, Miracle?"

"Yes, Darling?"

"Where are we going?"

Digby's ears perked up as well. "Yes, Miracle, where are we going?" he said.

Miracle smiled. "It's time we get right to the heart of this mystery," she said. "Darling, takes us to Trenton."

Silence. Darling had expected a shipping port, or an airship lifting station, or perhaps the Tube in New Amsterdam. Trenton was unexpected and perhaps a bit of a disappointment.

A moments hesitation, and then she called out, "Ok, Miracle," she called, cracking the reins and calling out gently to her horses. "Trenton. Right away."

In moments the three friends were headed out of the stable, away from the orange glow of the still burning buildings of their university and out onto the cobble stone streets. They were hardly the only cab heading out of the university and more than once they had to move aside to allow steam powered firetrucks to pass, heading in the opposite direction.

It was a little less than an hour to Trenton from the university, so Digby Ross closed his eyes and rested. Miracle was doing her best to deduce exactly what their next move should be, her mind a swirl of thoughts as she gazed out the window of the handsome cab. She knew full well that the devastation at the university was an attempt to convince her to seek out her father's assistance, something she was simply not prepared, nor willing, to do. She needed more information about exactly what was going on and what, if any, involvement her father might have in it. Two strange visitors in a single day, both suggesting that her father knew something about the mysterious "Professor Nettles" who may or may not be dead, and who, according to one of the wealthiest men in the country, may (or may not) have misappropriated something which didn't belong to him. It was all very confusing and Miracle was having trouble knowing exactly what to believe. For this reason she was determined to first learn as much as she could about Professor Harold Nettles; what the good professor was working on and what exactly were the circumstances of his disappearance or death. From there Miracle hoped to have a better grasp of the situation and be better able to determine her next course of action.

While Miracle contemplated and Digby rested, Darling sat in the drivers seat with a bright smile, softly humming to herself contentedly.

Chapter 6: Crosby

Immediately after being tackled by Digby, Patrolman Mark Crosby slipped away in the confusion of the moment, then sprinted away from the Princeton University campus as fast as his legs would carry him. His tall hat was crumpled and his finest suit stained with dirt, but that was nothing compared with the damage his pride had sustained. Knocked to the ground like a sack of flour, he had accomplished nothing in his effort to find Percival Lowell, except to do exactly what he had been warned not to do: make a spectacle of himself and attract unwanted attention.

Exiting the university on the cobblestone roadway, he quickly diverted to one side where he had tied up his horse a short time earlier. He had ridden this horse from the Princeton Saddlery where he had exchanged the horse he had ridden from Trenton. He could have rented a steam carriage, or even hired a driver but he believed that the horse made him less conspicuous, and was more difficult to trace should someone ever wonder where he had been and what he had been up to on his "sick day."

He had packed very lightly, just one change of clothes for riding, because he hadn't expected to be here long. He was of the belief while packing that Miss Miracle Lowell would succumb to his charms and readily offer him whatever information he needed. He had seen police detectives do this all the time. He was going to be a police detective one day – of that he was sure – but so far he had done little to prove it.

On the ride back to the town of Princeton he cursed himself furiously. His heart continued to race, not just from the thrashing he had taken from that college kid, but also at the thought of the response his failure would receive when he returned to Trenton.

He fumbled inside his vest pocket for the tiny box of enhanced snuff he kept secreted there. His fingers shook as he slipped the little bronze square open, lifted it to his nose and had a sniff. Immediately he felt the opiates flood his system; felt the tightening in his chest loosen its grip, and the feelings of anxiety at his own failure float away. Having been using snuff for so long the head rush was much lessened, but the calming effects remained. His failure no longer worried him. He would handle this situation. He would get the information required. He still had an ace up his sleeve. There was no need to report this incident; he didn't even have to bring it up. All he had to do was what was expected of him: find Professor Percival Lowell and retrieve the "package."

But how? he wondered. He had a tenuous lead, at best. He knew Professor Nettles had sent some sort of package to Percival Lowell not long before disappearing in a fireball that engulfed his dockside laboratory. Crosby knew this because he got the word straight from the kid Nettles had hired to deliver the package to the post office. Crosby had no way of intercepting the package, already en route, and the kid said he couldn't remember the address. Just the name: Percival Lowell.

It had been a fluke of luck that he had managed that much information. The kid had tried to cash in a gold Atlantean dollar at the grocers and the owner there had become suspicious. Not many of those coins around, and they were worth far more than the head of lettuce, sack of potatoes and jug of milk the kid was trying to purchase. Fearing the coin was a fake the grocer had held the boy and called the police. That's when Crosby showed up. He didn't even have to ask the kid any questions. As soon as he saw the police the kid started explaining exactly where he got the coin. Crosby recognized immediately that this kid might know even more than he was telling, even if he didn't know he knew it. Crosby told the grocer not worry about the coin, paid for the groceries himself and offered to walk the kid home. On the way he asked the kid more about what he knew about Professor Nettles, and if he had any idea about the explosion. The kid swore it was a total shock to him; he knew nothing except that his friend was dead and he needed to find a new job. The coin, he had said, was all he had to last him until he got a new job, working for someone else.

Crosby almost felt sorry for the kid. Almost. These emancipated kids were nothing but trouble. They all thought being free from their parents of the orphanages would make life easier. Instead they almost all ended up going on federally funded assistance, or taking jobs away from adults who had families to feed and bills to pay. The only real freedom these kids enjoyed was the freedom to be a burden to the rest of society, or to fill the ranks of an ever growing underground gang system.

It was true that some joined apprenticeship programs with the Steampunks or the Gearheads or even the Alchemists, but for the most part they were just a burden to regular folks who were also trying to survive.

Better to round them all up and re-open the orphanages, Crosby thought to himself. Whenever he was feeling down it always made him feel a little bit better to put down someone else. And who would be a better target than a dirty little leech on society?

His horse was sure footed, if not fleet, and Crosby made his way back to the Princeton Saddlery in short order. There he ignored the innkeepers offer of a "night's stay and a good meal" and instead rented another horse to take him back to Trenton.

Back on his new horse Crosby's thoughts returned to Professor Nettles and his mysterious package. He knew that retrieving the package was his first priority. Finding Nettles (assuming he didn't actually die in the explosion as Crosby's employer believed) would come later.

It was only an hours ride back to Trenton. When he was almost there he heard the silent rumbling of a steam powered carriage approaching from behind and moved his horse to the side. The horn blasted as the vehicle rumbled by, startling his horse. He recognized the vehicle immediately as belonging to Charles Paulson, the industrial magnate and richest man in Trenton, in fact, all of New Jersey, maybe even the entire East Coast of the Federated States. As Crosby worked to settle his horse and keep his seat a voice boomed out of the vehicle passing him, "Roads are for cars! Keep your damn horse, and its shit, off the roads!" Then the vehicle passed beyond earshot. Crosby carried on, this time staying just off the side of the road.

He stopped at a saddlery just outside the city limits and turned in his horse. He walked to the corner and hailed an electric cab to his two room, downtown apartment.

It was getting on to evening and Crosby was hungry. He changed his clothes, grabbed a couple coins, had a sniff from his golden snuff box, and headed out the door to the corner diner. Crosby slithered up to the counter and had a seat. The waitresses all knew him and he had no need of a menu. He ordered a cottage pie, and a cup of coffee. He needed to collect his thoughts before he could make another move.

The doe-eyed waitress with the nice smile delivered to him a steaming hot cup of coffee and Crosby was just about to have a sip when he felt a heavy hand on his shoulder. He flinched because he knew who was on the other end of that hand, and they would want answers that he wasn't ready to give. It was Henry Penry, one of Calabricci's goons, his right-hand man, in fact.

"Crosby, glad to see you back so soon," he said. "The Boss wants to see you. Now."

He didn't need to emphasize the 'now' part, Crosby had no doubt about when. It was the 'what' part he was concerned with and his trepidation was beginning to grow. Tiny beads of sweat were already beginning to trickle down the back of his neck.

"Sure Henry, sure. I was just going to grab a bite to eat and come right over to see him, in fact."

"Right," Henry half-growled. "The Boss doesn't like to be kept waiting, so why don't we just go now and you can come back and finish eating after."

It wasn't a question. Henry never took his bear paw off Crosby's shoulder and instead used his grip as leverage to twist Crosby from his seat and manhandle him out of the diner. Not one of the diners looked up from their meals. This was business as usual in Trenton and people knew better than to involve themselves.

Out front an electric cab idled silently and Henry hustled him inside then squeezed in next to him. The driver was a man Crosby recognized as being a regular driver for the Calabricci business. He said nothing, asked for no directions or destination, just shifted the car into drive and sped silently away from the diner.

Crosby knew where they were heading so he wasn't surprised when they pulled up a back alley behind a nondescript office building that faced the docks. Henry motioned him out of the cab, then sidled out behind him. Crosby knew the way so he led the big man into the building and up a long set of stairs to the Calabricci offices that occupied the top floor.

At the top of the stairs was a small desk where Calabricci's secretary, Polly, sat. She was pretty, with bushy blonde hair and blue eyes, not even taking into account the way her corset pushed her bosom to death defying heights. Demure was clearly not what she was aiming for when she got dressed each morning.

"Officer Crosby, how nice to see you," she cooed sweetly as she rose to her feet. "Mr. Calabricci is anxious to see you. Henry, you know the way."

Crosby knew her sweet smile and quiet nature belied the truth: Mr. Calabricci was obviously not happy. And even if he was, he wouldn't be once he heard what had happened at Princeton.

With a subtle shove to his shoulder, Henry guided Crosby toward a large frosted glass door at the end of a long hallway that led away and behind where Polly was seated. There were numerous other doors at intervals down the hallway, but they passed them all without hesitation.

The words "Business Manager" was etched into the front of the frosted glass door. Henry pulled him to an abrupt stop in front of it, and rapped his knuckles against the glass three times in short succession.

"Come," came the voice of Nick Calabricci from inside. Crosby had already learned to recognize it.

Henry opened the door slowly and motioned Crosby inside, but he closed the door again without entering himself.

Nicolas Calabricci, Nick to everyone who knew him, was seated at an ornate oaken desk. Behind him a set or large glass windows looked out onto the river. It was dusk, and the gas lamps of the dockside cast an eerie glow on the opposite banks of the Delaware.

"Officer Mark, come in, come in," he sounded surprisingly calm, a state which Crosby felt certain wouldn't last. "Have a seat." Nick was known for his explosive temper and had a reputation for not dealing well with the failings of those who worked for him.

Mark Crosby was ostensibly a patrolman with the Trenton City Police, but he was also an employee of the Calabricci family business. He had to supplement his income if he intended to survive, and joining with the Calabricci family was also a way of solidifying his chances for advancement in city politics. Today, patrolman, tomorrow detective; next year chief and from there perhaps the office of Mayor of Trenton. Crosby was hardly the first patrolman to join with the Calabricci family, but he was definitely the only one with such lofty pursuits.

"So, I understand you followed up that lead I sent you," Calabricci said, opening a small wooden box on his desk and retrieving a plump cigar. The Calabricci family had made their fortune in the cigar business almost three decades earlier. They had long since branched off into other types of "business" but cigars remained a point of pride for them.

Calabricci offered Crosby a cigar, but the young man respectfully declined. He'd simply never developed a taste for smoking. His enhanced snuff was more than enough, although he refrained from retrieving it from his vest in front of Mr. Calabricci.

"Well, uh, I went to Princeton as we discussed but I'm afraid I didn't learn anything new," he said

Calabricci was leaning back in his chair, now puffing on his well lit cigar. The smoke wafted across the desk and filled Crosby's nostrils.

"Did you find Miss Lowell?"

"Yes," Crosby said. "I spoke with her but she was reticent to reveal a location for her father. Although she did admit to knowing Professor Nettles."

"That's interesting," Calabricci said, waving his cigar. "Well, this was just your first meeting. When you meet with her again she's likely to become more trusting, more willing to divulge what she knows about where her father might be."

Crosby felt an icy chill creep up his spine and a sickening feeling form in the pit of his stomach.

"Well, uh, I'm not sure that will be possible, Mr. Calabricci," he said.

"Mark, look, call me Nick, please," he said with a wry smile. He turned his chair to face him now, directly across the desk.

"Nick, yes sir, Nick," Crosby smiled, but his stomach was roiling and the icy chill was growing colder.

"So, um, why not?"

Crosby froze. "Sir?"

"Why no second meeting? The whole point of this meeting was a sort of introduction, setting up a relationship which would help you ingratiate yourself into her confidence and lead her to tell you – and us – what you – we-- want to know, right?"

Calabricci tapped the ashen end of his cigar into the large glass ashtray, but his eyes were locked with Crosby's.

For a moment Crosby thought he was going to vomit. His stomach was now a stormy mess and the ice in his spine was spreading across his chest. He stammered; his tongue betrayed him when he needed it most; he had no idea what to say.

Calabricci broke the silence.

"Henry," he boomed.

The door behind Crosby opened and he heard Henry's voice. "Yes, sir, Nick?"

"Tell me what young Mr. Crosby has been up to today. He seems to be unable to recall key details. Which might be of importance to us in this endeavor."

"Sure, Nick. He hired a horse outside the city limits and rode to Princeton where he changed horses and rode straight to the university. He got Miss Lowell's class schedule from the main office then waited for her in the courtyard, just outside her classroom, reading a newspaper. After her lecture finished—I mean, I guess it was a lecture, what do I know about college, right?- (Nick chuckled, but Crosby was frozen in place) he met up with her. He seemed all charm and stuff, like a real nice guy. They took a stroll, chatting like, then Crosby put his hands on her and the next thing you know some guy comes out of nowhere and takes our boy down like a sack of potatoes. He grabbed his hat, didn't even dust himself off, and lit out of there like a cat with its tail on fire. It was a sight, boss."

Crosby was staring straight at Calabricci, watching to see what effect the story was having on the man's face. He wasn't happy, obviously, but it was something else, some blackness inside Calabricci's head which was suddenly coming to the forefront that made the young man squirm in his seat.

"Thanks, Henry, wait outside," Calabricci suddenly snuffed his cigar into the big glass ashtray with violence.

Crosby couldn't see himself, but he could feel the blood drain away from his face.

"So, Mark," Calabricci said as he continued to stab his now blunted and stubbed cigar into the ashtray. "Had a little tussle, did we?"

"Well, a small one, yes, but -"

"But what? Did you not hear me when I told you to keep this whole thing low key?"

"I thought a little -"

"You thought? You thought! I don't pay you to think, I pay you to do exactly what I tell you to do and nothing more. Henry!"

The door opened again. "Yes, sir?"

"Henry, do I pay you to think?"

"No, sir."

"Right, Shut the damn door."

"You see that? Henry understands his job, of course he's been doing it longer than you have, so maybe that's the problem."

Calabricci stopped talking and leaned back in his chair.

Crosby sat, frozen in place, hardly able to breathe for fear of inciting the man before him to some form of violence.

"I'll tell you what we're going to do, Mark," Calabricci said, very calmly, very quietly, yet not without a hint of malice. "You've screwed this all up for us. I have no choice but to take you off this job, give you something else to do to keep you busy. But stay away from Miracle Lowell and stay away from this whole business. Understood?"

Mark nodded, "Yes sir, Nick, sir."

"That's Mr. Calabricci to you now, Mark. You ruined your chance at comfort and friendship. Trust has to be earned Mark, and so far you are off to a very bad start in that department."

Crosby sank a little deeper into his chair.

"Henry!" Calabricci called again.

"Yes, sir?"

"Our patrolman friend here had to take a sick day today to go out on his errand and screw everything up for us, didn't he?"

"Yes, sir."

"Then I suppose, in order to maintain his cover he needs to be sick, doesn't he?"

Crosby felt his stomach churn.

"Yes, sir."

"Take care of that for me, then, will you please? See to it he gets to a doctor, then gets home alright, and can make it back to work in a day or so, but definitely has a good reason for missing work."

"Yes, sir. Maybe he should have an accident? I hear household injuries are on the rise."

Calabricci laughed. "Sure, that's a great idea. In fact, I think he might have fallen down some stairs. What do you think, Mark. Stairs ok with you?"

Crosby was completely paralyzed with fear now. He could say or do nothing, except sit.

"Stairs it is, then. Henry- handle this for me if you please."

"Right away, sir."

Crosby felt Henry's heavy hand grab him by the shoulder and haul him up and out of his chair. Henry outweighed him by at least 150 pounds of muscle, and stood at least a head taller. Crosby, by comparison, was not much more than a rag doll.

"Oh, and Mark," Calabricci said. Henry stopped, and swung Crosby away to face his boss. "Next time I tell you to do something, don't think for yourself; don't re-evaluate my plan, just do it. Ok?"

Crosby nodded, but his effort at mustering up something to say in his own defense failed in his throat.

Henry hauled him out the door, dragged him down the long hallway of doors to the top of the staircase.

Chapter 7: Paulson's Plan

Henry Paulson seemed relaxed and calm as he pulled away from Princeton University in his steam powered carriage, basking in the luxury of his leather seats and mahogany wood, but inside he was furious. He was the wealthiest man on the East Coast and would not be thwarted in his efforts by a young girl with more bosom than brains.

Paulson flipped a switched on the armrest.

"Callis," he said.

"Yes, sir," came a crackling reply.

"Bring me to my lawyer's office, straight away."

"Very good, sir."

Paulson settled back in his seat. He knew exactly how to handle this situation in such a way as to force the unwilling to willingly divulge what they knew.

Paulson was an avid hunter, known for his ability to flush the prey he sought, so as to have the best shot. He never returned from the hunt empty handed, and he did not intend to spoil his so-far perfect record now.

Paulson's steam powered carriage was much faster than a horse, and much more reliable (not to mention comfortable) than the newest electric cars roaming the streets. And even the electric cars, powered as they were with small steam driven dynamos, relied on his company. He made money no matter sort of motorized vehicle people chose to travel in. He relaxed and enjoyed the ride.

On the trip back to Trenton, Paulson considered the implications of what he was about to do. He chuckled to himself, knowing full well that the public would believe that what happened was simply the result of an overzealous utility attempting to squeeze every last penny from its customers. In the wake of what happened in Trenton the natural gas utility would find its reputation further tarnished and

Paulson would see his own stocks rise. In fact, this might be the perfect time to increase his investments in alternative fuel sources. Steam was steam, after all. It didn't matter so much how you made the steam, so long as it was captured and put to good use, generating electricity or powering manufacturing or helping people get from place to place.

Natural gas, on the other hand, was dangerous. It was explosive, after all, and anything explosive was inherently dangerous. This was an incontestable point. Natural gas burned, that's why it had once been used exclusively to light the streets and homes of people in all parts of the civilized world. But with the recent advent of the use of electrical lights, people suddenly had a viable alternative. Gas mains could be replaced with electrical wiring; dangerous natural gas could be replaced with safe, and Paulson would argue more effective, steam powered electricity generation.

It had taken him decades to build his steam empire. As the natural gas utilities had struggled to hold on to their empires, he had struggled to keep up with the explosive growth of his own. Finally the day had come when the war between the day was at a tipping point. Every new natural gas disaster was more ammunition in his argument against it. So too, did every steam boiler explosion hurt him, but they were fewer, more isolated, and less likely to make the national press the way a natural gas explosion would.

Paulson needed to dominate the natural gas utilities one way or another. True, he already had enough money for his own and several more lifetimes of extreme luxury, but this mattered little to his over-achieving nature. He would settle for nothing less than total dominance, no matter what the cost.

A sudden thought crossed his mind and he grabbed the tele-communicator from the armrest. "Operator? Paulson here. Get me Michael Carmichael, 225, if you please."

Carmichael handled all his investments and right now, he needed to make some subtle trades.

The office receptionist picked up first and Paulson introduced himself then demanded to be connected to Mr. Carmichael directly. "Carmichael? Paulson, here. I need you to buy another 1000 shares of that Brazilian company—yes, yes, the one with the trees. I predict we'll be selling more newspapers very soon and I want to get ahead of the trend. What? Hemp? No, man, good god, what are you thinking? Those people need to be run out the country on a rail! I won't be giving them any of my money any time soon!"

Paulson disconnected without a goodbye then returned to his thoughts. After his conversation with Carmichael he was thinking about the hemp growers. They were holding sway over a great many industries he wanted a stake in. His efforts at wresting control from them had so far been thwarted by their environmental lobbyists; a bunch of tree hugging, animal lovers who had descended on Washington like vultures looking to pick clean the bones of Industry before it had fully delivered on its promise to transform the world. This was similar to the problems he was having in Pennsylvania, where efforts to increase his holdings in coal production were being stymied by labor groups hellbent on delivering something they were calling a "living wage" for anyone in the mines. This made costs associated with coal production much higher than they needed to be, making natural gas a more reasonably priced alternative. Coupled with the fact that at least two of the major coal producing entities in the region were still holding out for more money, left Paulson with just a few small coal producing mines, and little alternative but to buy the coal he needed from them. These problems in Pennsylvania had led him to invest in an idea brought to him by one of the many researchers in his employ: Professor Harold Nettles. The mans ideas were arguably beyond mortal imagination, but Paulson thought they were worth the few thousands he said he needed to test his theory. Once the initial test showed the concept was valid, Paulson had ponied up the money Nettles said he needed to finish his project. Of course he had requested absolute secrecy and his own laboratory in which to work, neither of which was a problem for Paulson. He rented the top floor of a warehouse down by the river and stocked it with all the raw materials the professor had requested.

After almost two years work Nettles was due to deliver the finished project when something happened.

The newspapers claimed it was a natural gas explosion, but this was due to gossip and rumor started by operatives working for Paulson. Yes, the explosion had been caused by natural gas, but it seemed highly unlikely a leak or faulty system was to blame.

The headlines read: "Natural Gas Claims Another Victim!" but the reality was that no body was found. It was as if Professor Nettles had simply vanished in a puff of smoke. It was a parlor trick to be sure and one which Paulson did not appreciate. He expected a return on his investment and he was bound and determined to get it, if he had to chase Nettles to the ends of the earth.

Lost in thought he almost didn't notice when Callis slowed the vehicle.

Paulson grabbed for the switch: "Callis, what's going on?"

"It's a horse sir, and rider, in the road ahead. Just a precaution so as not to startle the horse, sir."

"Damn the horse, man! Accelerate now and sound the horn! I have an appointment to keep and I won't be delayed by some backward bumpkin!"

Callis blasted the horn and as they passed the man Paulson slid across the seat to be closer to the rider, opened the window and shouted at him: "Roads are for cars! Keep your damn horse, and its shit, off the roads!"

The steam carriage rumbled by, leaving the rider to struggle with his horse on the side of the road.

Paulson chuckled to himself at the sight, then offered more silent curses at the man.

"Dumb animals! The horse and its rider," he said to himself. He settled himself into his seat and delved deeper into his thoughts again.

The steam carriage slid against the sidewalk in front of the office of "Steersman, Lyle and Hardwick, Esq." These were the official attorneys of Charles Paulson and his assorted holdings. Paulson was their only client, and he gave them as much work as they could handle. Or course Lyle and Hardwick had died years ago, so only Steersman remained to handle the work. He just never bothered to change the sign.

Callis opened his door and Charles Paulson climbed out, crossed the sidewalk and strode into the office as if he owned the place. In fact, since he was their only client he practically did own the place after all.

The receptionist at the front had just enough time to say "Good day Mr. Paulson" before he hustled across the marble floor and into the office of Robert Steersman.

Steersman was a short, large man, with a dark brown handlebar mustache he kept delicately curled up and nearly around his eyes like a furry pair of spectacles. Though it was odd, Paulson allowed him to keep it simply because it amused him. Not much in life made Charles Paulson laugh so when something did strike his funny bone he considered it precious.

"Steersman," he boomed as he walked into the office.

"Mr. Paulson," Steersman said, as he hurriedly rose from his desk, shuffling some papers to the side. "I wasn't expecting you. Is there a problem?"

"Damn right there's a problem," Paulson said. "I cornered a quail and I need to flush her out of the bush she is hiding in."

Steersman looked confused for a moment. Then, "I assume we're not talking about birds, sir?"

Paulson stared at him a moment, smiling at handlebar mustache in spite of the seriousness of the business at hand.

"Very astute Steersman," he said. "I knew I kept you on retainer for a reason."

Steersman smiled, and took his seat behind his desk, motioning for Paulson to do the same at the chair opposite him.

"Well, I'm sure something can be arranged. What did you have in mind."

Still smiling Paulson looked right into the eyes of his attorney and said, "I want to blow up Princeton. Well, not the town, just the university. Tonight, if at all possible. Starting with the men's dormitories."

Steersman didn't blink. "Very good, sir. Shall I contact our usual man?"

Paulson, still smiling, said, "Yes, that will do nicely. See to it that the ladies quarters are completely untouched, however, and emphasize this point with him. I won't tolerate any mistakes."

"Understood, sir. Of course you won't-you never do. I'll make some calls immediately. Say nothing more about it. It will be done as you request."

Paulson stood abruptly.

"I expect it to be, Steersman. Nothing less from you, of course."

Steersman rose as rapidly as he could to follow Paulson's lead, but by the time he was to his feet Paulson was already out the door, grunting goodbye to the receptionist, and out the door.

Steersman sat down. He turned and looked out his window at the busy street beyond. This was a slightly more audacious request than Charles Paulson had ever made before, but no less possible. He wondered briefly what the larger impact would be, then dismissed the thought. Surely Paulson had good reason to go to such lengths. Steersman's job was not to question, merely to do as he was instructed.

He pressed a button on the side of his desk and a buzzer rang in the outer office. His secretary came hurrying in, buttoned up in a very professional looking dress.

"Yes, sir?" she said.

"Send a courier to fetch Jaxon Price. We'll be needing his services immediately. This evening in fact. If for any reason he is unavailable notify me immediately, otherwise I expect him in my office within the hour. Oh, and tell him to bring his kit."

"Yes, sir," she said, and backed out of his office, closing the door behind her which Paulson had left open.

Steersman turned back to face the busy street again.

Whatever Paulson had planned had better produce big rewards if the route there was through the decimation of one of the continents most prestigious universities. There would surely be a more thorough investigation of this than any previous attempt to make the natural gas companies look bad. At least he assumed that was the goal. In reality, Steersman had no idea exactly what Paulson had planned, and it was better that way. It was enough that he was responsible for arranging the various acts. Having too much foreknowledge would be simply too much risk.

Once inside his steam carriage Paulson was much more relaxed than he had been just minutes earlier. He was so relaxed, in fact, that he ordered Callis to make a brief stop before heading to the office.

"Let's swing past the Calabricci Cigar Factory first, Callis," he said.

"Very good, sir."

Flipping off the intercom to Callis, Paulson grabbed the tele-communicator once again.

"Operator? Get me the publisher of the Trenton Morning News."

While he waited for a connection Paulson fumbled his pocket watch from his vest pocket and checked the time. No wonder he was hungry, he thought, it's well past dinner.

Suddenly there was a voice on the other end of the line.

"Emory?" he said. "Charles Paulson here. I have a scoop on what might be the biggest story of the year for your little rag. Tomorrow morning your headline will be 'Princeton Tragedy Linked To Lowell Heiress.' Yes, you heard me right. Yes, that Lowell heiress. Trust me, all will be revealed sooner than you think. Now don't go broadcasting anything yet. I'll get you more details later—off the record, of course. Just consider yourself warned."

Paulson hung up the communicator and settled back into his luxurious leather seats, stroking the beautiful mahogany wood paneling, and chuckling ever so softly to himself.

"Miracle Lowell, you clearly have no idea who I am and just what I can do."

Chapter 8: Jaxon Price

Jaxon Price was attending to his bees in the backyard garden when his wife called from the porch.

"Jaxon! Courier here for you!"

Jaxon set down his smoker and casually walked away from his buzzing insects. He liked the bees. Yes, they did sting him quite often, but usually because of some mistake he made – moved too fast, or wasn't cautious about securing his suit. The bees had no interest in him, after all, if they sting they die, and nothing on earth is in a hurry to die. No, it was all about patience. When he was patient he could tend his bees, collect their honey and walk away unscathed. But if he was in too much of a hurry mistakes were made and he paid the price.

It was a good reminder and helped him maintain focus while working with high explosives. To rush, he told himself, is to die. Safely away from his hive of bees he stripped off his bee keepers gear and leisurely walked to the porch. Whoever was waiting for him would simply have to wait, he told himself, or they wouldn't. Made no difference to him either way.

He walked up the porch, slipped one arm around the waist of his wife and kissed her gently. She smiled and twirled out of his grasp. "Jaxon! The courier is out front." She swished away from him, off the porch into the backyard.

Jaxon walked through the kitchen to the parlor. The courier was a young man, seated in a cushioned arm chair, looking small and insignificant in the overstuffed seat. At the site of Jaxon Price he rose immediately.

"Mr. Price, sir," he stammered. "Message for you." He handed over a wax sealed envelope. Jaxon took it, turned around and slipped it open, breaking the seal with a calloused finger.

He read the note in a moment and turned back to the courier. "I presume you have a carriage waiting?"

"All-electric, sir," he said. "It's right outside. Ready when you are."

"Very good. Give me a minute and we can go."

Jaxon walked to fireplace, still holding the note. He slipped a match from his pocket and struck it against the bricks. He lit the note and tossed it into the ashes.

He went to the back porch where his wife was just coming back from feeding the chickens. The moment she looked into his eyes her sweet smile faded.

"Not more work?" she said.

He stepped to her, arms open, but she turned aside.

"I thought this sort of thing was over for you."

He sighed. "It's just -"

"One more job," she said, rolling her eyes. "It's been 'one more job' for the past three years. It's always 'just one more job' isn't it? And it always will be." She turned her back on him and walked into the house. He heard the screen door slam behind him but didn't turn around. He knew she had a point. It was always one more job than he expected, but what choice did he have? This is what he did. This was all he knew how to do. This was the result of his service in the Federated Militia fighting in the Caribbean War against the Spanish. It was the Federated States of America Militia and English Navy, against the French and Spanish combined military might. For three years they fought, hopping from island to island; on the Florida shores and the Jamaican coast. When the dust finally settled the Federated States of America gained four new members (Cuba, Jamaica, Haiti and Dominica) and the English gained a dozen or more islands stretching from Bahama, to Puerto Rico and all the way down to the coast of Venezuela.

Jaxon was there in Santo Domingo when they raised the Stars and Stripes with the four new stars representing the new federation members.

During the war the New Jersey 12th Regimental Militia taught him how to do one thing and do it well and that thing involved blowing stuff up. After the war they gave him a small monthly stipend and sent him home, back to rural New Jersey. His parents had died while he was away, and the family farm had been sold to pay off their debts. He returned to a small town where everyone was a stranger, but he was determined to find a way to make something work. He met a girl, Penelope, and married her. They had a small house in town and he took whatever work he could find on local farms. The work was hard and the pay was barely enough to keep the bill collectors at bay. Penelope was happy just being with him, being together, but Jaxon wanted more. He didn't like doing manual labor for someone else; watching them get rich off the sweat from his back.

But the fact was that a man with his specialized talents could only find so many ways to make a living. After the war the nation was primed for growth. Industrial growth was happening everywhere. Factories were sprouting like mushrooms after a spring rain. Most of the factories were powered by coal and getting the coal meant digging for it. Or blasting.

With nothing but his talent for blowing things up, Jaxon Price set off across the country to find his fortune. He kissed Penelope goodbye, promising her he would return a wealthy man or die trying. She just asked him to return with all his limbs.

First he tried his luck in Kentucky, blasting the tops off mountains to reveal the rich coal deposits beneath. It was a simple job and paid good money, but he found conversation with the locals less than stimulating and the work itself was dreadfully boring. So off to California he went, in search of blasting opportunities in the gold mines. Turns out most of the good blasting opportunities in the search for gold had already been exhausted, so he headed back east, to Utah, where he worked the Bingham Canyon Mine, blasting away the rock to reveal the green globules of copper beneath.

It was during his time in Utah that his calculated precision and exquisite perfectionism when it came to handling high explosives came to the attention of Charles Paulson. It seemed that Paulson was one of the largest providers of steam on the East Coast. His holdings in coal were going to make him a rich man, if only he could do something about his major competitor: natural gas.

Paulson made him a lucrative offer which included a nice sized piece of land back in his hometown. In return Price would put his specialized talents to work on projects Paulson felt were crucial to his success. It didn't matter to him that the work was illegal, or that in some cases people might get hurt. By now Jaxon Price had one thing on his mind, getting rich, and whatever he had to do to accomplish it, he was willing to do.

In the past four years he had used his skills to topple churches and courthouses; a couple factories and a hospital. From Pennsylvania to Vermont; New York to Virginia and all the way up to Maine. Wherever Paulson had holdings which weren't growing as fast as he needed them to, Price was soon there to lend a hand. Because of his deft touch and careful planning, Price had avoided anyone being seriously injured in the blasts. No one had as yet been killed, either. Natural gas was dangerous stuff, but it was also abundant. By comparison coal was dirty and much harder to transport around. It was also less likely to cause your building to explode. Paulson exploited this danger by having Price set charges which triggered a natural gas explosion. In the aftermath of the destruction the conclusions were always the same: a natural gas leak led to an explosion.

Price got paid. Paulson got rich. Nobody was the wiser.

Penelope had no idea what Price was doing for Paulson, or even that he was working for Paulson at all. All the work had been commissioned through an intermediary, Paulson's attorney, Robert Steersman. Steersman contacted Price, gave him his instructions and whatever funds or resources he felt he needed to get the job done, and settled up with him when it was time to get paid. Now that Paulson Steamworks had a stranglehold on the entire East Coast work had slowed down. Not much need in proving the same point over and over again. People had learned about the dangers of natural gas and cast their vote for politicians who were willing to tear out the pipes and switch to steam. Steam for heating their homes and steam for powering the electric dynamos that turned on their lights at night. Paulson controlled it all.

For his part Price thought his work had served its purpose and was looking forward to retiring to his bees and his farm and Penelope. His last job had been almost three months earlier and he fully expected the lull to continue. Although he was surprised to get a call to Steersman's office, he had no choice about going. All he had was due to the largesse of Charles Paulson. Price knew better than to bite the hand that fed him.

Walking back into the kitchen, past Penelope who stood gazing out the window at the field, he went to his bedroom and changed his clothes, throwing another change of clothes into a small bag. From under his bed he pulled out his tool kit – specialized fuses and concentrated blasting caps he needed especially for this type of work.

He walked back downstairs and went to the kitchen. Penelope was still there, still staring out the window.

"I'll call you if I won't be back within a day," he said.

She didn't turn around. He didn't bother kissing her goodbye, just turned and walked back to the parlor. The courier was still sitting in the over-stuffed chair, still looking none too comfortable.

"Let's go," Price said.

The courier popped out of the chair like a shot. "Right. Yes. Would you like me to take your bags?"

"No. I've got these. You just drive."

"Sure thing, Mr. Price. Sure thing."

He was out the door and into the electric car before Price made it down the front porch.

Staring out the window on the way into Trenton, Jaxon Price was amazed at how much it had changed since the last time he was here. It had only been a year or so, but new buildings were everywhere on the outskirts where a year before only farms were to be found. In the industrial district groups of goggle-eyed steampunks with long black leather coats were gathered here and there, most likely on break from the tunnels beneath the city or the Steamworks factory itself.

In the downtown, well-dressed ladies walked the sidewalks with brightly colored parasols while in the financial district well-dressed men hurried from block to block. Trolley's zipped along with electric cars. He noticed there were no piles of horse manure about as there used to be. No more horses were permitted within city limits; Jaxon had read the news story about the new city ordinance but hadn't been in the city since it was enacted. Now being in the city he definitely approved of the change.

The driver spun through the city with alacrity, waving to passerby and taking the occasional alley short cut to avoid stopped traffic. Rather than pull up to the curb in front of Steersman's office Jaxon instructed the driver to take him around the back and wait. He knew his way from there, having been this route many times before. He exited the car without a word, cases in hand, and walked through the back alley entrance silently.

Down the long hallway he came up behind Steersman's secretary without announcement and startled her.

"Mr. Price," she said. "I didn't hear you slip in. Let me ring Mr. Steersman."

In moments he was sitting in front of Robert Steersman as the man finished a phone call.

"Yes, that's right, I heard she was a member of some neo-revolutionary group called, uh-" he glanced out the window behind him at a passing movers truck. "-the Anti-Federalist Movement. Been giving soap box lectures to groups of students, spouting some really radical ideas about bringing down the government. I heard she has been telling students that even the institution they attend is fair game in what she called "the war against the established autocracy." Yes, you can quote me on that. My name? Right, it's-" he glanced out the window as a flock of pigeons exploded from the sidewalk. "-Byrd. Montgomery Byrd. Yes, I'm a student. Well, I'll be a freshman there next semester. I heard her speak whilst taking a tour of the university just last week. Terrible stuff she had to say. My mother and father were none too impressed, to say the least. Well, that's really all I have to say about the matter actually. I'm afraid I have to get back to my studies. Or my chores. Yes, my studies first and then my chores. Goodbye now."

Steersman hung up the phone. Pulling a white silk hanky from his vest pocket he dabbed it across his brow. This latest scheme of Paulson's was much more complicated than anything they had been tasked with previously. Having to phone the local newspaper and impersonate a student to implicate a young lady in what is likely to be a devastating event that will gain nationwide attention, was more involvement than Steersman would have preferred, but Paulson had demanded it. So too had he demanded that Price be told exactly what was going on and be given further instructions than he might normally expect.

Despite his reservations Steersman had no choice but to get right to it. So he did.

"Mr. Price," he said.

"Mr. Steersman," Jaxon said.

The pleasantries out of the way, Steersman got right to the point.

"Tonight your target is Princeton University. Begin with the male dormitory, target a few other buildings of note, perhaps the political sciences lecture hall and the chapel, but under no circumstances are you to target the girl's dormitory. Do you understand?"

"Princeton University? Tonight? That's not much time for me to plan. Normally a job like this requires weeks of planning, learning the routines of security and personnel, anticipating contingencies..."

"I don't care what it takes to get it done by tonight, but it must be done tonight," Steersman said.

Jaxon settled back into his seat and set his jaw.

"Not possible," he said.

Steersman knew from experience this was a negotiation he could win. He pressed the buzzer on the side of his desk and in a flash his secretary came rushing in.

"Yes sir, Mr. Steersman?"

"Pull the deed on Mr. Price's property holdings please."

"Yes sir," and she disappeared again.

"What are you playing at Steersman?" Jaxon said.

"I'm afraid I'm not playing at all Jaxon. Mr. Paulson wants this job done tonight. Period. If you won't do it we no longer have any need of your services. That means you're out of a job, and we take back that nice little farm of yours."

Jaxon thought a moment.

"You know nobody is going to be able to do this job for you tonight," he said. "It's not that I don't want to, it's that you are asking me to do the impossible."

Steersman brought his fist down hard on his desk.

"I don't want to hear what's not possible! I want this job done tonight, the way I requested it. And if you won't do it I'll find someone who can." He lowered his voice. "It's that simple. No work, no farm. What will your pretty little wife think of that, I wonder?"

Jaxon knew what she would think of that. Penelope loved the farm. The countryside had been good for them both and he didn't want to lose it.

"Fine," he said. "I'll do it. But I can't promise it'll go off without a hitch."

"Meaning?"

"Meaning I can't promise we won't have a chain reaction of explosions, or maybe just a single explosion. Or I'll blow myself to bits. I don't know. Like I said, I can make no guarantees. I'll do my best, that's all."

"You do the job Mr. Paulson expects of you, and nothing less. You hear me Price?"

Jaxon nodded agreement, his mind already awash in thoughts of exactly what he would need to make this all happen in the time frame requested, in the safest possible manner. The idea that he was likely to kill innocent university students and staff members wasn't lost on him. But his time in the war had already numbed him to regrets such as those. Nobody was completely innocent. Work was work and this was the work he did.

He chose, right then and there, the safety of his life, his wife Penelope, and their life together over anything or anyone else. Steersman was still talking and Jaxon had to thrust his conscious mind to the forefront to acknowledge him.

"I imagine you'll be needing certain supplies. You can no doubt find everything you need at the usual place. If you need help, bring whomever you'd like, but you'll be responsible for their actions."

"Of course," Jaxon said. His mind was already slipping back to the job.

"Good. I took the liberty of pulling a map of the university grounds. It includes infrastructure details such as gas and electric lines. I imagine that will be useful to you?"

"Yes, of course. I'll need all the help I can get. And a little luck wouldn't hurt either."

Steersman peered at him. "You up to this job Jaxon, or not?"

"Of course I am."

"Because if you screw this up there will be hell to pay."

"There always is," Jaxon muttered, turning to go. "I'll need to get started right away-"

"Oh, Jaxon, one more thing," Steersman said.

Jaxon stopped, turned back.

"There's a girl on campus. A Miss Miracle Lowell. She will be staying in the ladies dormitory. Be certain you leave that building completely untouched. Start with the men's dormitory, progress in any direction you choose, but be sure that the ladies dormitory, and Miss Lowell, remain secure. Understood?"

Jaxon nodded. "Sure. Just add it to the list of ridiculous requests and near impossible duties I've been assigned. What if she isn't in the ladies dorm? What if she sneaks out in the night and goes to the men's dormitory for something and she dies in the initial explosion?

What then?"

Steersman smiled. "That would be an unfortunate turn of events, especially for you, Jaxon. As I said before, you do the job Mr. Paulson expects of you. No exceptions. No mistakes."

Jaxon considered this for a moment. "Do you at least have a picture of this girl, so I can make sure she isn't where she's not supposed to be?"

Steersman shouted for his secretary. "Do we have a copy of that Trenton Evening Times paper with the honors students at Princeton University? From a couple weeks ago, I believe. Yes. Bring it in here right away."

Steersman's secretary returned a short time later with a folded up newspaper and handed it over. Steersman spread the paper on his desk and started flipping through it. He came to a section in the middle with several large photos of students. There in the middle was a smiling photo of Miss Miracle Lowell.

Steersman tore the image from the paper and handed it over to Jaxon.

"Here. This should help you identify Miss Lowell."

Jaxon glanced at the photo. Pretty girl, he thought. I wonder what she did to deserve this sort of treatment. What did Paulson want from her and why didn't he just take it?"

"Anything else," Steersman was saying.

"No. I'm done here. I know what you want and I'll do my best to deliver it, as usual."

"Good man, Jaxon. You do just that and we'll be all settled up."

Jaxon knew better than to believe he would ever be done with Paulson, or Steersman for that matter, but at least he could keep them happy. For now.

Without another word he turned on his heel, walked out of the office and back the way he had come in. When he was gone Steersman called for his secretary again.

"Yes, Mr. Paulson?" Steersman had swiveled his chair and was gazing out the office window.

"I think I need some insurance," he said, without turning around. "Get me Mr. Calabricci on the telephone."

"Right away, sir."

When she left, Steersman sat staring out the window. "I have a bad feeling about this. All of this. But especially about Jaxon Price."

Chapter 9: Awakening

The next time Digby Ross opened his eyes it was still dark outside. His forehead felt cool and it was only with some effort that he managed to raise his hand and find a cool compress sitting just above his eyes. He tried to sit up but found himself not quite ready for the challenge.

"Mr. Ross, don't try to move. It is enough that you are moving-at last!"

He recognized the gentle timber of the voice, and his eyes moved in her direction, but they were not quite ready to focus. And he was not quite sure whose voice it was he heard – just that it was familiar and female.

A shadow came close beside him and he felt her touch on his shoulder.

"You are back among friends Mr. Ross," she said. "Don't try to sit up. You've had a rough time of it I'm afraid, and you no doubt still need some rest. Though you have been sleeping for a day."

Digby tried to speak but found his throat dry, his tongue as rough as sandpaper in his mouth.

As he attempted to say something a hand brought a small glass to his lips so he could drink.

The water tasted like metal, residue from a rusty pipe, he thought. His mind was slowly beginning to clear away the clouds even as he struggled to collect his thoughts and remember where he was; what was going on.

He squinted his eyes shut and felt a nagging ache on the back of his head. He reached up again, slid his hand to the aching spot and felt a bandage. It was carefully wrapped around his head, with thick padding at the back, right in the spot where the aching resonated. He shrank back a little from his own head.

"Relax, now, don't touch it," she said. "You had a rather nasty bump on the head. I don't know how you managed to stay upright for so long, in fact. We were afraid you might have cracked your skull."

The cool compress was removed and Digby managed to turn his head and watch as it was rung out in a nearby basin, the drips of water making a gentle sound in the porcelain bowl, each one causing just the slightest reverberation in his head.

The compress was pressed against his head once more and he felt the cool of the water seep into his forehead. She slipped it softly down across each cheek, and across the bridge of his nose and then his neck. Gently cooling and washing him.

The water was refreshing and he tried again to lift himself up onto his elbows, this time managing a slightly more upright position.

His eyes were becoming more accustomed to the dim light of the room and his brain was slowly clearing. He recognized Miss Kinder now. Darling Kinder, Miracle's roommate.

Quickly images came flooding back into his mind at the thought of Miracle.

The strange visitor in the fancy dress and hat; the mysterious Mr. Paulson in his steam powered carriage; the explosion.

His throat refreshed from a swallow of water he managed to croak out her name, "Miracle?"

It was a feeble attempt at a question, but Darling got the point.

"Don't worry Mr. Ross. Miracle is safe. She is right now arranging our passage somewhere, she hasn't yet told me her full intentions. Just that we are traveling soon."

"How long?" he croaked.

"How long until we go? She asked.

He shook his head, using his arm, now more freely his own to indicate his head.

"Oh, yes, how long have you been asleep. It seems you must have slipped unconscious during our carriage ride here, likely more injured in the explosion than any of us first believed. It has been a full day since that dreadful night, Mr. Ross, and we have been staying here at this - " she glanced briefly around her - "hotel, hiding in fear for our lives, while Miracle took to finding the answers she sought and I stood constant vigil at your side."

He managed a smile at her, though his mind was already racing with worry for his friend. "Thank you," he whispered.

She smiled, his eyes now accustomed to the darkness and more focused he could make out the slight look of worry lingering in them.

"I'm feeling much better," he continued. He pushed himself up into a full sitting position. He felt as he did the night his football team won the championship and he spent all that night drinking beer.

Technically, that actual night was still mostly a blur to him, but the feeling he had now was the feeling he had the morning after that night.

"Where is she now, Miss Darling?" he managed as he struggled to get comfortable.

"Who?" she asked.

"Miss Lowell. Miracle, of course. Where is she now?" he glanced around their small room. "Clearly she is not here at the moment."

"Oh, yes, indeed she is not. Sorry for my confusion but during the past day you have often spoken names and asked questions which I tried to answer only to find that you were simply speaking out loud in your delirium."

This gave Digby pause as he wondered what sorts of things he had said and what answers he had received in response.

"I'm sorry, Miss Kinder. That was rude of me. Of course. And I thank you for keeping such vigil; for caring for me. I am appreciative."

She smiled, and in the dimly lit room her perfect white teeth shone like a beacon.

"Of course Mr. Ross," she said.

Digby reached back and rubbed his aching head again. He pulled the bandage free, easing the ache somewhat while Darling fretted about him doing so.

"Has Miss Lowell left you some knowledge about her whereabouts now?"

"Why yes, yes she has. She has been out all evening to meet with assorted individuals who she believes might have some knowledge of Professor Nettles: where he is now, what he might have been working on, oh, and what was in the package he supposedly sent to her father."

"I see," he said. "Why is she out now, at night, alone?"

"So as not to be spotted by the Coppers, of course," she said, and turned to walk back in the direction of the little table where she must have been sitting when Digby finally roused himself.

Digby reached for the glass of water she had refilled and set on the small table next to him. He was still very thirsty, and as his brain continued to chase away the cobwebs he suddenly became aware that he was also quite hungry.

His hunger could wait for now. What he really needed was to get out of this bed, get dressed and find out what the devil was going on now, he thought.

As he guzzled his water, Kinder returned with a folded-up copy of the Trenton Evening News and handed it over to Digby.

He set down his glass and took the paper. There on the front page were pictures of himself, Miracle and a smaller one of Kinder with the caption: "The three bombing suspects escaped with the help of a Miss Darling Kinder....."

Digby stopped, shook his head to clear away what he thought was still a fog in his brain and read it again. The article which accompanied the photos of the three went on to explain how police were searching for them, believing they were responsible for the bombing at Princeton. Fortunately it made no mention of where the trio may have fled to, but did say authorities across the state had been advised and police in all surrounding areas were being notified. The paper also reported that Federal authorities were already on their way from Philadelphia to investigate.

He set the paper down, his fists clenching the newsprint fiercely. "These are damned lies!" he said. "We had nothing to do with this. What ever would have given them this idea?"

Kinder patted his shoulder. "Miracle says it was likely Mr. Paulson who 'tipped' them to us, believing that she would be forced to flee to her father where he could then follow and find whatever it is he's looking for."

"Blast!" Digby said, shoving the paper aside. He could feel his strength returning with every drawn breath. His heart was nearly racing now as he thought of Miracle out on the streets alone, at night, a wanted felon—or suspected felon, but wanted by the police nonetheless.

"Darling, er, Miss Kinder, I'll need my boots, if you please."

"Are you going somewhere? And please, call me Darling. I realize it's a ridiculous name but I've grown accustomed to it over the years."

He looked up at her. "Fine, Darling, my boots, assuming I still have my boots."

"Oh yes, they're here. Miss Lowell instructed me to also buy you some suitable clothes should you awaken enough in time to travel with us."

"Travel where?"

"Why, to see her father, of course. Miracle says she should conclude her investigation this evening and then we'll need to leave."

"Her father? But didn't you just finish telling me that is exactly what she believes Paulson wants us to do?"

"Yes, I suppose it is."

"Then why are we doing it? Why are we doing any of this? Why don't we just go to the police and sort this whole thing out now before one of us, like those poor souls at Princeton, ends up injured or dead?"

"Shhh—you must keep your voice down Mr. Ross. These walls are quite thin and I'm certain your voice is now strong enough to pierce them."

Digby hadn't even realized his voice had risen. He swung his feet off the bed and felt his head spin quite a bit more than he had expected. "Oh, Mr. Ross, I don't think this is the time for you to be up and about," Darling said. "Perhaps you should just rest a bit more. Let me get you something to eat. Build your strength back up. Miracle will return soon and she can sort it all out for you. She did explain it to me in more detail, but I was so focused on caring for you I must admit I didn't pay close enough attention."

Digby had made up his mind, however, and although he was ravenously hungry, he fully intended to get dressed and head out the door in search of his friend.

"My boots, if you please, Darling," he said.

She looked at him. "Hadn't we get you into some trousers first, Mr. Ross?"

He looked down at himself and noticed he was dressed in only a small nightshirt.

He looked back up, embarrassed, but she was smirking at him.

"Yes, of course, trousers then, if you please."

She turned and strode quickly to a nearby closet where she retrieved a complete set of clothes for him, quite well pressed and starched.

As Digby struggled to get them on she waited as far away from him as she could manage in the small room with her back turned toward him. She was fidgeting and lifting her feet and putting them down softly, yet somewhat frantically.

"I'm not wholly convinced you should be going out, Mr. Ross," she said, back still turned.

"Darling, if I am to call you such, by your first name, then I suppose you should do the same. You may call me Digby."

"Oh, of course Mr. - I mean, Digby. But Digby, I still don't believe you should be going out. You've been half unconscious for the past day, lying here in delirium, haven't eaten and have only had what little water I could force into you."

Digby, with one foot barely into his trouser leg stopped. He looked at himself, suddenly realizing in addition to desperately needing food he also needed a toilet. He rubbed his face and felt the stubble of a full days growth.

"I suppose there is some merit to what you are saying," he said. "In fact, have we a private bath in this room?"

She lifted one arm and pointed to a small door adjacent to the closet.

"Right," he said. "Let me just attend to a few things." He started to rise, swayed unsteadily on his feet and sat back down. She half turned at this, then turned back again, her foot stomping silently. Digby tried again and made it to his feet, one hand on the wall nearest him. He moved slowly toward the lavatory, inching his way across the floor and along the wall as he went until he reached the door.

Closing the door silently behind him he looked at his face in the mirror. Instantly he understood why Darling had made such a fuss. He looked very much like a cadaver just risen from a freshly dug grave. His eyes were sunken with a somewhat glassy look and dark circles in rings around both. After a couple days of not shaving he was desperately in need of a razor and now, in this confined space, he could smell himself for the first time. A mixture of sweat and sickness, it was not pleasant.

He glanced around at the wash basin before him as a slight rapping came at the door.

"I took the liberty of securing you a razor," she said. "It's behind the mirror. And you've forgotten your clothes, but I have them here for you. I hope I chose the correct sizes."

Digby pulled open the tiny door and took the clothes she proffered him. Then he turned back, opened the mirror, found the razor and began shaving. His hand was unsteady at first, the throbbing in his head still somewhat strong, but he managed to get through it without too much bloodshed.

He washed his face and dried it on a nearby towel. He pulled loose the shirt, suspenders and slacks from the hook where they were now hanging on the back of the door. There were also a pair of clean socks and underwear and a small baby blue bow tie. The bathroom was slightly smaller than he would have liked for getting dressed, but he made do. Once he struggled into them he checked his look in the mirror and found that although his eyes were somewhat sunken and dark he could easily pass for overly tired as opposed to half-dead. It was only then, gazing at himself in the tiny bathroom mirror, that he realized he hadn't been dressed.

Someone had stripped him naked, out his pajamas – where were his pajamas? – and been caring for him, half-naked, these last few days. Miracle. Surely it had been his friend, Miracle. Not Darling. He hardly knew her. It simply would not have been proper for her to see him in his altogether, even under such dire circumstances. Yet surely, that is what must have happened for Miracle has been out doing god-knows-what and for god-knows-what-reason.

He looked at himself in the tiny mirror one last time, straightened his bow tie, then pulled open the bathroom door. Darling was standing right there and was slightly startled at the abruptness with which he had opened the door.

"Oh," she said. "You were quiet and I was concerned." She turned away, a slight pink blush beginning to color her cheeks.

"Quite alright Darling," Digby said. "I have the feeling you and I have become quite close today. Well, perhaps you've been close, as I was unconscious. Someone disrobed me and I can't help thinking it was you."

She said nothing, but the pink blush of her cheeks turned a deeper red and began to spread down her neck and across her chest. He took her reaction as affirmation and decided for her sake to quickly change the subject. He was suddenly very hungry.

"Would it be possible to get something to eat?" He asked, smiling.

She exhaled sharply, then, "Oh, yes, of course. I have some fruit and nuts or some cheese; I could pop down to the shop and get you some soup if you prefer; whatever you feel you could eat."

"Honestly, I feel as if I could eat a horse," he said. "Whatever you have is fine. Then we best be off to find Miracle and start sorting this entire thing out."

Darling rushed to a small cabinet while Digby sat back down on the bed to catch his breath. While she rummaged around, he considered something, then –

"Thank you, Darling," he said.

She stopped and turned slightly toward him. He was smiling at her.

"Thank you for caring for me while I was unwell," he said.

She smiled, but quickly turned back to what she was doing, replying over her shoulder. "It's quite alright Mr. Ross," she said, forgetting to address him by his first name as he had asked. "My father insisted I learn some general nursing skills. 'Never hurts to be prepared,' he told me. And apparently he was right."

She turned back to Digby smiling, with a tray brimming with assorted fresh fruits; a small bowl of nuts and a little block of cheese wrapped in cloth. She placed the tray in his lap then poured him a glass of water from a nearby pitcher.

While Digby ate, Darling talked about the day's weather (quite warm for Autumn) the latest news (other than their fugitive status, of course) and what they knew about the injured and dead at Princeton (many that Digby knew, including his roommate.)

When he finished, Darling took the tray away, setting it on the top of the little cabinet. She turned toward him, pressing her dress down as if fearing it was wrinkled, while Digby rose to his feet, steadier than he had been not so long before.

"Alright Darling, are you ready?" he asked.

She looked unsure of herself; of him; of the plan to go out looking for Miracle in the dead of night, but she nodded anyway.

"Alright Digby," she said. "If I cannot talk you out of this then I suppose I am."

Digby smiled at her. "That's the spirit old girl!"

She smiled back.

With three tentative steps Digby reached the door to their little room, and with one hand on the doorknob turned to Darling.

"Now, let's go find Miracle Lowell," he said and pulled open the door.

Standing in the hallway in front of him was his friend Miracle

Lowell.

"Oh," she said, slightly startled. Digby was speechless. "I see you've finally decided to get out of bed. Just in time, I might add. Well, come along Digby. We've work to do."

Then she turned on her heel and strode away down the hall.

"Oh, and best to have Darling collect our things," she called over her shoulder. "We won't be returning here."

Digby looked at Darling, who was already rushing about the room, throwing things into a little bag.

"Nice to see you, too Miracle," he muttered. Then he held the door for Darling as she scuttled out of the room after Miracle, pausing only a moment to straighten his bow tie. Digby closed the door behind her and quickly followed after.

Chapter 10: An Angry Man

Jaxon Price knew all there was to know about explosives. How to use them, what to expect from a half stick of dynamite or a vial of nitroglycerin; how to blow the top off a mountain or how to collapse a cave tunnel. His years in the military and his experience since the war had given him an uncanny ability to know exactly how to do exactly what he needed to do, without error.

But tonight at Princeton University something had gone wrong. Something terrible. Price had been meticulous in setting charges on the men's dorm which would have made a great deal of noise, caused quite a bit of damage, but resulted in no injuries (unless someone had wandered down to the basement for some reason.) He hadn't been given enough time to do much more than that, even if he had chosen to disregard the lives of all the students and faculty. Time was his biggest enemy, so he did the best he could with what he had available.

Standing just outside the men's dormitory as the first explosion blew the top off the building he knew immediately that something dreadful had gone wrong. He had placed no explosives there; no reason for that to have happened at all.

That first explosion shook the very foundations of the building, sending debris 100 feet into the air like a geyser. Jaxon struggled to keep his feet as roofing materials rained down in the darkness. As he struggled to get a grasp of what had gone wrong there was another explosion on an entirely different building. The explosives he had set in the basement went off just as he had scheduled them, but they only added to the noise; they had nothing to do with the devastation he was witnessing all around him.

This, he thought, has nothing to do with me. Someone else has been at work here tonight.

Before he could wrap his mind around who was doing what, the university began erupting into chaos. Buildings were exploding and fires were burning. Almost immediately he could hear screaming; people were running around the quad, some on fire as they ran. Jaxon was aghast. He had seen so many things in his life, so much tragedy, but this – this was something altogether different. These weren't soldiers. These were children. Innocents.

Jaxon moved away from the men's dormitory, grabbing a man who was stumbling toward him in the darkness, blood running down his face and neck, his hair smoldering with soot. He helped the man to a patch of cool lawn far enough away from the building to be safe and sat him down. Then he went back for someone else. He could hear more explosions and saw pillars of fire rising up into the night sky all around him, but he was closer to the men's dormitory so he stayed there.

He had helped several young men to the lawn and sat or laid them down as he scrambled back to find others. The front wall of the building was a shattered mess—beds were hanging out windows and fires raged throughout the wooden interior, blasting up into the sky, lighting the grounds all around. Thick black smoke was being blown away from the front of the building by a strong wind which gusted up every now and again, so he could at least see. But the damage was incredible. The entire building would come down, sooner or later, he thought. How many people have died? How many more are going to die?

He cleared his mind and went back to grabbing whomever he could from what he considered the danger zone around the building and dragging them away to the lawn.

As he worked frantically to save as many young men as he could he became aware of a single voice rising above the din of screams and roaring fires. It was a woman's voice.

The front of the building was lit by the glowing orange flames. A young woman was standing at the foot of the building shouting up to someone. He heard her call a name: Digby Ross.

Price knew immediately who she was. He recognized her from the picture he had in his pocket. The picture of the girl he was to follow should she leave the campus. He finished setting another young man down on the lawn and rushed closer to the girl, Miracle, yet still with his eyes on helping anyone in need. Miracle twice tried to get inside the building but the stairs had collapsed and fire licked at the entry way.

She stood at the front of the building again, calling up to her friend Digby. Price assumed whoever he was he had been sleeping in one of the upstairs bedrooms. He scanned the windows above where Miracle was standing. One room, on the third floor, had a bed half hanging out the shattered window. It seemed Miracle was shouting toward it – at least that was the best Price could make out from his distance. It was a good bet that whoever had been in that room had died from the fire, the explosion or was dying from the smoke, Price thought.

Just then a shadowy figure suddenly arose from the bed, like Lazarus, and Price swore under his breath.

"Cripes! He's still alive."

Price stood a short distance away from Miracle – she had no idea who he was and took no interest-- and watched as she shouted orders up at her friend; as the man disappeared inside the smoke and fire filled room, then reappeared with something wrapped around his waist. Price was astounded to see the man jump from the window, unroll like a fluffy window blind, then jerk to a stop like a knotted yo-yo. Within a minute the man had worked the knots of his makeshift rope free and plummeted the remaining 10 feet or so to the ground.

Price considered moving to help them both, but before he could move another explosion shook the grounds. He whirled and saw plumes of orange fire erupting from another building on campus. Whoever was doing this is still here, he thought. They are still blowing up buildings, these poor kids be damned. I've got to put a stop to this.

Price began moving in the direction of the latest explosion, with one eye on Miracle who was helping her friend up. Back lit by the burning men's dormitory he saw the pair moving off, away from the building. As he made his way through the chaotic campus he was able to see that they were heading directly for the young ladies dormitory. Steersman had given him strict instructions not to damage that building. Price wondered if whomever was blowing up Princeton tonight had similar instructions.

He shook his head free from thoughts of Steersman as he stood in what he took to be the central garden of the university. He glanced around him at the burning buildings, noting in his mind which buildings had exploded in what order. Within seconds he was able to determine the movement of the person or persons responsible, and knew which building was their likely next target. Without a moments hesitation he took off at a sprint in that direction.

Like all the buildings on campus this was a large, administration building, likely empty this time of night. Brick on the outside, but with a dry timber infrastructure which would welcome the touch of any flame and no doubt burn easily. The front was dark except for the orange glow of the other burning buildings. Price quickly moved around to the side, expecting to need a fire escape or backside exterior stairwell to access the roof. In the darkened alley he collided headfirst into someone, knocking himself and their shadowy form, to the ground.

"Oooofff! Hey, watch it!" came a voice in the darkness.

"Who's that?" came another voice, several feet away in the shadow. Price had only moments to react. He leaped into the air and brought his boot kicking out in the direction he had heard the first voice.

There was a crunching contact and a howl of pain.

Three bright flashes of light and three matching pops! told him the second voice was armed with a gunpowder pistol and shooting wildly in the dark.

Price spun away in the darkness, then made again for the shadow he saw in the still darkened alley. He grabbed at it, clutching a coat or shirt – he didn't know which – and throwing the form over his shoulder and down to the ground with a thud. The gun went off a fourth time, but the voice was silent. Unconscious.

Price heard moaning from the direction of the first voice he had heard – the one who had already tasted his boot. His eyes were more accustomed to the darkness now and he could see a man lying there. With a quick leap he was straddling the man's chest, his hands around his neck, holding tight.

"Who sent you here!" he shouted. He leaned his face close to the man to get a better look. It was no one he recognized.

"Got off me! I ain't sayin' nothin'! Get off me!"

Price tightened his grip and the shouting voice became a strangled gurgle. Price released his grip slightly and the man gasped for air.

"You're trying to kill me!" he croaked.

"What the hell do you think you're doing to these kids?" Price shouted back. "This isn't a game. People are going to die here tonight and it's your fault. Not mine, you hear? Your fault."

The man was trying to get his hands under Price's to free his throat from the steely grasp, but it was no good. Then suddenly he stopped struggling.

"You – you're Price, ain't you?" the man said.

Price was frozen.

"How do you know who I am? Who sent you here?"

Even in the darkness Price could see the man's icy stare and vicious smile.

"Look, this is just a misunderstanding Price, we're working for the same guy, you and me. Us." he said. "We're all here just doing a job – the same job – for the same guy."

Price stared down at him. "Who? What guy?"

The man kept smiling up at him and said one word: "Steersman."

Before Price could think it through, make sense of what the man was saying he felt a sharp pain on the back of head. The second man must not have been unconscious after all, he thought, as he fell to his side.

"Forget him!" the second voice said. "Let's go. We done enough, we need to leave now."

"Nyah—this guy broke my nose," said the man who Price had been strangling, still gasping for air. "I owe him a little somethin'"

Price tensed himself, but there was little he could do in his groggy state to prepare for the steel toed boot that crashed into his ribs.

"There, how d' you like them apples," came the voice. Then they were gone.

Price struggled to his feet. His ribs were sore, probably cracked, maybe broken. He looked around, but in the darkness at the end of the alley he could see nothing. Whoever that had been was now gone.

Good. No more buildings should spontaneously erupt, he thought. With one hand holding his ribs he made his way back out of the alley in the direction of the ladies dormitory. There were now more students gathered here, some lying down, some standing, some helping and some dead. Young ladies were streaming out of the dormitory with bandages or sheets; blankets and pots of water. They were trying to help whomever they could. One of them approached

Price, seeing his disheveled appearance; blood on his mouth and one hand seemingly holding his ribs in place. He waved her off, insisting she help another man nearby who was badly burned.

All the while Price was scanning the crowd, looking for Miracle Lowell. She was the key to all of this – whatever 'this' was. He had to find her, find out what Steersman, no, Paulson, wanted with her and why he was willing to kill so many people to get it.

Stumbling around, slowly scanning, Price looked like one of the dozens of other young men still in shock from the circumstances. So when Miracle Lowell, Digby Ross and Darling Kinder came hurrying out of the dormitory they never noticed him. His was just another face in the crowd.

They were in such a hurry to get to Darling's carriage and get far away from the university that they didn't see him follow them to the stables; didn't notice a lone rider set off behind them; didn't notice him still when they stopped outside Trenton to sell off Darling's cab and horse and get a car into the city.

Price was careful and skilled enough to keep his distance and remain unseen by the trio the entire time. He followed them into the city, right to the dirty hotel they decided to stay in, right up to the tiny room. He noted how the boy, Digby, seemed to be injured, maybe even unconscious, and how Darling seemed to be caring for him while Miracle was busy making calls from local phone stations.

Price knew he couldn't just keep watch on them forever, he had to get back to warn Penelope. But at the same time he also knew Miracle Lowell was the key to finding out what was going on. He couldn't just lose sight of her for a day while he went home.

His ribs hurt. Each breath was a stab to his side, and he wondered just how bad the damage was. Didn't matter, he told himself. This is now a battle, and I'm in the midst of it.

When Miracle returned to the room it was Price's turn to use the local phone station. He dialed the number for his home and waited breathlessly while it rang.

"Hello," came a sleepy voice on the other end. It was not quite dawn and Penelope, who always rose with the sun, was no doubt still in bed.

"Penelope, it's Jaxon," he said.

"Oh, Jaxon. What's wrong?"

No time, he thought. No time for explanation. He was angry, and scared, but he had to focus.

"I need you to do something for me, and I need you to do it without asking me any questions."

Silence. Then, "Go ahead. I'm listening."

He consciously relaxed his breathing, and spoke calmly.

"Pack a bag. Leave the house. Go to your parents—directly to your parents—and wait for me there."

"Ok," she said. "How long will you be?"

He paused.

"I don't know. I just – I don't know."

"Is it bad, Jaxon?"

He paused again, thinking. He had never lied to her before and he wasn't about to start now.

"Yes, Penelope. It's very bad, and very dangerous. I'm into something, and I can't come home until I find a way out of it. Will you do as I ask?"

Now it was her turn to pause.

"Of course. I can be there within an hour."

"Penelope, one more thing. In the chicken coop, under the third bed, there's a case. Take that with you."

"What is it?"

"No time to explain everything, my love. Pack only a small bag, take the case and be out of that house before the sun rises, ok?"

"Of course."

"I've got to go now dearest," he said.

"Jaxon?"

"Yes?"

"Will I see you again?"

He could hear the emotion in her voice. Knew the thoughts and worries which were likely racing around her head.

"I'll do my best, love. I'll do my best. Now, go, please, and hurry."

He hung up the phone. Then he stepped out of the phone station and disappeared into the shadows.

Chapter 11: Steampunk Rules

"I'm not saying 'no' I'm simply asking why we need to walk into that cesspool of depravity before we do so!"

Miracle could tell from the tone of his voice that Digby did indeed mean "no" and so she would have to explain just enough to convince him it was in their best interest.

Digby, Miracle and Darling were huddled in the shadows of an Eastside alleyway, watching the pub across the street. The dirty wooden sign above the door read The Jack. A steady flow of local steam plant workers, more commonly known as steampunks, had been streaming into the place. The place was obviously popular with this crowd. The twanging of guitars and tinkling of a piano, along with the raucous laughter and cheering, could be heard even where they were standing.

"I need to speak to a man about a ship," Miracle said quietly. "A steamship, to be precise. And I know he can be found in there, tonight. In fact, he's waiting for me."

"Yes, you've said that already," Digby said. "But you haven't explained how you know him, who he is, or why we need to go in there tonight instead of waiting until tomorrow and meeting him someplace, well, less disreputable looking."

Miracle looked into the eyes of her friend and saw the young boy who used to chastise her for climbing too high in the old tree, or throwing rocks at the hornets nest to see what would happen. She had grown a great deal since, and while Digby was taller, stronger and certainly wiser than he was in his youth, he still seemed overly protective. She secretly thought it was cute most of the time, but at this particular moment she found it annoying. She took a deep breath, then said:

"Digby Ross, we have been framed for an incredible act of violent domestic terrorism because we refused to help people interested in finding my father, who they in turn believe can help them find a missing scientist who these same people believe has stolen something of considerable value from them. Are all these people connected? Are the people we know of the only ones involved or are there more people acting behind the scenes who are also bent on finding Professor Nettles no matter what the cost?"

Digby tried to open his mouth to retort, but she raised a gloved finger to his lips.

"In the meantime we are trapped in a city where every newspaper headline screams our names and every cop has been told to shoot us on sight. We have to get out of here, get to my father and find Professor Nettles before anyone else gets hurt. And to do that we first need a ship. And the man waiting for us inside that quaint little pub can arrange it for us."

She pressed her finger a little harder against his lips. His eyes were wide, then slowly his lids dropped and he nodded acquiescence.

"Well, I for one am excited!" Darling said. "I've never been to an actual pub before, my father said they were no place for a lady. But he did teach me how to hold my liquor – just in case."

Miracle turned to her friend and smiled. Digby too looked her way, Miracle's finger still pressed to his lips, his eyes now wide with surprise. Darling never ceased to amaze them both.

With Digby resolved to accept her reasoning, and Darling near giddy with excitement, Miracle led her two friends out of the darkness of the alley, across the street and into the pub. The music was much louder inside than it had been across the street. Someone was banging away on a piano, a joyous old bawdy tune, while a guitar and drums, cymbals crashing, collaborated. The air was thick with the smell of cigarette smoke, stale beer and soot. The floor was covered in ground-in coal dust and general dirt.

The place was crowded, with every table taken and folks just milling about in small groups. Long black trench coats, goggles and boots seemed to be the acceptable attire, as most patrons were dressed alike, with a few in just suspenders, trousers and boots with shirt sleeves rolled up. The bartender looked as if his last job had been as strongman at the circus. He had slicked back black hair and an unwaxed handlebar mustache that stretched across his face like the world's largest caterpillar. Here and there a busty waitress squeezed through the crowd with a tray of fresh beer, or fended off the gropes of a pub regular, laughing as she twisted and turned her way back to the bar, or to the table where she was headed.

Miracle and her small group squeezed through the crowd as quietly as possible, straight to the back. Digby was trying not to look too out of place, but he felt sure he was failing miserably. His face was a steely frown and he struggled to not make eye contact with anyone. Darling on the other hand was all smiles. Her bubbly personality was simply too much for her to contain and she found herself quickly inundated with an abundance of "Good evening Miss!" and "Fancy a drink?" and "Quick turn on the floor, Miss?" She politely declined, flashing her brightest smile, seemingly incapable of hiding the delight in her eyes, and hurried after her friends.

Miracle approached a table in the darkest corner of the back of the bar. A single jack booted young man sat astride his chair, turned backwards, with a hand rolled cigarette dangling from his lips. His face was dirty, his hair straight and black and pushed back from his forehead, held in place by a small black leather cap and a set of brass framed goggles. The collar of his trench coat was turned up, and the shirt he wore beneath, once likely white or gray, was covered with black smudges. His boots looked thick enough to crush concrete but he was tapping his toes gently in time with the music.

Miracle approached him directly, Digby and Darling close on her heels.

"Bernardino?" she said, above the din of the music.

His dark eyes were focused on the music, and he seemed not to notice her. But he held up a single finger to signal she wait just a moment. Digby was in a hurry and leaned past his friend to call the man out, but as he did the music stopped and the young man jumped to his feet, clapping wildly and whistling like a steam locomotive. In fact, the entire bar was cheering and calling for more. Digby glanced over his shoulder and noticed the musicians were setting down their instruments, the piano player standing up, reaching for a fresh beer. As the applause settled down Bernardino looked at Miracle, a bright smile on his lips.

"I see you made it ok, and you brought your friends," he said. "Very good."

Digby noticed that Bernardino spoke with an Italian accent. The dark hair and dark eyes made sense.

"Come sit down, please," he said. "Let us drink and talk. I think I have found what you have been looking for." He motioned for the three to join him at the little table, offering his own chair to Miracle, grabbing a chair from a nearby table and motioning to Digby to do the same at another table nearby. Since the music had stopped people were moving about, so there were more empty chairs than there had been a moment earlier.

The four sat down together at the tiny darkened table. Bernardino snubbed out his cigarette on the floor, then whistled again, this time for the waitress who immediately jiggled her way over.

"Another beer, Bernie," she said. "And what about your friends?"

"Nothing for me, thank you," Digby said without looking up, and Miracle shot him a look.

"I'd love a beer!" Darling called out.

"You got it, darling," the waitress said. "And for you, miss?" looking at Miracle.

"I'll have a beer and so will my joyless friend here," Miracle said, stabbing Digby with her eyes.

The waitress shimmied away, Bernardino actually turning his head sideways to keep her posterior in view as she made her way back to the bar.

"Bernardino, can we please do this as quickly as possible," Miracle said. "As you might imagine we must limit our exposure. The sooner we can get out of Trenton, the better."

"Relax, relax," he said. "I told you, this place is safe. Nobody but us Steamies in here and we have rules, you know."

"Rules," Digby said, glancing around at what he considered a pub full of unsavory types. "What kind of rules?"

Bernardino pulled a little pouch of tobacco from inside his trench coat and began rolling a new cigarette. "Steampunk Rules, fratello. Nobody sees nothing, nobody knows nothing. The City, she don't care so much about what we do down there-" pointing to the floor – "so we don't care so much about what they do up here. We come up here to have a good time; eat, sleep, drink, smile, that is all."

This last he said with eyes on Darling, and she instantly blushed, hiding her eyes.

"Glad to hear it," Miracle said. "Now, do you have the information we need?"

Bernardino meticulously spread the tobacco into his sliver of paper, and carefully began rolling it between his fingers. "Yes, yes. I said I had it, so I have it," he shrugged.

"Well?" Digby said expectantly, although he had no idea what information this man might have which they would need.

Miracle rested her hand lightly on his sleeve. It was enough to quiet his mouth, but it also set his pulse to quickening.

"Bernardino, please don't keep us in suspense," she said.

His cigarette now finished, he slipped it between his lips and reached back into his coat for a shiny lighter. He flipped open the lid and a flame erupted immediately. He drew a deep breath of smoke and blew it straight up above their table. With the cigarette now dangling between his lips he smiled at her.

"You have something for me, yes?" he asked.

Miracle reached her hand beneath the table, into her lap, and brought back up a small satchel. She handed it across the table to Bernardino and he took it quietly, slipping it into the folds of his coat.

"Don't you want to count it?" Miracle asked.

Bernardino smiled. "Signorina, please," he said, shrugging again. "What sort of a gentleman would I be if I were to display distrust to a lady such as yourself?"

His smile was disarming, and even Digby felt himself relax. This man, he thought, this dark and dirty man can be trusted. He wasn't sure how he knew it, but he did. Bernardino was trustworthy if for no other reason than because Miracle trusted him.

"You need a ship, I found you a ship," he said, puffing on his cigarette. "No questions asked, room for all three of you, destination of your choosing to be revealed once you get aboard."

"Is it safe," Digby asked. "Can you guarantee our safety?"

Bernardino frowned. "Nothing in this world can be guaranteed, fratello. Sorry. The best I can do is tell you that I am a man of my word, and this ship and her crew are as safe a place as any you might expect at this time. Safer surely than our fair City of Industry is for you at the moment, I'll tell you that."

The waitress arrived with a tray of beers. Leaning across the table, setting down the sloshing glasses she pressed her bosom into Digby's face. He tried to turn away but as he did, his nose was caught in the top of her blouse and he pulled it slightly down lower than it already was.

"Easy there handsome," she cried, laughingly. "I'm still on duty, you know." She set down the last beer, leaned close to Digby's ear and whispered, "But I get off in a coupla hours if you'd still like a peek-a-boo."

Before Digby could respond she turned and strutted away. He was left gaping in her direction. When he turned back to the table, Darling was staring straight at him, eyes like daggers. He blushed despite his best efforts.

Bernardino was sliding a slip of paper across the table to Miracle when Digby had composed himself. Miracle took it, glanced at it quickly, then secreted into her lap.

"Nothing until tomorrow morning, I'm afraid," Bernardino said. "It was the soonest, and safest, I could arrange for you. I will take you there myself."

"It will do," Miracle said.

"Now," he said. "We drink to your good health and safe travels!" He raised his glass. "Salut!"

Miracle raised her glass to sip, Digby fumbled his glass to his lips and took a swallow. Darling raised her glass with a look of sheer desperation. She brought the glass to her mouth, closed her eyes and started chugging. As Miracle, Digby and even Bernardino sat amazed, Darling drained her glass, slamming the empty vessel back down on the table.

"One more for the road!" she called.

There was shocked silence from her friends, but Bernardino cried, "Buono! Buono! Yes, another round here. Come my friends, we drink tonight, you travel in the morning."

Digby looked at Miracle, who shrugged a silent reply. Bernardino moved his chair around the table, closer to Darling, and summoned the waitress again.

The four of them sat drinking for a time, and soon the piano player struck up a tune again. Not long after the piano started Bernardino swept Darling onto the dance floor. Digby and Miracle sat awkwardly at the table still nursing their original beers. The music was loud again, so Digby leaned close to Miracle's ear to whisper - "You have what we need?"

She looked up at him and nodded, her eyes focused inwards. "I think so," she said.

She laid a hand on his sleeve again and leaned in closer.

"I'm sorry for all of this, Digby," she said.

He could see in her eyes she was. She was worried, about her father, about their friends at Princeton, about their current situation. He knew his friend, he knew how she thought.

Digby put his hand on hers.

"It's not your fault, Miracle," he said. "How could you have predicted any of this? And now you're doing what you do best – fixing things for everyone."

When the music finally stopped again Darling had consumed three beers, on top of the first which she had drained as easily as Digby might a glass of cool water on a warm summer day. She had danced with Bernardino and at least a half dozen other young men, twirling and laughing and thoroughly enjoying herself.

Digby and Miracle remained at the table, laughing and smiling at their friend. Digby's head had finally stopped aching, and he felt himself starting to relax. He was tapping his foot to the sound of the music and swinging his finger in the air like an orchestral conductor. He was having fun.

Darling sauntered back to the table, plunked herself down on a chair and exclaimed, "What a fabulous time I am having!"

Miracle smiled at her friend. Digby reached across and patted her sleeve with concern. "Why not settle down just a bit, Darling," he said, with a smile.

Darling frowned. "Oh, Mr. Ross, I assure you, I am just fine. In fact, I am better than fine. I feel – free! – for the first time in my life I feel free!" She threw her arms up in the air, jostling a man standing right behind her. He jumped back, cried favor, and promptly ordered Darling another beer.

In no time, Darling's new friend was seated at the table with the three friends and Bernardino. Their table was now the center of attention as Darling switched to shots of whiskey, and challenged the men to a drinking contest.

Digby expressed his concern to Miracle, but she smiled and told him not to worry.

Soon enough the piano player started up again, the guitarist and drummer seated behind him, and began a moving dirge.

Darling was drawn to the dance floor by yet another young man, and Bernardino reached out for Miracle's hand. She looked up at him and smiled, letting him lead her out to the floor. Digby was left alone at the table, watching his two friends slowly move about the dance floor. His eyes moved back and forth between the two women, finding himself suddenly on edge. These two young women, his young women. At least, he suddenly felt that way, that they were his—not his property, but his responsibility. That's what it was. He felt responsible for Miracle, of course, but now he felt responsibility for Darling as well.

And for the last couple days it was these same two young women who were responsible for him. It was Darling who had helped them all escape from the university, sold her carriage and horses for money they could use to hide, and survive; gave them time to resolve this situation they now found themselves in. It was Miracle who was planning, plotting; attempting to solve this mystery and rescue them all.

And there they were, dancing slowly across the wood floor of a dirty pub with a bunch of steampunks, in the city known as the technological hub of the Western world.

And he was sitting and watching them. Nursing the same warm beer he had been served hours ago.

The waitress sidled up alongside him, leaning her soft hip against his shoulder.

"Not dancing tonight, handsome?" she asked.

"I'm afraid not," he said, sheepishly.

"Good," she said with a wink. "You should save all your dancing for me."

Digby felt the smile creep across his face. She smiled back and sauntered away again to the bar. He momentarily thought she looked familiar, but decided he was simply imagining the familiarity.

He was feeling better. His friends were feeling better. He felt sure this whole situation would be resolved in short order, so he grabbed his half empty beer glass off the table and drained it in one swig. Suddenly he had a thought. He would go over there and cut in on the ladies dancing – one of the ladies. But which one, he thought.

He rose to his feet and made to move in that direction when there was a loud crash at the front of the bar. The doors burst open and Trenton police were suddenly streaming in the door, whistles blowing, batons raised above their heads. Leading the charge was someone he recognized. Crosby! Only he was dressed in a police uniform, with a bright brass-covered arm he raised over his head and brought crashing down on the closest lad. At his side was a pair of mustachioed men in bowler caps.

"Nobody move, this is the police!" Crosby cried. More shouts rumbled across the pub like cannon fire. Digby froze. The bartender jumped over the bar and landed with a crash against the first few coppers through the door, barely missing Crosby who was swinging his brass arm madly from side to side like a club. Steampunk patrons and coppers fell to the floor in a mass of arms and legs and whistles. The crowd suddenly erupted into a chorus of shouts and fists. Trench coats swirled, and boots were kicking out in all directions as more police rushed through the door.

The waitress screamed. The lads on the dance floor charged into the mass of police. Suddenly Miracle was at his side.

"Where's Darling," she shouted as a bottle went flying just above her head. Digby glanced around and saw Darling swinging a chair at a policeman who had her cornered near the piano. Digby said, "Stay here!" and charged across the crowded room, dodging batons and chairs. He brought his fist down on the shoulder of the police officer and the man crumpled to the floor like a rag doll.

Darling beamed at him. "Digby!"

"Come on," he grabbed her hand and pulled her back to the table, although as he did he realized this wasn't perhaps the smartest move. Miracle was there, watching the fighting with eyes wide open.

The three friends huddled around the table, when Bernardino flung himself in their direction.

"We must go!" he gasped at them. "Now!"

Digby, Miracle and Darling were all too ready to leave but all three noticed their exit was currently blocked by a dozen police officers, with more trying to squeeze through the door with each passing minute. The steampunk lads engaged them as they tried to work their way further inside, but slowly the defensive wall was giving way.

"My friends will hold them as long as they can," he said. "We must go while we still have a chance."

Miracle turned to him. "But where?" she said.

Bernardino whistled and four men from the back of the crowd positioned themselves carefully in front of the small group. Crosby and the rest of the police, still at the front of the pub, disappeared from view for a moment. Bernardino reached across their table and turned it over, revealing a trap door in the floor beneath.

"There, there," he said. He reached down for the metal handle and drew the door up, revealing a long dark staircase down.

"Come, come!" Bernardino said. "Per favore—we must exit these premises post-haste."

Darling went first, hurling a chair over the heads of their impromptu steampunk wall in the direction of the chaos before she went.

Miracle was next. Bernardino followed Miracle, while Digby lingered. Suddenly he felt hands on his hips turning him around. He raised his fist to strike but stopped short as he locked eyes with the busty waitress.

"I didn't even catch your name," she said, smiling.

"Digby," he said. "Digby Ross."

Then she grabbed him, pulled him down to her height and kissed him right on the lips.

"Pleased to meet you Digby Ross," she said, still clutching his lapels. "I'll see you later!" Then she spun him back around and pushed him toward the hidden staircase. He stumbled, caught himself and started down the steps.

The waitress definitely seemed familiar to him, and he looked up to say something about it, but she was already closing the door behind him. Down the steps he went, although they were more like a ladder. He dropped down to a dirt floor, and glanced left and right. There was a dim light to either side and for a moment he was frightened that he wouldn't find his way after his friends. Suddenly, to his right, a voice in the darkness. It was Miracle.

"Come along, Digby," she called. "And do be quick about it!"

Chapter 12: Into The Tunnels

Desk Sergeant Paul Pearcy had a sore bottom from sitting at his station all day and now late into the night. His wife would no doubt be waiting up, angry because she mistakenly believed he had gone out for drinks with his friends rather than come straight home after his shift. But the reality was that just as he was about to clock out for the evening his relief reported in sick and the detectives turned up with a couple dozen or so angry steampunk lads they had pulled out of The Jack on the Eastside. Part of some late night raid to catch the three fugitives wanted for blowing up the university a couple nights back.

Sgt. Pearcy knew all the details of that crime, and knew how the higher-ups had been busting everyone's hump to find the three and lock them up fast before the public had an outcry.

Trenton was a world class city, after all, and it just wouldn't do for a bunch of so-called anarchists to think they could blow up a nearby school, a world class university to boot, with impunity.

Sgt. Pearcy thought the whole thing sounded like a frame-up which would likely turn into a police cock-up, but then, what did he know. He was just a Desk Sergeant. Check them in, lock them up; answer the phones, take messages. His job was less than exciting but it was exactly what suited him.

No sooner had Sgt. Pearcy finished processing the last dirty steampunk, and was grabbing the phone to call his wife, when Patrolman Mark Crosby strutted up to the desk. His left arm and hand was covered in brass sheeting, the result of a recent accident. He looked like some sort of half-dressed rusty knight, Sgt. Pearcy thought to himself.

"Sgt. Pearcy, sir," Crosby said.

"Patrolman Crosby," Pearcy replied, the phone receiver first dangling from his outreached hand then being slid silently back onto its cradle. "And how may I help you this fine, fine evening?"

"I thought, since I was here, I might check on our little guest," Crosby said, his eyes shifting side to side, his voice a husky whisper.

Sergeant Pearcy never cared much for Patrolman Crosby. There was just something unsavory about the man. Too eager for recognition, maybe. Or, something else.

Pearcy knew exactly who Patrolman Crosby was talking about. The "little guest" in question was not the youngest person ever incarcerated in their jails, but he certainly was the quietest. Hadn't said more than a simple "please" and "thank-you" in the past few days. The charge sheet said the boy was arrested for defrauding a shopkeeper, but Sergeant Pearcy suspected something much more complicated was afoot. Especially since Patrolman Crosby had been the arresting officer. Sergeant Pearcy doubted anyone else in the station was even aware of the young man now sitting in a darkened isolation cell. Patrolman Crosby had been his only visitor.

"I'm willing to lay better than even odds he's still there, Patrolman Crosby," Sergeant Pearcy said. "But by all means don't take my word for it. Please feel free to check for yourself."

Crosby's arm clicked as he clenched his fist, staring now straight at Sergeant Pearcy.

"I think I will, Sergeant," he said, raising his shiny brass arm from the desk and turning away.

"Very good Patrolman," Pearcy said. "Do let me know if he isn't there, will you."

Crosby turned on his heel and walked away toward the jail cells, while Sergeant Pearcy reached again for the telephone. Dialing through to the operator Sergeant Pearcy was muttering something about "the whole thing's a little suspicious if you ask me..." when the operator picked up and asked him what number he wanted.

Crosby strolled down the hallway, his good right arm rubbing his brass encased left arm. The doctors told him his arm was fractured in at least three of places. (The story he told was the he suffered it during a "fall" down the stairs at his apartment when he was ill.) The brass sheath allowed him to return to work, and offered protection for his damaged arm to continue healing. It also made for a nasty club if needed, Crosby had learned.

Crosby passed a few cells, now crowded with steampunk lads, kicking the walls and shouting about "lawyers." He ignored them all and made for the two isolation cells at the end of the hall. The one to his left was empty. His little sneak-thief was in the cell on the right. Crosby slid the pass-through slot open and saw the boy sitting quietly on his cot, awakened no doubt by all the recent commotion. Crosby slid the pass-through slot closed, unlatched the cell door and walked inside.

Jeremiah Maddy looked up from his sitting position, a momentary gleam of hope in his eye. This was quickly extinguished as his eyes adjusted to the light and he recognized Patrolman Crosby.

Crosby looked down at his little felon and smirked.

"So, enjoying your stay?" he said. "Eating well, I presume? Likely a whole lot better than you would on the streets."

Jeremiah said nothing. His face was expressionless.

Crosby crossed the cell floor and sat himself down on the cot beside the boy.

"Are you ready to get out of here?" he said.

Jeremiah wanted to remain stoic but he couldn't hide his obvious relief at the thought of escaping his iron box.

"Indeed, I would sir," he said hurriedly. Although he doubted very much if the offer was genuine.

Crosby took a deep breath, extended his brass arm until it clicked and clacked into place. He worked the fingers like nut crackers, enjoying the look on the face of the little boy beside him.

"Good boy," he said. Crosby felt like a spider inviting the fly to his web for a feast. "I'm prepared to get you out of here young man," he continued. "I just need you to do one little thing for me. Do you think you could do that for me?"

Maddy was immediately suspicious, but he nodded agreement nonetheless. He had nothing but loathing for Patrolman Mark Crosby, and he seriously doubted the man truly had his best interests at heart.

"That's a good lad," Crosby said, stretching and clicking/clacking his arm again. "Word on the streets of Trenton is that nobody knows their way around the city of Trenton quite like Jeremiah Maddy. Is this true?"

Jeremiah nodded again, and said, "Like the back of my hand, sir."

"Good," Crosby said. "So, if I needed you to find someone for me –

and quickly, mind you – you could do that for me?"

Jeremiah ran a hand through his shaggy hair. Then, "I s'pose I could, sir. Indeed I could, sir."

"Good, good," Crosby said. "I'll tell you what, young man." He reached his right hand into his uniform pocket and fetched out the Atlantean dollar he had confiscated from the shopkeeper as evidence of the crime. "If you can find this person for me, and do it before dawn, I'll not only get you out of this cold cell you've called home these past few days, but I'll also sweeten the deal and give you back these ill-gotten gains of yours."

"But that was my earnings," Jeremiah cried suddenly, reaching for the coin impulsively.

"Now, now, young man," Crosby said, snatching the coin back against his chest. "Don't spoil it with your ragamuffin lying now." Jeremiah settled back.

"Good," Crosby said. "Now, do we have a deal?"

Jeremiah nodded.

"Right," Crosby said. "Let's go."

Bernardino lead the way through a maze of underground tunnels with Miracle, Darling and Digby trailing close behind. Every turn added to his companions confusion but he seemed quite sure of where he was going. It seemed as if they had already walked for miles, but no end was in sight. Every now and then Bernardino would turn back to them and say "Just a little farther now." They just followed quietly.

Suddenly the wooden beam lined dirt tunnel gave way to a brick lined tunnel. A little further along and they came to a big iron door. Bernardino turned to them again.

"This door will take us into the steamworks, the tunnels that run beneath all of Trenton," he said. "Everyone we pass will be like me, steampunks who work here. No worry. They won't say nothing. We can pass right through."

Everyone nodded agreement, though they weren't quite sure what to expect. It just seemed the thing to do.

Bernardino turned the latch and pulled the door. It opened easily, but loudly, and a warm burst of air buffeted them from within.

"And don't touch anything," Bernardino cautioned. "Everything here is very, very hot. Yes?"

They all nodded again.

Bernardino stepped through the door, followed by Miracle and Darling and then Digby. On the other side of the door they found themselves in a large, well-lit, concrete tunnel. There were large pipes running along the top and sides of the tunnel. Every now and then they could see brass gauges, and vents embedded in the joints between pipes. There were a few steampunks walking by just as the small group stepped into the tunnel. They raised a hand to Bernardino but said nothing as they passed.

The tunnel was warm, hot in fact, no doubt from the steam flowing through the pipes all around them.

Digby gazed around him. He had been to Trenton and a few other cities, but he had never considered the infrastructure which was just below the streets. These pipes, he thought, they carry the steam that runs the electrical generators that power everything. From the coal-fired plants on the outside of the city, the steam moved silently beneath the streets, tended by these lads here, these steampunks as they were called.

Bernardino was pulling off his trench coat and handing it to Darling. "Here," he said. "Put this on. It will protect you from the steam vents. Molto caldo. Very hot." Darling was wearing a skirt which left his shins and feet exposed. Miracle and Digby were wearing slacks and boots.

Bernardino pulled off his goggles and handed them to Miracle. Then he passed her his cap.

"Please," he said. "Try to cover your hair with these."

"I thought you said it would be safe here," Digby said, understanding now that it was a disguise Bernardino was thrusting on his friend.

Bernardino looked at him. "Not unsafe, exactly," he said with a smile. "Just being cautious. Better safe than sorry, eh?"

"It's alright Digby," Miracle said, donning the goggles first and using the strap to pull her shock of red hair back from her forehead, then covering the rest with the leather cap.

"Buono!" Bernardino said. He ran his hand along the closest steam pipe, not seeming to mind the heat on his calloused hands. Then he pushed his now dirty hands across first Miracles face, then Darlings. He reached for Digby, but Digby backed away, reaching his own hand toward the pipe. Bernardino grabbed his wrist.

"Molto caldo," he said again. "Very hot."

Digby wrested his hand away and reached for the pipe any way. He gently smudged his fingers across it, feeling the burn of the heat instantly but refusing to cringe. He quickly moved his fingers along the pipe, then smeared the soot across his own face and forehead. He turned to Darling.

"How does that look?" he asked.

She smiled at him, her eyes shiny from the alcohol still working its way through her system. "Handsome," she said. "And dirty. Dirty handsome!" Then she laughed.

Digby frowned then smiled in spite of himself. Miracle turned and brought her finger to her lips to shush her friends.

Bernardino was already leading them away down the concrete tunnel.

They moved through four or five separate junction points where tunnels intersected, turning sometimes left and sometimes right and sometimes not all; past at least four other groups of steampunks, but nobody said anything to them and they walked quickly with their heads low.

Digby was hopelessly lost. Every now and then the group passed a steel ladder leading up and he was tempted to climb it and have a peek outside, get his bearings, but he resisted the urge. Besides, he thought, it is dark outside and I don't really know my way around Trenton anyway.

Walking through the concrete tunnel, Miracle's mind was racing. She was trying to put together what few pieces of the puzzle she had available to her and not getting very far. True, she had some irons in the fire which would likely yield more information, sooner or later, but she was impatient for information. She didn't like not knowing something, anything, especially when that thing was clearly having a dramatic impact on her life and the lives of those closest to her, not to mention all those who had perished in the anarchy which had rocked Princeton. Something big was going on, she told herself. It was bigger than her, bigger than the world she had been living in. Forces were at work which wielded more power than she had ever dreamed of, and these forces were seemingly aligned against her. She resigned herself to simply wait until she had more information before trying to solve this puzzle, but also steeled herself for more trying times which undoubtedly waited just ahead of them.

For her part, Darling Kinder was marveling at all the adventure she had seen so far and greatly looking forward to what was yet to come. And she was thirsty, parched in fact, from all the beer and liquor she had drank. Her head was swimming but she chose to let her mind drift a little ways while her legs carried forward.

The phone rang and Charles Paulson answered it himself.

"Yes," he said gruffly. "I see. Don't expect a bonus for this type of blundering. How can you not find them in your own city? Damn your eyes! Find them and find them now you buffoon."

He slammed the receiver down and turned in his office chair to his wireless communicator. It was dark outside, after midnight, but he didn't care. He pressed the broadcast button and waited.

There better be an answer before I count to three, he told himself. Then -

"Uh, yes?" came a crackling stammer through his wireless communicator speakers.

"Damn you Steersman," Paulson bellowed. "Are you sleeping?" He already knew the answer, but waited for the lie.

"Uh, no, no, of course not," came the lie.

"I should hope not," Paulson said. "I ask you for one little action and you blow up half of Princeton. I ask you to bring me a girl and you deliver nothing. I should have your head for this!"

Silence blasted from the speakers. Paulson continued.

"The police raid tonight turned up nothing," he said. "Miss Lowell and her friends seemingly vanished without a trace. We're running out of time and your failures are trying my patience."

"I see, yes, well, I'll make a call of course, Mr. Paulson," came the crackling reply.

"Damn your calls, man, I want action!" Paulson cried. "I want a solution and I want it before the sun rises this morning. Do you understand me?"

"Ye-yes, sir, of course Mr. Paulson," came the stammered reply. "Of course. Before sunrise I'll have her delivered to your door."

"See that you do," Paulson said. "I pay you a great deal of money to sort these types of issues out for me Steersman. I expect action and I expect results. I don't expect, and I will not tolerate incompetence. You should know this full well by now. Paulson out."

He clicked off the speaker and swiveled his chair back around.

Miracle, Digby and Darling, led by Bernardino, wandered the tunnels beneath the city for what seemed like days, but was closer to a couple hours. At different points Bernardino would point above them and call out sights of interest.

"This is the City Hall," he said with glee, placing a finger to his lips and pretending to tip-toe. Further along he pointed out the "Gear Heads up there who make all their teeny-tiny wind-up machines." He shrugged at this, obviously unimpressed with the true mechanics involved in the industrial mechanized automation advancements being developed there. Miracle and Digby were well aware of what was happening in the factories above them. At least they had a good idea. Digby felt himself wishing desperately he could simply climb the nearest ladder and seek safety among those who would soon (after graduation, of course) be his peers.

Suddenly Bernardino ducked into a small tunnel to one side. The trio followed him and came up short, finding themselves in a small brick walled room with cots and hammocks, a wooden cask, and a small shelf with cups. There was a heavy steel door at the far end of the room and like the tunnels themselves, pipes snaked across the ceiling disappearing into the abyss above them.

"We're almost where we need to be, so I thought we would rest here," Bernardino said. "You must be tired, no?"

"A bit, yes," Miracle said, pulling a chair free and slinking down into it.

Darling nearly fell into a chair opposite her, obviously too tired to even speak.

It occurred to Digby that while he had slept the day away his two friends had not rested since the day before. He looked at the girls and noticed now the sheer exhaustion etched on their faces. They were each going on 48 hours of wakefulness. They desperately needed sleep.

Miracle rested her head in her hands, lost in thought or falling fast asleep, Digby couldn't tell which. Darling slouched in her seat, her head back and her eyes closed.

A sudden clanging noise shook them all. Digby whirled around and saw Bernardino with a large wrench in his hand, tapping on a nearby pipe.

"Quiet please!" he shouted. "The ladies need rest."

"Mi dispiace – sorry," Bernardino said. "I thought you might want some food, and some wine, to rest."

"No wine," Darling groaned, now leaning forward, her head on the table.

"Food would be very nice, Bernardino," Miracle said, her eyes still closed.

"Why were you banging?" Digby asked.

"Ordering delivery," Bernardino said, and smiled. "It should be here shortly."

Bernardino clearly knew what he was doing. Within minutes two young boys came rushing into the room with two bags of food. Some cheese and bread, a thick sausage and a jug of milk. The three ate heartily. Bernardino declined their offers to share.

When everyone had finished eating Bernardino rose and walked toward the tunnel, motioning Digby to join him. With his thick gloves he reached up and loosened the light bulb, darkening the room.

"Ladies, why not rest yourselves more comfortably on the cots," Bernardino said. "Your friend and I will take a walk and be back soon. You are perfectly safe here. Rest. Sleep. You'll feel better."

Miracle and Darling rose from the table. Darling took two steps and collapsed onto the nearest cot, instantly asleep. Miracle thanked Bernardino for his help, smiled at Digby, then crossed to the cot closest to Darling and laid herself down.

Bernardino led Digby out into the tunnel again. Digby was not tired at all and happy to leave the girls to rest. He was slightly worried about leaving the girls alone, but Bernardino assured him not to worry, saying "Steampunk Rules, fratello. Steampunk Rules."

Bernardino walked along the tunnel for a bit, turning first right, then left, ending at the base of a steel ladder. He climbed the ladder, motioning Digby to follow him. At the top he released the clamp locking the lid in place then pushed it aside. Digby, hanging beneath him on the ladder felt a rush of cool air from above, then the rush of warmer air coming up from beneath him. He climbed up and out, behind Bernardino, and found himself standing in the middle of an alley, surrounded by large brick walls.

Bernardino was fishing into his pocket for his tobacco and papers again. Digby looked around him. Digby glanced around but recognized nothing. Not that he expected to. Trenton was the technological and manufacturing hub of the Federated States of America. It stretched for miles in all directions. Although Digby had been to the city many times he had no doubt that there was much more to see than what he had so far seen.

"Where are we?" he asked as Bernardino was lighting his cigarette. Bernardino took a drag and spoke as he released the smoke from his lungs. "Toy market," he said. "They make those little wind-up things in there-" pointing to one side of the alley "-and they make bicycles over there-" pointing to the other side. "Over there they build dynamos for homes, to keep the lights on, and over there, across the street, is a place where they make wireless communication equipment. They say, Trenton makes, and the world takes. This is so, I think."

It all looked the same to Digby. To his right was a brick wall. Across the street was another brick wall. All around him were matching brick walls, in fact. The darkness didn't help.

"So, what do you do?" Bernardino asked.

Digby pulled himself up straight.

"I'm a university student," he said.

"Ahh-this I know," Bernardino said. "But for what do you go to university, this is not so clear to me."

Digby thought a moment, considering. "Well, I suppose in your vernacular I would be studying to be a Gear Head."

Bernardino laughed. "It's alright, fratello. We all have a burden to carry. Yours is a big brain, eh?

Digby smiled. "I never thought of it that way," he said. "I suppose some people might think that, but really, I'm just a farmers son with a knack for taking things apart and putting them back together."

"Mmm," Bernardino said between drags on his cigarette. "This is a good skill to have. We steampunks must have this same skill. Those lights you see out there-" pointing to the streetlights "-the generators that supply the power, the networks of pipes that carry the steam, the power plants that produce that steam, all those machines we are responsible for. Taking them apart, putting them back together, keeping the city humming along for all the people who work in these factories, or the cafes, or the hotels or the homes. We do all that. No winding required."

Digby considered this thoughtfully. It was true that everything that happened above ground did so only because of the work which went on below ground. That didn't mean that the work the steampunks did was any more important than the work done by anyone else, however. In fact, he thought, what good would it be to have all that steam, all that energy, all that power, without something to do with it? One gave meaning to the other was more like what he was thinking.

He changed the subject.

"So, tell me more about these rules you are always talking about," he said. "What are the Steampunk Rules, exactly? Is there a list or do you have to take a test?"

Bernardino laughed.

"No, no, fratello," he said. "Nothing in writing, of course. It's more like a philosophy, a bond between brothers and sisters who risk their lives in the dangerous tunnels and steam plants. We stick together because we rely on each other in all things. The power plant machines are enormous, much more than any one person could care for alone. It takes a team. Always a team. Working together is the only way to survive. And to work together we have to trust each other without question in all things."

Digby could appreciate this. It was much the same on the farm. One person could milk a cow, or bale the hay, or drive the tractor, but the entire operation required many people working together, usually family, but anyone who was hired to work the farm was treated like family, so, in essence, it was one big family. This made perfect sense to him.

He smiled at Bernardino and said, "I think I understand."

Bernardino smiled back. "Come, let's sit down for a bit, relax, let the girls sleep. I can tell you more about the Steampunk Rules and you can tell me more about the burdens of having a big brain."

They both laughed, and settled back into the darkness on the cool concrete.

Chapter 13: Gathering Forces

Patrolman Mark Crosby stood in a small alley, across the street from The Jack, where an earlier police raid had somehow allowed Miracle Lowell and her two fugitive friends to escape. Crosby's little helper had decided to start here, said he needed to check his contacts in the area to see if they might have a lead, know something, anything about where their targets might have disappeared to.

Crosby was impatient. His arm ached from the pitched brawl he was in earlier, and his heart was racing. Mr. Calabricci had made it quite clear that he would not accept failure again, and Crosby had no intention of failing. The consequences from last time were just about all he could bear.

He rubbed his brass covered arm again at the thought of it.

Crosby had no idea what this entire affair was about. Why was Miracle Lowell the only person who knew where her father, the famous scientist and former ambassador, Percival Lowell? What did Mr. Calabricci want with Percival Lowell in the first place? And what did any of this have to do with the supposed disappearance of Professor Henry Nettles?

Clearly Miss Lowell was guilty of something. Why else would she have decided that now was a good time to blow up Princeton University and attempt to flee the area with her gang of Anarchists? Then again, the Eastern world was on the brink of war, perhaps Miss Lowell was somehow a part of it.

Crosby had wracked his brain trying to deduce a connection between these people and what Calabricci might gain from it all. Other than the fact that Lowell and Nettles were both professors, Crosby couldn't see as they had anything to do with each other for more than a decade. And whether or not Miss Lowell could lead him to her father, who may or may not know something further about Professor Nettles, seemed entirely beside the point. Why not just find him without her? Why not just send out an alert for Professor Nettles. If he was alive then someone had surely seem him, been in contact with him, passed him on the street by now.

For the past several days Crosby had been consumed with trying to decipher the workings of this entire affair, hoping to somehow gain the upper hand, come up with a better plan; work out a better deal for himself. But then his mis-step two days ago and subsequent trip to the doctor, had quickly satisfied his desire for knowledge and left him to re-focus on doing exactly what Mr. Calabricci had asked him to do—regardless of what it was or what questions he might have about it. And right now Mr. Calabricci wanted him to locate Miss Miracle Lowell and bring her to his office before she and her friends were taken into police custody. Once Mr. Calabricci had finished with her Crosby was free to take her into official police custody, and receive all the acclaim that would come with it.

"Detective, sir!" came a shout from the opposite end of the alley. Crosby turned and recognized a small silhouette. He started in that direction.

"Quiet, quiet now, before we are noticed," he said, somewhat louder than a whisper but not a shout.

"Sorry, sir, truly I am," Jeremiah said. "But I got some good news, good news indeed, sir."

"Have you found them?"

"Not quite sir, but I know where they're heading."

"Do tell, boy."

"The word is they are using the steam tunnels to cross the city; headed for the docks to meet a ship in the morning."

Crosby considered a moment.

"How sure are you of this?"

Jeremiah pulled himself up straight.

"Very sure, sir," he said. "The word is good, as it comes from someone I trust. One of my boys who's been down to the tunnels, seen them, and knows exactly which direction they are heading. There's only one place they could be going, and there's only one ship due in at the docks in the morning that is planning to leave again straight away."

"What ship is this?"

"She's called the Platypus, sir, can't say as I ever heard of her before," Jeremiah said. "Mighty strange name at that, if I do say so myself."

Crosby stood thinking, right hand stroking his brass arm silently. "Tell me again how sure you are this is where they are, that this – Platypus – is where they are heading."

"I'd stake my life on it, sir," Jeremiah said without hesitation.

Crosby smiled. "Good," he said. "Because you are. Now, come with me first, I have to make a call, then you'll take me to this dock, and this ship, and we'll see how right you are."

Paulson had no sooner disconnected his line when Steersman's wireless communicator rang again. This time it was Mr. Calabricci.

"Steersman, I have some news you might be interested in," came his voice through the radio speaker.

"Well, don't keep me in suspense, damn you!" Steersman learned long ago that as good as he got from his superiors was as good as he gave to his inferiors. The harder Paulson made it rain on him, the more torrential the rains that poured down on those who served Steersman.

"I have some information about that girl you've been looking for," he said.

"So—what is it?" Steersman was losing patience.

"I'm afraid I had to pay a stiff price for this news, which I'll have to pass along to you. You understand, of course."

Steersman sighed. "Name your price Mr. Calabricci and I'll have it to you by the morning."

By the time Steersman stood up from his wireless table he was giddy with excitement. "We have you now Miss Miracle Lowell. And through you, your father. And through him, whatever it is that Mr. Paulson desires."

He sat back down at the table and dialed in the connection to Paulson, nearly beside himself with joy, and not a small amount of relief.

When Digby and Bernardino returned to the small room inside the steam tunnels Miracle and Darling were awake. The dark sky of the night had started to lighten above the pair of young men seated in the alley, with dawn likely fast approaching. Digby was unsure exactly how long they had been gone, but apparently it was long enough for the ladies to get some much needed rest.

"Ah-ladies!" Bernardino said. "Better now, no?"

"Indeed Bernardino," Miracle said. She was sitting at the table with Darling. There was a freshly sliced apple on the table and she and Darling were eating eagerly.

"Yes," Darling said between bites. "The cots were quite, firm, but very restful. We are grateful."

Bernardino bowed low, half jesting, but half in serious recognition. "I am honored," he said.

Digby felt the sudden pangs of hunger and snatched the last slice of apple from the table, barely beating Darling to it. She gave him a sideways glance, made to slap his hand, but smiled.

For a moment it was as if the group was a simple gathering of friends. Digby looked around at the small brick room, the steam pipes, Bernardino, and was quickly reminded of the desperate straits in which they remained.

Miracle stood from the table and motioned Bernardino to join her in the steam tunnel, outside the room.

She looked at Digby and smiled slightly. Her eyes looked weary, but Digby was confident she was still in control. Miracle had a plan, and he would play his role willingly, he thought to himself.

Digby took the chair Miracle left empty. He looked at the empty plate before him and frowned. He looked up and found Darling smiling at him. Suddenly, as if by magic, she produced a new shiny apple from the bag she had packed and brought with them from the hotel. Digby reached for the knife, but darling snatched it first, and with dexterity he was surprised to see from her (though he wondered why anything she did still surprised him) she peeled cored and sliced the apple in a flash.

Digby did a poor job of hiding his surprise, but Darling just laughed. "Eat, Mr. Ross," she said, sliding the plate closer to him. "I mean, Digby." She smiled again, this time looking slightly away, a pinkness rising to her cheeks.

Outside the brick room Miracle took Bernardino some distance down the tunnel, where she could see a great distance in either direction to be certain no one was within earshot.

"I just wanted to confirm our destination this morning, if you please," she said.

"Of course," Bernardino said. "The ship you seek, she is called the Platypus, though I do not understand what means this "platypus", some mythical creature perhaps. Regardless, she is to dock this morning for precisely one hour, no more, no less, then leave again for Philadelphia. She will carry passengers and cargo, though exactly whom or what, this I do not know."

"And she is the first such ship in or out of the harbor in the past week?" Miracle said.

"Si, Senorina," Bernardino said. "It is exactly as you asked. I have friends who work the harbor steam facility and they assured me no other ships have been or gone for such traffic as this."

"Can you trust these friends of yours Bernardino," Miracle asked. "Truly?"

"Steampunk Rules, Miss Lowell," he said and smiled as he gave a slight bow. "They would not lie to me, nor I to you. Your money and reputation has earned you the information you seek, and my honor to my friends has earned me mine."

Miracle smiled. She knew this man, Bernardino Abatangelo, could be trusted for much the same reason he now presented to her that his sources could indeed be trusted. She was not without resources herself, friends who could be trusted, friends who were even now working diligently to free her and Digby and Darling from this predicament while simultaneously assisting her in her attempts to solve the mystery in which they had become ensnared. Bernardino came highly recommended, and that recommendation was enough to ensure her trust.

Miracle placed her hand on Bernardino's shoulder. "Thank you," she said. "Your word is good enough for me. My apologies for the questioning, but there is so much at stake."

"This I understand," Bernardino said. "These are strange days in which we live. Across the ocean the world is at war, while over here my city is turned upside down in some crazy search for a half-mad, probably dead anyway, professor - and this business at your university, so many dead there for sure." He shook his head. "Terrible business. I do not envy you."

Miracle sighed. She was, of course, fully aware of what was going on in Europe these days. The alliance between Germany and Austria-Hungary had resulted in a huge imbalance in power in the entire region. The Russian Czar has already said he would welcome an invitation to ally with the Ottoman Empire, with many in the region claiming his true goal is a new empire, something they are calling a Super Russian Empire. The result of such a further alliance or a larger empire, would result in a massive power block in Eastern Europe which would undoubtedly lead them to war with each other or their Western counterparts. The Federated States of America would likely side with its allies, Britain and France, Belgium and Italy, but its ability to participate would be limited by the wide Atlantic Ocean. How quickly they could become involved and to what affect was debatable. And that was presuming the various members states would actually agree to participate in unison rather than squabble over who would pay for what and whose blood would be most heavily shed. It seemed unlikely that any involvement by the FSA would include the fiercely nationalist Cherokee State, while the citizens of the Texas Republic would no doubt be first in line to volunteer ground forces. The Federal Congress would debate and debate, while protesters would march and picket—it was a wonder anything ever got done in this nation, but somehow it always did. This was all true, but unfortunately, not at the top of her priorities list at the moment. She needed to focus on the moment, solve the mystery, save her friends, clear her name and most of all, keep her father out of danger.

Miracle shook herself from her dark thoughts and focused again on the problem at hand. There were further steps she must take to bring her plan to fruition.

"Bernardino, how much time do we have left before the Platypus arrives?"

Bernardino shrugged his shoulders. "I am not quite sure, maybe an hour, maybe more. These things, with ships; it is not my area of expertise, the sea, so I cannot tell you exactly. I know only where she will dock and shall be sure you are there to greet her."

"Very well," Miracle said. "Then I need a few more things before we leave. Can you arrange these for me?"

Bernardino stood straight. "Tell me what it is you need and I will do my best to make it so for you."

Miracle smiled.

Chapter 14: Brawl at the Docks

As dawn broke over the Delaware River at the Trenton City Docks, Mark Crosby found himself once again on the verge of something he felt was glorious. Like rats in a trap he knew that any moment now Miracle Lowell and her friends would be stumbling onto these docks to board a tiny steamer. As soon as they did, Crosby and his army of thugs would storm out of hiding and take them all by force. He felt confident that not much force would be needed for the fugitive trio, but just in case he had gladly accepted the two dozen men Mr. Calabricci had sent him.

Looking around him now, Crosby saw a parade of broken faces; tough men who had known tough lives that had broken them down, left them shadows of the men they could have been. They were all armed with baseball bats and brass knuckles, some with pistols and knives. Their eyes were dark in the shadow of the dawn, but he didn't need to see their eyes to know they were eager for blood. He could practically smell the violence they were eager for.

"Sir, might I have my coin now?"

Crosby looked down into the eyes of Jeremiah Maddy. The beggar boy had been quite useful, just as he had thought he would. He certainly was due his coin, but not yet, Crosby thought.

"When the ship arrives, you'll have your coin," he said. "Not a minute before, and certainly not if it doesn't arrive. In fact, if it doesn't arrive as you've promised I'll set these men loose on you, so take care, and hope to god your information is correct."

Jeremiah shrank back against the wall of the warehouse, into the shadow where the group of thugs, led by Crosby, was waiting, somewhat impatiently.

He didn't trust Crosby, and he certainly didn't trust anyone else in his vicinity, but he was stuck. He had no chance of sneaking away now, but maybe once the action started – once Crosby's attention is on his prize and not on Jeremiah – then perhaps he could slip out of sight, take to the tunnels and make his way out of the city. Make his own way in the world, truly in the world, out of Trenton. Somewhere West, perhaps, or maybe South, where the winters never grew cold. He could join with the Cherokee, become a farmer. His options were nearly limitless as he had no ties to keep him here, and frankly, no better options at the moment. Might as well dream big, he told himself.

Crosby meanwhile was thinking of his forthcoming promotion. Detective for sure, initially, then it was only a matter of time until he was named Chief of Police in Trenton. From there, maybe he would seek political office. Eventually, perhaps, the governor's office. Might as well dream big, he told himself again.

"Look, there, smoke!" came a cry from the midst of his group of ruffians.

"Quiet there," Crosby said harshly. But he could hardly hide his own excitement. There, just around the first bend in the river he could see the pillar of smoke. There, in the river, black smoke like that could only be from a steamer, he thought. It would take the ship another fifteen or twenty minutes, at least, to come to rest at the docks where he stood.

"Alright you bastards," Crosby called over his shoulder. "Ready yourselves. I want all of you to keep a careful watch on the docks. Remember who we're looking for. And advise me the moment you spot them. And nobody make a move without my explicit instructions."

"But, I'm not a bastard," came a call from the back of the group. "I know who my father is." The group broke into spontaneous laughter, which Crosby quickly silenced.

"Silence!" he said. "Keep your mouths shut and your damn eyes open."

The men shuffled their feet and grumbled but remained for the most part silent. They didn't normally take orders from anyone not in Mr. Calabricci's employ, but in this case, this man – Crosby – was taking orders from Mr. Calabricci himself, so they were forced to obey him. For now.

The minutes passed, more slowly than Crosby preferred, but gradually the steamer came into view. It was a small ship. It had two smokestacks rising up from the center of the top deck, as well as three tall wooden masts. Clearly it was some sort of refit from the last century, Crosby thought to himself. A sailing ship converted to run on steam to meet the demands of the 20th Century. A god-awful ugly sea going vessel, in his opinion, but then, he knew nothing of ships and sailing. He didn't care much for airships either, preferring to feel his feet always planted firmly on the ground.

Crosby could hardly stand the waiting. He slipped his good right hand into his vest pocket and withdrew a small tin of enhanced snuff. He brought it to his nose and took a deep breath. Instantly his heart quickened, the blood rushing to his extremities, his pulse pounding in his temples; the ache in his brass coated arm diminished and he suddenly felt as if he could simply jump across the dock and gray waters of the Delaware itself, right to the deck of that oncoming steamer. He took a deep breath of the dank river air, the morning still crisp and cool, the morning sun risen to bless the day in golden sunshine.

Crosby was lost in a reverie all his own, his mind adrift with thoughts of his forthcoming grandeur. So lost was he in his own mind that he hardly noticed the steamer coming to rest at the dock. Dockside workers rushed to tie off the moorings, as the ship lowered its gangway.

Jeremiah tugged at Crosby's sleeve. "Sir," he said. "Shouldn't we be headin' that way?"

Crosby started, looking down at Jeremiah, then focusing on the steamer. He glanced over his shoulder again, at the group of thugs. "Anyone see anything?" he said.

There was murmuring, and shrugging, but nobody was quite sure what they were looking for. They saw lots of things: the docking steamer, the dock men rushing out to greet her, tying off the starboard lines; the sailors at the railing shouting down happily; cargo being brought out to the ship for transport; cargo being unloaded; dozens of men and women moving toward the ship. Nothing like what he had told them to watch for, however.

Crosby was getting anxious. From his vantage point he had a clear view of the comings and goings, but he hadn't expected so much activity. He thought they would be able to clearly identify who was a passenger, and simply pick out Miracle Lowell and her friends from the line, but this was not what was happening.

There were a few passengers making their way down the dock now. An old man walking slowly, pulling a wheeled shipping trunk; a young couple with a small child in a stroller, a few other well to-do men, walking in a group, talking excitedly. Now that the gangway was fully deployed passengers started streaming off the ship. Dozens of people, fresh to the shore after their trip; small children screaming and yelling, came racing down to the dock, their mother calling after them to "be careful!" There were others, too many for Crosby to keep track of. He hadn't been prepared for this. He hadn't expected so many people coming and going. He was confused, but the adrenaline rush forced him to act without hesitation.

"C'mon!" he called to his men. "Search everyone. She's here somewhere. Find her, dammit!" He strode out from the alley, marching straight to the newly docked steamer, forcing his way through the crowds of workers and disembarking passengers, and the passengers waiting to board; his men pushing and shoving their way through behind him.

"Search everyone!" he shouted to them again. "Don't let her get through here."

As Crosby made his way through the crowds, he forgot all about Jeremiah, who had seen this as his opportunity to escape. He slipped to one side as the gang of men streamed by him, circled around to the side and dropped down off the edge of the dock. From there he crawled along the edge, his hands taking hold of the slippery wood that lined the concrete dock as best he could, inching his way closer and closer to the ship.

Crosby and his men meanwhile were grabbing everyone who passed, pulling off hats, and turning faces to the sun to get a better look. In the midst of this crush of people, some trying to work at their business of loading and unloading a steamer, others disembarking, others arriving for boarding, Crosby and his gang of thugs made their way closer and closer to the ship. Suddenly one of his men shouted, "Hey, you there, let me get a look at you!" Crosby turned to look and saw a flash of red hair tumble from beneath a dock workers cap.

Now he had her, he thought, and shouted: 'There, there men! Get her!"

His men, as he called them, were somewhat slow on the uptake, and only those closest to what was happening responded initially. Fists were swung, but like a slippery fish Miracle Lowell disappeared beneath their feet. Crosby, who was several yards away from where she was quickly lost sight of her. There was a rush of men in his direction now and he was struggling to get through them.

"Out of my way, damn you!" he shouted, using his brass covered arm as a wedge. Panic stricken passengers scurried out of the way as best they could, but the dock had become so crowded now that there was little room to move. Passengers trying to disembark were stopped by the crowd of thugs. Dock workers, confused by what was happening had started to gather, further clogging the entrance, and passengers arriving to board were also stopped by the crowd. The crowd was now so large one man dropped off the edge of the dock into the water, shouting that he "couldn't swim!" Only the first old man, pulling the wheeled steamer trunk had made it safely to the gangway, just now slipping inside the ship.

Crosby didn't care. In fact, emboldened by the panic and the confusion, he began swinging his brass covered arm in a wider and wider arc, bringing it crashing against anyone, man or woman, who had the misfortune of being too close to him. It was mayhem, and Crosby was in his element.

Suddenly Crosby heard a different cry from a man behind him.

"Here! Here! I've seen her right here" he called.

Crosby turned and spied a mass of red hair twisting in the fist of one of his men. Crosby couldn't get a good look at the girl's face, but the hair was the right color. He turned, pausing only to push a man off his feet in front of him. Swimming through the crowd, Crosby made his way closer to the man who had the girl by the hair. Suddenly he saw the man drop to his knees from a sudden kick by his prey and the girl vanished into the crowd.

"Get her! Get her!" he shouted at the men nearest him and they rushed in that direction.

Crosby stepped forward, and tripped, almost falling to the dock. He looked down and saw a small child, cowering at his feet. He swung his brass covered arm back meaning to swipe at the pitiful creature when he felt a mountain crash into him, knocking him aside like a rag doll. His head hit the concrete dock and he saw stars. As he shook the darkness out of his eyes he heard a familiar voice and looked up in time to see Digby Ross standing over him smiling.

"Well, fancy bumping into you again!" Digby said. Then he dashed away through the crowd, toward the steamer. Crosby struggled to his feet, looking for his men, but by now the dock had erupted into a vicious brawl, a bar fight without the bar. Most of the passengers, either coming or going, had fled the area, but the dockworkers were not to be trifled with. This was their turf, and they didn't take kindly to being pushed around.

Within a few short minutes the otherwise quiet and calm, mostly deserted dock, had turned into a wild free for all.

Crosby struggled to his feet, being jostled from every side by thugs and dock workers, dodging fists and clubs and kicks, searching frantically for some sign of his prey or her friends, but finding nothing as he was able to see almost nothing through the fighting crowds.

Suddenly his ears heard the familiar clang of a police steam wagon. He twisted his neck, both hands furiously shoving others aside, and saw the wagon come roaring onto the docks near where only a few minutes earlier his rag-tag group was hidden in the alleyway. It screeched to a stop, skidding several feet before finally halting precariously near the edge of the dock. The rear doors flung open and Trenton police forces began streaming out. Each uniformed officer carried a baton, raised above his head, blowing whistles loudly as a warning they meant business. No sooner had this first wagon disgorged its belly then a second and a third police steamer wagon came roaring in behind it. The officers who came streaming from their rear doors also had whistles, but instead of batons they carried iron shackles.

Soon the first wave of blue uniformed officers joined the fray, batons swinging, whistles blowing. Both dockworkers and thugs fell before the swarm, as they fought their way through. Those that fell before this first wave of officers were summarily cuffed in iron and dragged back to the wagon by the second wave of officers.

Crosby was momentarily shocked. Why were the police here? He wondered. Who had called them? Were they simply attracted by the near riot he had caused here? No. Too soon for them to respond. Most of the Trenton officers were more interested in avoiding fights rather than rushing to join them.

Crosby only had seconds to make a decision. He threw his arms in the air and shouted over the heads of the thugs and dock workers to the nearest officer.

"Here! Here! All officers to me!"

Crosby had no authority over anyone, but the police force responded, recognizing one of their own and sensing his need. The blue swarm moved as one, batons swinging, bringing down thugs and dock workers alike. Passengers who put up no resistance (as most did) were bustled off in irons to the steamer wagons. Crosby recognized this as a clearing action, but he also noticed that passengers went to one truck while thugs and dockworkers went to another.

Crosby began swinging at the backs of his own men, much to their surprise. His brass arm came crashing down on the shoulder of the nearest man and he crumpled easily. The thug to his side turned and saw what Crosby had done. He swung a piece of lumber and Crosby easily ducked beneath it, kicking out a foot, and catching the man in the solar plexus. He was not so lucky with the third man who hit him in the side of his face with what felt like a hammer. Crosby was stunned, staggered, and slipped to the ground. The crowd closed over him and he felt the kicks and stomping from dozens of feet, but was unable to do much to protect himself short of wrapping his arms around his now aching head and face.

The police force was strong, but their opponents, with backs to the open water and many with police records they did not want revealed, fought fiercely. Crosby, caught beneath it found himself further kicked and broken by unnamed feet. He tried to roll himself away and was too successful at it for his own good. He rolled off the edge of the dock, splashing into the still cold Delaware River water between the dock and the steamer ship. The ship itself was rising and settling on the waves, swaying to and fro, sometimes closely approaching the dock. Crosby knew this was no place for a man, fearful to be caught between the steel ship hull and the hard concrete of the dock. He dog paddled to the surface, his brass arm weighing him down, struggling with every stroke. He was frantically trying to avoid the ships hull and the dock, and crying out for help to those above him, but receiving no answer.

His fingers closed on a length of rope dangling down from above and he hauled himself slowly up it. His brass arm was little help, mostly weighing him down. His brass fingers offered no grip on the slippery rope, his right-hand taking on all the weight. As he pulled his lower body free from the water he used his legs to wrap around the rope, feeling it tight against his skin, and trying to use it as a step to boost himself higher.

The ship's hull came crashing close against the dock, and he swung himself away on the rope, like a child on a tire swing, frantically pulling himself higher on the rope. His urgent swing to the side, however, had created a counter swing which again brought him perilously close to be squeezed between ship and dock.

He pulled himself, now so close to the dock his eyes could peer above it. He brought his right hand up and used it to grab at a nearby cleat. He pulled himself up, his torso now laying sprawled on the dock, and released a sigh of relief. But no sooner had he thought he was safe than a wave from the Delaware brought the giant steamer up and against the concrete dock right where he was. He felt the pinion of the ship on his legs and cried out, but the instant agony was too much. His eyes grew dark and he lost consciousness.

Chapter 15: Steamship Stowaways

Digby Ross found himself deep within the bowels of the Steamship Platypus, sitting on a small wooden chair. His knuckles were bruised and still bloodied from the brawl; his chin ached and he rubbed his jaw with his sore hand. A wayward elbow from some dock worker had nearly laid him out, but he had recovered quickly to join his friends here inside the ship.

As the police wagons had rolled up, Digby, Miracle and Darling, disguised as dockworkers, had used the resulting confusion to slip aboard the ship. Looking back briefly Digby had seen Crosby fighting his way toward the police, then crumple to the ground, disappearing beneath the crowd. Digby had turned away, slinking up the gangway, slipping past the crowd of sailors who had gathered to watch the dockside fighting. He saw Miracle standing at an entryway to below decks and quickly followed her down. Once in the hold the trio collapsed in exhaustion.

The police had gathered all passengers, thugs, and those dockworkers who had made the mistake of inviting arrest, into their steam wagons. There was some sort of commotion outside, the sirens of a steam ambulance, Digby thought, but the three friends were unsure what exactly was going on, too fearful to show their faces above decks. They stayed below, as Bernardino had advised them, and sought shelter in the hold. There was plenty of cargo down here, chairs to sit on, blankets to sleep on and even clothes to change into. Several crates of men's and women's apparel headed for Philadelphia was stowed here and they helped themselves to whatever they needed, and fit properly.

It had been hours since the brawl on the docks and the ship was only now on its way. They felt the slight sway of the ship as it slipped down the Delaware. The ride itself would be quite short, so whatever Miracle had planned, Digby thought to himself, we should get busy doing it now. So that's what he said.

"Whatever you've got planned, Miracle," he said. "Shouldn't we be about it?"

Miracle had just finished fastening up her leather bustier and was slipping on a pair of long sleeve leather gloves. Then her coat. Then for effect she slipped a fashionable ladies feathered bowler on her head, tucking her waves of red hair underneath.

She looked every bit as stunningly beautiful as she ever did, Digby thought.

She looked up at him, caught him staring at her, and smiled. He blushed in spite of himself and looked away.

"What's your hurry, Digby?" she said. "I've always enjoyed a nice river cruise."

Digby sighed.

"It seems to me, if we're here for some reason, we should get busy doing it," he said. "We can't simply hide for the duration of the trip. Eventually someone will come down here, looking for something, the ship will arrive in Philadelphia and this cargo will need to be unloaded. Hadn't we be somewhere else by then?"

Darling Kinder, who had been busily dressing behind a makeshift screen on the far side of the hold, came striding up, her leather boot heels knocking against the steel floorboards. She was wearing a pair of black leather trousers and a loose fitting blouse covered with a red leather vest and a pair of long black leather gloves. She too had adorned herself with a ladies hat—a tall hat that made her appear much taller than she actually was, but looked fabulous nonetheless. Women do so love their accessories, Digby thought. He had grabbed a pair of khaki trousers with suspenders, a white shirt and a khaki vest. He topped off his garb with a tweed drivers cap. There was a wooden box nearly overflowing with shoes, but he couldn't find any quite large enough for his enormous feet. The ones he settled for were the least tight fitting.

"First things first, Digby," Miracle said. "Now, thanks to Bernardino, we have proper attire. Next we'll ingratiate ourselves with the crew and then, on to the passengers."

"Need I remind you, time is precious," Digby said. "This ship will make port in Philadelphia in the next couple hours. Does your plan include us staying aboard then, as stowaways, or going ashore as wanted fugitives?"

Darling, standing near where Digby and Miracle were talking, was having some trouble adjusting her vest. Her ample bosom was threatening to burst free at any moment and Digby did his best not to stare as she first shifted it one way, then the next. She caught him watching her and smiled. Then quickly blushed and looked away.

"Do try to contain yourself Darling, please," Miracle said. "Before Digby's eyes fall onto the floor and we have to waste precious time searching for them."

"Oh, I'm sure it's nothing Mr. Ross hasn't seen before," Darling said, as she quickly turned her back.

"Digby, if you please," Miracle said.

"Oh, sorry," Darling said, spinning back around, now properly dressed. "Digby."

He felt his cheeks burning with embarrassment, but Digby met her gaze and smiled. She smiled back. He was not above taking a ribbing from a friend and he was just as deft at returning the favor.

"I wouldn't say I've ever had this particular view, however," he said, indicating her bosom.

They laughed but Miracle suddenly seemed unamused. She turned on her heels, calling over her shoulder with a heavy sigh.

"Come along Digby," she said. "And you too, Darling, provided your bosom doesn't get in the way." She smiled to express her humor, but Darling blushed nonetheless.

It wasn't a large ship, but it wasn't a rowboat either. The trio of friends made their way carefully through the hold to the ladder up. Up was the only direction they could go from here any way, so Digby was confident they would end up where they needed to be if they simply followed it. He had never been fond of ships. His father and mother had taken him many times to the shore, and they had even taken a cruise up the East Coast to Maine once when he was a small child. He remembered the trip quite clearly because he had spent most of it sick to his stomach, heaving over the railing into the crashing gray waves, watching the coastline pass slowly by, praying for death.

The waters were much calmer here in the Delaware, and for that he was quite glad. He didn't relish the thought of being a wanted fugitive and being sick to his stomach at the same time.

Two decks up from the hold was a lower deck. A rush of hot air swept Digby's hair back from his forehead, nearly dislodging his cap, and he surmised this was where the steam engines were kept. The trio had stepped up to the deck and began making their way up the next ladder, when a crew member suddenly ducked through a nearby passageway, nearly walking straight into Miracle.

"E're, what are you three doing down here?" he asked.

Miracle never missed a beat.

"I'm afraid we're desperately lost," she said, moving her coat aside, and stretching her cleavage with a deep breath. "Can you please show us back to the first class passengers quarters?"

He quickly rubbed the sweat from his brow and smiled, haphazardly. His front teeth were long missing, and his lips curled uncomfortably around them. "Aye, Miss -"

"Lowell," Miracle said. "Miracle Lowell."

Digby instantly prayed that this man had spent the last month trapped down here, without access to a radio or a newspaper.

"Miss Lowell," he said, smiling in his strange way. He looked suddenly smitten and willing to do anything for Miracle at the moment. "I can't go up to the passengers quarters, of course, being a steamie, stuck down here I'm afraid. But I can show ya' the way, of course."

He motioned for the trio to follow him back down the corridor he had just emerged from. The steel ship clanked and rang around them. As Digby suspected they soon came to the heavy steam engine, with it's coal fired furnaces blasting heat into the room. Digby pulled the hat from his head to wipe away the sweat from his brow. The sailor who led them motioned them through the engine room quickly, apologizing for the noise, and the smell and the heat.

"No place for a lady, I'm afraid," he said hurriedly. "My apologies to you both."

Miracle and Darling looked admiringly at the big steam engines, smiled at the sailor and hurried after him.

It seemed to Digby they walked the entire length of the ship before finding a new set of ladders which rose up one deck to a steel staircase. The sailor stopped at the foot of this and told them crew wasn't permitted any higher.

Miracle thanked him for his time. Darling smiled and leaned out to take his hand in thanks, exposing herself just a bit more, much to his obvious pleasure. As the trio climbed the steel staircase, the sailor hurried off, a big wide smile spread across his face.

Up the flight of steps the trio found themselves first on the deck for coach passengers, then up another flight of stairs to the deck reserved for first class passenger quarters. There was another flight of stairs leading up from there and Digby felt a cool breeze drafting down, telling him they were just one deck below the open air. He fought the urge to sprint for the stairs and rush up to the top deck, but Miracle and Darling were headed in a different direction, so he suppressed the urge and followed.

Down a long hallway they walked, passed an assortment of cabin doors to where first class passengers could leisurely relax during the trip. There were only a couple dozen of these, quite expensive for a simple trip down the Delaware. Most passengers were one flight down in general quarters, where everyone was grouped together, with bench seating. At the end of the hallway they came upon a set of double doors, opening to a large dining room. The table was spread with a large buffet and a dozen or so passengers were lined up to it, plates in hand. The floor of the room was filled with an assortment of tables and chairs. Large windows offered a glorious view of the river. One side, to Digby's right, offered a view of the Pennsylvania riverside, green and tree lined, while the other offered a view of rural New Jersey, and its seemingly endless farmland. To the north he could still see the Trenton skyline, it's dockside warehouses and factories looming like dark monsters on the banks of the Delaware. Above the city, plumes of black smoke rose into the air like dead trees in a burnt forest.

Digby turned the other way, toward the green farmland which stretched outside the city of Trenton. He was staring out at the New Jersey riverside, remembering his parents farm, and the days of his youth spent there, working on the tractor and farm equipment; tasting the fresh tomatoes and corn, and the delicious rhubarb pies his mother baked. Digby walked to the window lost in a daydream, staring into the distance, while Miracle and Darling hurried to the buffet. They were undoubtedly famished having only eaten a small meal late in the night.

Digby was watching the riverside pass slowly by when a man ambled up alongside him.

"Lovely view, isn't it?" the man said. "No matter how many times I see it I always see something new."

"Yes, yes, it is lovely," Digby said.

"I imagine you've driven through much of it though, haven't you?" the man said.

Digby turned. The man who was addressing him was smartly dressed. Old as Digby's father, quite likely, but obviously much more wealthy. His suit was tailored. His hat rising nearly a foot above his own head, matching Digby's height where the man's own growth had long since stopped. He had in one gloved hand a porcelain plate from the buffet table loaded with bread and fruit and cheese. In his other hand he held a champagne glass, filled to the rim.

"Beg your pardon?" Digby asked, confused.

"As a driver, I mean," the man said, stuffing his face with some cheese, while trying not to spill his champagne. "I imagine drivers see much more of the countryside than anyone else these days. Other than the airship pilots, I suppose."

"Oh, well, I think you have it all wrong-" Digby started, but was interrupted by Darling who had approached from his other side.

"Sorry, but I'm afraid my driver is quite new to this area," she said to the man. "He hasn't seen much of the countryside at all. Yet. But my sister and I plan to soon put his skills to the test. Isn't that right?" Miracle approached behind her.

"Indeed," she said. "We'll have young Mr. Savor here knowing this countryside like the back of his hand in no time."

Miracle held out her gloved hand to the older gentleman.

"I am Miss Monica Kingsley and this is my sister, Christina Kingsley," she said. The gentleman was caught off guard, both hands filled with food and drink. He struggled to take her hand, jostling first the plate, then the glass, finally stepping quickly over to a nearby table and setting both down, wiping his hands quickly on his suit pants before rejoining the ladies. Digby slid back a step, allowing Darling and Miracle to move to the front.

Savor? Digby thought. What sort of name was that? And what was his first name? He'd never even driven a real steam carriage, so he hoped desperately that the subject would not come up in conversation.

The gentleman returned and took Miracle's proffered hand in his.

"I am Reginald Givens," he said. "It is a pleasure to make your acquaintance." he released Miracle's hand and took Darling's, offering a similar greeting.

"Consider me at your service, ladies," he said.

"The pleasure is ours Mr. Givens," Darling said without missing a beat. "Do tell me, what brings you out on the river today?"

"Business, I'm afraid," Givens said, turning back to the table with his plate and glass. He snatched a piece of fruit from the plate, popped it into his mouth, then took a swallow of champagne to wash it down. Digby thought the man quite rude, but Miracle and Darling simply smiled.

"I'm in the clothing business," he continued. "Ladies clothing, in fact. Perhaps I might entertain the two of you at one of my stores today. We should be arriving in Philadelphia within an hour. I am most certain I could help you find the latest fashions from Paris, or Milan. Something much more – er, um, well much less, leather, if you please."

Miracle and Darling laughed.

Miracle did a small twirl. "Do you not think 'steampunk chic' is fashionable Mr. Givens?" Her skin tight pants and impressive cleavage made the sight more than somewhat remarkable, Digby thought. Apparently Mr. Givens thought so too.

"Now that you mention it, it is quite becoming," he said.

Darling stepped up. "And what of my choice today?" she said, leaning forward slightly. "Do you not find it to be quite becoming on me?"

Givens was nearly sweating at this point.

"I must admit, you ladies seem to be on the verge of something here," he stammered. "I might need to revisit my stock when we arrive in Philadelphia."

"Indeed you should Mr. Givens," Miracle said. Then she turned to Darling. "Come Christina, let us head to the deck and take the air. If you will excuse us sir. It has been our pleasure to make your acquaintance."

Miracle offered her hand once again and Givens took it. Then again he took Darling's hand, and bid goodbye. He said nothing to Digby, merely watched the young ladies walk away.

The trio wandered back down the walkway and to the steel staircase which led up to the open deck. Darling and Miracle had loaded their plates with an assortment of everything so they had plenty to share with Digby once up on deck.

Digby was glad to be in the fresh air once again. The air was fresher here than it had been in Trenton, cooler, but the sun felt warm. The ship had been delayed hours from the dockside brawl and arrests. Hours he had spent in that cramped hold, hoping against hope that they would not be discovered. Now, up on the deck, standing at the railing with Miracle and Darling, eating bread and fruit and watching the shoreline drift calmly past, he could almost believe it had all been a dream. One long, dark, terrible nightmare from which he might awaken at any minute.

Darling broke his train of thought with a small belch. Digby looked aghast but Miracle laughed.

"Glad you're enjoying yourself, Darling," she said with a smile.

"Please, pardon me," Darling said. Then she laughed herself.

Just the sight of the two girls laughing brought a smile to Digby's face. Once again, he could easily forget their troubles and just enjoy the moment.

"Don't look now Darling," Miracle said. "But it seems you have an audience."

Miracle motioned for her to turn around and when she did Darling saw a small pair of eyes gazing at her from a darkened corner of the deck behind a chair.

Darling cooed. "Hello," she said softly and started walking toward the boy. He shrunk back against the steel wall, further into darkness. "Don't be afraid. Are you hungry? Come here, we have plenty to share." She waved him over but he remained where he was.

"Miracle, I might need help with this one," she said over her shoulder.

Miracle strode forward, right up to the boy who in turn seemed to disappear into the shadow behind the chair.

"Come out of there right this instant," she said sternly.

Digby shook his head. "You have such a way with children," Digby said. "Not much for nurturing, are you Miracle," he laughed.

Miracle was undeterred.

"You heard me," she said. "Come out of there and get something to eat right now. Don't make me ask you again."

"Don't frighten him so, Miracle," Darling said.

But the boy moved. He shuffled himself up from a crouching position and did his best to straighten his clothes before stepping into the sunlight. He stepped closer to Darling who held out a piece of fruit. He took the fruit and jammed it into his mouth, juice dribbling down his chin, then held out his hand for another piece.

"As you see Mr. Ross, I do indeed have a way with children," Miracle said.

Darling, still holding the plate, had dropped to a crouch to be closer to the boy's level. "What's your name?" she asked.

The boy choked down the piece of cheese he had just popped into his mouth, then said, "Jeremiah, Miss. Jeremiah Maddy, if you please."

Miracle stepped closer to the boy, then she crouched too. "And tell us Jeremiah, what are you doing on this ship – a stowaway, no doubt."

The boy looked momentarily frightened.

"Don't worry," Darling said. "You're among friends. Are you here with your parents? Are they below decks?"

"No mum," he said, still helping himself to whatever he could snatch from the plate. "I'm emancipated, see. Self-employed, too."

"I see," Miracle said. "So what are you doing aboard this ship?"

Jeremiah stuffed one more piece of bread into his mouth, choked it down, then said, "I'm here chasing a ghost."

Digby laughed, Darling frowned, but Miracle suddenly became very serious.

"Tell me more," she said.

Chapter 16: Steamship Ghost

Jeremiah Maddy had seen a ghost. At least, he assumed it was a ghost, since everyone was saying that Professor Harold Nettles had died in an explosion at his laboratory. So the old man he saw dragging the rolling trunk up the dock toward the waiting ship must have been a ghost because it was most definitely Professor Nettles. Jeremiah never forgot a face.

Jeremiah didn't know who these people were, or why they were being so nice to him, but they were definitely upper class. In his experience the upper class folks weren't very nice to people like him. In fact, they weren't usually very nice to anyone who didn't have as much money as they did. He had sneaked aboard this ship during the fighting. Now that someone had seen him, no matter what their intentions, he thought it best to oblige them. For the moment.

As Jeremiah's mind raced to explain exactly why he was here – weighing the pro's and con's of revealing too much or too little information, Miracle took the lead.

She looked at him very seriously, then said, "Was this the ghost of someone you knew?" she asked.

Jeremiah nodded slowly.

Miracle smiled.

"Was this the ghost of Professor Harold Nettles, by any chance?" she said.

Jeremiah's eyes opened wide and his mouth fell open a little, revealing a partially chewed piece of bread mixed with cheese and fruit.

"Do close your mouth, Jeremiah," Darling said smiling. "It's not very becoming for a young gentleman."

He closed his mouth and swallowed hard.

"Well?" Miracle asked.

Jeremiah nodded.

"I thought as much," she said. "You saw him coming aboard this ship? Today?"

"Ye-yes, Miss," Jeremiah stammered. "Just this morning I seen him, plain as day. And so I followed him."

Hearing all of this Digby had come closer and crouched down as well.

"Nettles? Here? Now?" he exclaimed, popping his head up suddenly and looking around as if the professor might be somewhere close by.

"Yes, sir," Jeremiah said.

"How do you know it was Professor Nettles?" Darling added softly.

"I'm his assistant, Miss," Jeremiah said. "More like, I run errands for him and such, but I've been doing that for a year now so's I know the man when I see him. And that definitely was the Professor I seen getting on this ship this morning."

Miracle stood up and turned to Digby.

"I expected as much, and now we have confirmation," she said. "All that's left is for us to find him, somewhere, on this ship."

Darling was standing now too. She handed the plate of food to Jeremiah who was now eagerly stuffing the last remaining bits and pieces into his mouth, unconcerned with what was being said above him.

"But wait, are you saying you expected this all along?" Digby asked.

"Well, I didn't expect to find this boy who would confirm what I suspected," she said. "But otherwise, yes, I did indeed expect that Professor Nettles would be on this ship, at this precise moment."

Darling stood there, seemingly unsurprised in the least by what her friend had said. She just smiled knowingly, nodding her head.

"Did you know as well?" Digby asked her.

"Oh no," Darling said. "I had no idea. But I trusted enough in Miracle to know wherever we were heading was the right direction."

Digby shook his head. "Why am I always the last to know?"

Meanwhile Miracle had crouched back down to face Jeremiah.

"Now, Jeremy-" she started.

"It's Jeremiah, Miss," he said, wiping crumbs from his face.

"Right, sorry," Miracle said, smiling. "Jeremiah. I don't suppose you'd be willing to come work for us, now would you?"

Jeremiah stood a little taller. He fingered his pockets, noting just one coin.

"Of course," he said. "How may I assist you, Miss"

"Well, to begin with, my name is Miracle Lowell," she said. "This is Darling Kinder and Digby Ross. And we desperately need to find Professor Nettles as soon as possible."

"Pleased to meet you all," Jeremiah said. "I'll help you any way I can. I saw the professor get on this ship, that's for sure, but I ain't been able to find him no where."

Miracle smiled. "That's alright," she said. "If we know he's here then all we need is your help to spot him. Seeing as none of us knows what he looks like you are just the help we need right now."

Miracle stood up.

"In my estimation there are about 36 first class passenger cabins aboard this ship," she said. "I suggest we start there."

"Oh, and what, simply go knocking on doors, asking for Nettles?" Digby said.

Miracle turned to him. "Precisely," she said. "Now, come along Digby. And bring Jeremiah, if you please."

Miracle started walking away and Darling rushed after her. Digby looked at his friend, then down at Jeremiah. "Well, you heard the lady, young man," he said. "Come along."

Despite the fact they were all stowaways, Miracle walked right back down the steps as if she belonged there. Passing crew members and first class passengers alike, she waved when appropriate and ignored others just the same.

Darling followed close behind her, side by side when there was room. Digby, still in the guise of their driver, and Jeremiah, followed a respectful distance behind the ladies. Darling made a quick trip to the buffet table again where she loaded another plate with food, then returned to the small group. The dining room was more crowded now, as first class passengers came up from their cabins for brunch. Miracle leaned down to Jeremiah and whispered in his ear. He craned his neck around, scanning the room, but shook his head to her in response.

The quartet had now cleared the dining room. Digby expected they would all make their way down to the first class passenger cabins, but Miracle stopped him.

"I need you to wait here," she said. "If Professor Nettles should be strolling above decks, or in the loo, or wherever, and return here while we are searching cabins. Well, as you can see, we need to be in multiple places at once. Stay here, if you please, Digby."

"But how will I know what he looks like?" Digby asked. "Shall I start asking everyone for their name when they walk in?"

"Digby," Miracle frowned. "Professor Nettles is an older gentleman, traveling alone. If someone matching that description comes in, simply keep an eye on him until we return. Surely you can manage that, yes?"

Digby frowned back, but agreed to wait behind while everyone else went further into the ship.

He watched as Miracle, Darling and now Jeremiah, walked away, then turned back to the dining room, looking for a quiet corner in which to wait. Someplace where he could see both the main dining room and the entryway simultaneously. He found such a spot near the back of the room, and even a chair on which to sit. So he sat. And waited, wondering how long it might take his friends to search all the cabins. And what if the professor was not traveling first class? If they had to search the entire ship they would never finish before they arrived in Philadelphia, or were caught as stowaways by a suspicious crew member. Digby didn't want to think about what would happen if they were caught. It didn't matter whether they were innocent or not. Right now the city thought they were anarchists. That means a likely death sentence or life in prison, at best.

Digby was entirely lost in thought, deep inside what he considered a very gloomy future he and his friends were facing. Even if they found Professor Nettles, the man could do nothing to help exonerate them for the crimes they have been accused of committing. Digby was beginning to believe it was all quite hopeless.

Though lost in thought, Digby still scanned the room regularly for old men looking suspiciously like they might be a professor. He sat for some time, scanning the room, turning over his thoughts, one by one. So intent was he on his search for the old man he never noticed the young lady now standing to his side, until she tugged on his sleeve, and cleared her throat.

Digby was so startled he nearly fell off his chair, instead pulling himself upwards to his full height. He found himself gazing into a pair of beautifully familiar eyes, atop a fabulously bright smile. He felt sure he knew her from somewhere, but was unsure of exactly where.

She leaned close to him and whispered in her ear, "Digby Ross, whatever are you doing here, of all places?"

He was flummoxed. He didn't know exactly what to say. She continued, "Don't say anything. We don't want anyone knowing you are here, after all. Am I right?"

He nodded at her, still speechless. An old, lost and afraid look crossed his face. She reached for his hand, holding it in her slender fingers. Then she leaned close again.

"Don't worry," she said. "Your secret is safe with me. Why don't we take a walk and you can tell me all about your adventures."

She turned to lead him from his chair and walk him toward the door, but he hesitated.

He leaned closer to her and whispered, "I appreciate the offer and the discretion, but I'm afraid I cannot leave at the moment."

She smiled. "I understand," she said. "A man of your particular – talents – and current occupation, must be wary at all costs. Perhaps I might sit with you for a few moments?" She pulled out a chair beside him and sat down. Digby was confused, he didn't know who she was, but she clearly knew him. And he wasn't exactly sure how to handle this current situation, so he simply sat perfectly still as she eased into the chair beside him.

She rested her hand on his leg as she leaned in close. "Do tell me dear Digby, how you came to be involved in this, well, shall we say, situation?"

Digby's heart raced. This young lady had him at a disadvantage. She was fully aware of his current circumstances, and yet he knew nothing of her except her familiar beauty. Was she a classmate? He thought. Could be. She was about his age, and clearly a young lady of means. Her dress line plunged at the neck, revealing ample cleavage and skin so clear and smooth, like a bowl of sweet cream. Chances are that she is in university somewhere, and Princeton is (was, he reminded himself) the most prominent university in the region.

"Are you here alone," she asked.

Digby paused, perhaps a moment too long, then, "Yes," he said. "Just me."

"I see," she said, smiling. "I had expected to see your friends, what are their names? Miracle and Dottie, or something."

"Darling," Digby blurted out without thinking.

"Yes, that's it," she said, smiling. "Darling. I expected they would be with you seeing as you are all part of the same, shall we say, organization."

"We're not part of any organization," Digby said. "We're just friends. And no, they are not here with me. They are busy trying to clear our names, let people know that we had nothing to do with what happened at Princeton. Nothing at all."

The young lady patted his leg. "Relax Digby," she said soothingly. "Don't be tense. I understand how it is. It is easy for a young man such as yourself to fall under the allure of a beautiful woman, find yourself saying and doing the most dangerous, terrible things."

"No, no, no," Digby said. "It's not like that all."

"Oh?" she said, still smiling. "How was it then? Do tell me."

Digby paused a moment, trying to think. But it was difficult to think with her so close. Her hand, as it was, on his leg. Her ample bosom so – there, right there. He could smell her perfume now, just a hint of sweetness in the air between them. She shifted ever so slightly and moved an inch or two closer to him, leaning over expectantly, waiting for him to say something. But what could he say?

"Framed," he said finally. "We were framed."

She gasped. "Framed? By whom and for what reason would they have to frame a handsome and bright young man such as yourself?"

These were questions he had no answer for, and he regretted that. But he blundered on anyway.

"By evil men, that's who," he said. "Evil men up to their own evil enterprises."

She smiled. "It's always evil men, isn't it? Rich and powerful men who rule the world; think they own everything and everyone."

"That's right," Digby said, agreeing because it made perfect sense to him at the moment.

"These evil men must be stopped, Digby," she said, leaning in closer. "Don't you agree?"

"Yes," he said, reciprocating with a lean in her direction. His heart was racing now. "Yes, they must certainly be stopped."

"And you are just the young man to stop them, aren't you?" she said, her hand now squeezing his leg, her lips now coming dangerously close to his.

"Yes," Digby said. "Indeed I am. Just the man."

She closed the distance between them in an instant, pressing her lips hard against his. He was surprised, but accepting. He didn't push her away. He thought perhaps he should, but she smelled so sweet and her lips felt so soft. He was lost in a moment.

Then all hell broke loose in the dining room.

First, he heard his name shouted at him from a distance.

"Digby Ross!" He broke away from the kiss immediately, twisting to look in the direction from whence it came. As he did, his young lady friend, taken by surprise, fell over and down.

Miracle and Darling were standing in the doorway to the dining room. They looked quite perturbed. Shock and disappointment converging on their faces. Digby jumped from where he was sitting, and turned back to the young lady. She had recovered nicely, tumbling down, rolling and springing back up on her feet to face him.

"Why Digby Ross," she said smiling, a short blade suddenly appearing in one hand. "I thought you said you were here alone?" She lunged at him with the knife, but Digby twisted again, off to one side, sprinting for a nearby table to position it between the knife-wielding young lady and his mid-section.

He thought he was safe there until he felt two strong hands grab him by the shoulders and spin him around. There was a well-dressed man facing him. Digby felt the first punch crash into his solar plexus doubling him over. The second fist came crashing onto his back, sending him sprawling to the floor.

Miracle and Darling, still in the doorway, saw the room erupt around him. A few men who they had believed were ordinary first class passengers, now began tackling Digby. A few others started for the doorway where Miracle and Darling were. Miracle wasn't going to wait for them to come to her. She launched herself at the first man, her right foot swinging up and out in a powerful kick. He went spinning away. Darling pushed her way past Miracle and made for the men on top of Digby. She grabbed the first man and pulled him off like a sack of potatoes, physically throwing him across a nearby table.

Normal first class passengers were scrambling for the door, and young Jeremiah simply shrank into a corner where he could watch from a safe distance. Crew members working in the dining room started blowing whistles and more crew members began rushing in, some from the main doors, squeezing past the exiting crowd, and some from the kitchen doors at the back.

Digby saw none of this from beneath a pile of three very stout men.

He was struggling just to breathe, when suddenly he felt the weight lifted off him as Darling grabbed the last man and tossed him aside. Next she grabbed Digby and hauled him to his feet.

"Are you alright," she asked, breathlessly.

"Yes," Digby said.

"Good!" Then she slapped him hard across the face, stinging his cheek and nearly dropping him to his knees. "Now come on, Miracle needs us!"

Digby was stunned, but his head was clear enough to know what was going on. This was some sort of trap and they were caught in the midst of it. Miracle was taking down men faster than a prize fighter. Her feet and fists were flying in all directions, yet each one finding its target perfectly.

Darling was across the room in a few long strides, grabbing men and shoving them aside as she went. Plain clothes men, crew members. They didn't know what to make of this. Unsure if they should strike a woman, their split second hesitation was enough for her to get the advantage and send them sprawling.

Miracle on the other hand was facing opponents who were ready, willing and quite able to strike her any way possible if it meant taking her down. Unfortunately for them, she was quite capable of parrying their blows and delivering her own in such a way as to momentarily, possibly permanently disabling them, before moving on to her next opponent.

Digby saw all this and decided the girls were handling themselves quite well, so he might as well stay right where he was. Which was good because at that exact moment he was struck in the head with a pineapple, no doubt lobbed from the buffet table. He turned and caught an apple square in his eye. He saw the man responsible and sprinted for him, tackling him backwards over the table, down to the floor. With one hand pinning the man down, Digby reached up to the buffet table and grabbed the silver serving tray, bringing it crashing down into the mans face. Digby jumped back to his feet and made for the closest crew member with a ferocious growl.

Despite taking down a few men, Miracle quickly realized they were outmatched. She looked up in the direction of Darling who was holding her own – and a chair – against two men. Catching her eye, Miracle motioned for her to start heading for the kitchen door. Digby was already in that area, Miracle thought to herself, and together the trio had the best chance of making it out of the room that way, rather than the main door. Perhaps from the kitchen they could disappear back into the bowels of the ship to re-group.

Then she remembered Jeremiah, and turned to call to him. He was pressed back against the wall of the dining room, watching intently everything that was happening. Miracle had worried he might be frightened, but he didn't appear frightened as she looked at him now. He looked excited.

Out of the corner of her eye Miracle saw Darling take a bad turn. One crew member had her by the arm and another grabbed her around the waist from behind. She was trapped, and Miracle was too busy to help. Digby too was facing off against two crew members, so he was in no position to help. But before her eyes Miracle saw young Jeremiah launch himself away from the wall to the top of a nearby table, then leap across two more tables to the back of the man holding Darling from behind. Jeremiah grabbed the man by his ears and yanked outward. The man, clearly in agony, released Darling to snatch at Jeremiah, but the boy instantly let go and launched himself to the nearest table, escaping the man's reach. Miracle saw all this even as she fought one man down to his knees, bringing her foot crashing into the side of his face, sending him to the floor unconscious.

Miracle spun around and started toward the kitchen door at the rear of the dining room. No sooner had she taken a few short steps when the young lady who had been kissing Digby leapt in front of her, knife in one hand, wicked smile on her face.

"Well, well, Miracle Lowell," she sneered. "I've heard so much about you."

"Delightful," Miracle said. "I'm afraid you have me somewhat at a disadvantage, however. Your name is-?"

"Putnam," the young lady said. "Violet Putnam. Special Agent for the Federated States of America. I've been sent to collect you and your terrorist friends." She lunged forward ferociously but Miracle was ready for it. She side-stepped, swinging Violet's knife arm aside, and pushing her to the floor.

"Nice to meet you, Violet," Miracle said, brushing a stray lock of hair from her face. Then she deftly stepped on Violet's back as she made for the kitchen door. "And don't let me catch you kissing Digby ever again."

Darling and Miracle worked backwards toward the kitchen door, bringing themselves close enough to Digby to drag him along too. Jeremiah was still hopping from table to table, distracting men toward him and away from the others more than he was actually fighting anyone, but this worked nearly as well.

The four of them were now grouped together, back to back. There were no more crew members coming in through the kitchen doors. Miracle wasn't sure if this was good news or bad. Perhaps all the crew in fighting condition was already here, or maybe there was no door to below decks in the kitchen as she surmised. One way or the other they would need to find out, quickly. Miracle was getting tired and Darling and Digby looked exhausted. She feared for young Jeremiah as well.

Punching down a man, Digby was now right beside her. He glanced at her and said, "I didn't kiss her on purpose, you know," he said.

"Not now, Digby," she said, kicking at a nearby crew member.

"Did you at least find what we were looking for?" he said.

"Yes. But I don't think that's going to do us any good at the moment."

Darling nudged against Digby's arm and he turned to her.

"I saw what you were doing, too, you know!" she said to him.

"What? I wasn't doing anything!" he started.

"Inexcusable," Darling said, and turned away to punch out a nearby plainclothes man.

The three friends, with Jeremiah safely behind the group, were backing slowly toward the kitchen door. They couldn't turn their backs on the still charging men, so when there was a brief moment Miracle turned to Jeremiah and said, "Go to the kitchen—see if there's a back door. Run!"

Jeremiah disappeared immediately. A few punches, kicks and broken chairs later, he was back. Miracle knew from the look on his face there was no back door in the kitchen. They were all trapped now. The situation was hopeless and Miracle knew it.

The men had gathered around the group in a semi circle, trapping them, cornering them as you might a wild dog. Suddenly they stopped moving forward, parting slightly to make room for Violet, who sauntered to the front, between the growling men and the four friends.

She still held her gleaming blade, but less threateningly. Her hair was disheveled, and her dress was torn, the top hanging open, exposing a leather undergarment.

"Enough!" she shouted, and the men quieted down. She reached a hand up and tore the top of her dress open and down. It fell to the floor and she kicked it away. Beneath the dress she was clad in a leather top and leather shorts. All eyes were now on her, even Darling and Miracle.

"Quite enough, Miss Lowell," she said. "As you can see we have you surrounded and outnumbered. If you push this forward we will have no choice but to force the issue with further violence. You might not care for yourself, Miracle, but which of your friends are you willing to sacrifice to make your escape?"

Miracle looked at her friends. Darling spoke up.

"I'm with you all the way, Miracle" she said. "This hussy is all talk and no action."

Digby was staring at Darling, but said "I'm in it 'til it's really over, Miracle, and this is definitely not the end."

Jeremiah, staring up at Darling with admiration, said, "Yeah—me too!"

Miracle smiled.

"Well, it's unanimous," she said.

Violet Putnam had a devious look in her eye. She smiled at the four of them. "I must admit, I was really hoping you would say that," she said. "Take them all, gentlemen. Dead or alive this ends here."

Chapter 17: Steamship Rescue

Miracle, Darling, Digby and even Jeremiah, braced themselves for the assault they knew was coming. Only it never came.
As Violet Putnam gave her order to attack, a voice called from the back of the room.
"I wouldn't do that if I were you."
The group facing Miracle and her friends all turned. Miracle, Darling and Digby looked up and over their heads. There was a man standing in the doorway of the crowded dining room holding a strange looking gun.
Violet called over her shoulder to Miracle.
"Another of your terrorist friends, Miss Lowell?" she said.
Miracle shook her head and said, "Can't say as I have any terrorist friends."
"No matter," Violet said. "Whoever you are, understand I am a Special Agent for the Federated States of America on official business.
"My name is Jaxon Price," he said. "And all that matters now is, I am the one with the gun, so that means I am in charge. Now everyone just move to one side of the room and allow my friends to come toward me. One wrong move, and well, let's just say I have an itchy trigger finger."
The men started to move aside but Violet told them them all to freeze where they were.
"Jaxon Price, you can now add your name to the list of wanted terrorists," she snarled. "As for your itchy trigger finger, I don't recognize that weapon you're holding. In fact, it looks more like a toy to me, so why not save yourself a great deal of heart ache and put it away before you get yourself hurt."
Jaxon smiled, pointed the gun at the nearest man and pulled the

trigger. Instead of the bang everyone was expecting there was a short flash of light and a strange zapping sound. The man gasped once then simply crumpled to the floor.

"Huhn," Jaxon said. "Seems to work ok to me." He stepped over to the man on the floor, raised his foot and shifted the man a bit. "He's still breathing, but I'm pretty sure he's gonna wake up with a mighty fine headache. So, who's next?"

As one, the men moved to the far side of the dining room, with Violet reluctantly joining them, standing in front, arms crossed, her knife now sheathed at her side.

Miracle, Darling, Digby and Jeremiah saw their opportunity and crossed the room quickly. Miracle didn't know who this man was but at the moment she might as well consider him a friend.

He motioned for them to keep moving, out the door and up the steps, but he grabbed Digby by the arm as he passed.

"Go below and grab some crew members, we need to get two lifeboats ready to drop," he said.

Digby had no idea who he would "grab" or how to ready a lifeboat, but for the moment the man with the gun was in charge, so he decided he might as well go along with it.

Miracle, Darling and Jeremiah went up the steps and Digby went down below.

Inside the dining room Jaxon stood guard over his charges, gun leveled.

Most of the deck crew had been wrangled by the FSA agents to help apprehend Miracle and her friends, but Digby found extra bodies, mostly porters, to help him ready the lifeboats. Canvas tarps were pulled back and the boats were made ready to lower into the water. When that was done he returned to the dining room where Jaxon was still standing guard over the FSA agents and crew.

"It's ready," Digby said.

"How many boats?" Jaxon asked.

"Two, as you said. But I don't see as we need more than one. There's only the four of us, well, five counting you. No wait, six counting, uh, a last minute addition. But still these boats are pretty big. Plenty of room for all of us."

Jaxon smiled.

"Nice work," he said. "But the boats aren't for us. And we'll need more of them eventually."

"You can't be serious," Violet said, having heard the entire conversation. "You'll never get this ship into port before we get to shore. We'll have an army of agents waiting for you wherever you try to go. Take it all the way to the Republic of Delaware if you'd like, we'll be ready for you."

Jaxon just looked at her. Then his gun flashed and buzzed and she dropped to the floor. As Digby watched, Jaxon gunned down every single man in the dining room until they were just one huge heap of bodies.

Digby suddenly felt ill. Jaxon saw the look and turned to him. "Relax," he said. "I call it a 'numb-gun' for a reason. It just knocks them out for a few hours, or so I've been told. That first guy I shot is still breathing just fine-see?"

Digby looked, and yes, the man was still breathing, but the pile of bodies in front of him, watching them cower as Jaxon gunned them down one right after the other, was still a little sickening.

"Ok, go up on deck and round up some of those passengers," Jaxon said. "Get them down here to help carry all these people into one of the lifeboats. Tell them this ship has been seized and they better play along if they want to live. They'll help."

It took some time, but Digby did as instructed and the passengers were very willing to help. Soon one lifeboat was loaded with all the agents and crew, nearly two dozen men and Agent Putnam, and set adrift on the river. As the ship sped away down the river Digby watched over the railing. The lifeboat just tilted slowly in the water. Nobody moved.

Jaxon said he had cornered the captain and the command crew before coming to the dining room, so the ship was still steaming down the river, full speed. Apparently the plan for stopping in Philadelphia was now scrapped. Digby didn't know what the new plan was, he had been too busy shifting limp bodies into a lifeboat to pay much attention. Miracle and Darling had joined Jeremiah down below. Digby assumed they were meeting with Professor Nettles. What he didn't understand was why, now that they had the professor, didn't they simply find out what he knew, get him to the authorities, or do whatever needed to be done to sort this whole thing out.

Once again, Digby thought, Miracle is playing the game six moves ahead of me. He surmised that although she claimed not to know Jaxon she likely did. Why else would he be helping them at such great risk to himself?

Digby was still standing at the railing when Jaxon Price walked up and stood beside him.

"They'll be fine," Jaxon said. "Relax. Lifeboats are sturdy. They'll drift there, maybe even drift to the shore, and when someone wakes up, they'll all make it to dry land. It's a busy river, likely some other ship will pass by here shortly and haul them in. Hopefully, whatever happens, we'll all be long gone by then."

"To where?" Digby asked.

"Frankly, I have no idea myself," Jaxon said with a smile. He put one hand on Digby's shoulder. "But wherever it is we'll have a much better chance of sorting this whole mess out than we would in Philadelphia."

Jaxon turned and walked away from the railing. Digby took one last look at the lifeboat then trailed after him.

Just as Digby expected, everyone was gathered in Professor Nettles cabin, except Jaxon. He told Digby he needed to keep an eye on the captain, and went back to the wheel house. Jaxon also told Digby that when the ship reached Cape May they would drop the remaining passengers into lifeboats and send them ashore. Presumably without knocking them out with the numb-gun first, but Digby wasn't sure. Professor Nettles was a kindly sort by Digby's estimation. He had been quite pleased to see young Jeremiah when they were reunited, and admitted he was sorry to have left the boy with the impression he had been killed.

"Do you still have that coin, Jeremiah?" he was asking as Digby walked in.

Jeremiah fished into his pocket for a moment and pulled out the shiny Atlantean dollar.

"I lost it for a few days, this rotten copper took it from me, said I stole it from someone, kept me locked up for days until he let me out to find these folks," Jeremiah nodded toward Miracle, Darling and Digby. "But I had the last laugh! When he was rushing out on the docks I slipped this out of his pocket. He was too busy acting like a tough guy to even notice. And he didn't even see you getting on the boat, but I did. That's why I'm here. I work for you, professor. Seeing as how you weren't blowed up after all I figure you still need an assistant, so here I am."

Professor Nettles chuckled and tousled the boy's hair. "Indeed I do, young man, Indeed I do."

"Professor," Miracle said. "As much as I appreciate the sentiment of this reunion there are a few things we need to clear up."

Professor Nettles looked up at her.

"Yes, I'm sure there are," he said. "How may I assist you?"

"To begin with, what's your business with Professor Percival Lowell?" Digby blurted out.

"One thing at a time, Digby," Miracle cautioned him. "But yes, professor. We understand you sent my father a letter. A letter which has apparently generated a great deal of interest, possibly resulting in an attack on our lives, and our subsequent pursuit by federal agents who blame us for a very serious attack on Princeton University. Whatever you can tell us about what you've been working on, what involvement my father has in all of this, and how we might be able to sort everything out, would be greatly appreciated."

Professor Nettles took a deep breath and let out a heavy sigh. He looked down at his shoes, then up at the ceiling.

"Where to begin," he said. "It's so complicated, and rather, well – I'm afraid I've made a serious mistake that has had far reaching consequences, consequences which I'm certain are still unfolding even as we speak."

Professor Nettles rubbed Jeremiah's head as he spoke. Just as he was about to begin, a young sailor came running for Digby.

"Mister Jaxon says he needs to see you in the wheelhouse, sir," he said to Digby.

Digby grumbled about leaving just as he was getting some answers, but Darling and Miracle assured him they would fill him in on all the details when he got back.

"Go ahead, Digby," Darling said smiling. "Perhaps you'll find another young lady in need of assisted breathing."

Digby frowned at her, but Miracle laughed. Even Jeremiah looked at him, laughing. Only Professor Nettles was confused, remarking that he also had trained in assisted breathing techniques if there was a need for it, which brought even more laughter.

Digby just trudged away.

The wheel sat on the very top deck, above the dining room. Digby had to climb a set of steel steps he hadn't noticed before to reach it.

Inside he found a very sweaty looking handful of sailors, including the captain. There five men inside the wheelhouse, plus the captain. It was full of assorted dials, gauges, levers and knobs. There were two main control panels situated in the center of the room, with a wheel at the front. There was one sailor manning the wheel, and the captain stood beside him. Nobody said a word when Digby entered. Suddenly Jaxon Price popped up from behind the control panel nearest where Digby had entered. He had his hands beneath the control panel, seemingly engaged with something, but Digby couldn't see exactly what he was doing from the doorway.

"Ah, Dingy-excellent, come help me with this would you?" Jaxon said.

"It's Digby," Digby said. "Digby Ross."

"Oh, Digly, right," Jaxon said, still mangling Digby's name. "Just come here a moment would you, and make it sooner rather than later."

Digby strode across the room to the control panel where Jaxon was standing so he could see what the man was doing. He stopped short. "That's, that's --" Digby said.

"Dynamite, yes I know," Jaxon said. "Take hold of these wires here, if you please."

Digby stepped forward and delicately took hold of the wires Jaxon handed him.

"What are you doing?" Digby asked as Jaxon disappeared beneath the control panel.

"Well," Jaxon said from beneath the control panel. "Before I saved your asses in the dining room I stopped by here and told the captain that I had rigged the wheelhouse with a wirelessly activated explosive device. Only I hadn't."

Digby looked at the captain, who had clearly heard what was being said, but didn't move. Digby just stood there, holding the wires as delicately as possible.

"Ok, hand me just the blue and green wires," Jaxon said from beneath the control panel.

Digby looked at the wires in his hand. There were four: red, yellow, green and blue. He gently separated the blue and green wires and handed them down.

"Ok, now the other two," Jaxon said. Digby handed those down.

"Bingo," Jaxon said, pulling himself out and up to his feet. "Now I really have placed a wirelessly activated explosive device in the wheelhouse. Aye captain?"

The captain said nothing, just kept his eyes out on the river ahead. "Right, well if you're done with me then I'll be getting back below decks," Digby said, and headed for the door.

"Wait for me, would you," Jaxon said. He stopped at the door and held something up for the captain to see. "Just stay the course old man. Clear?"

The captain just nodded at him. The man standing next to him at the wheel was visibly shaking, thick beads of sweat across his forehead. Outside the wheelhouse, before descending the ladder, Digby thought of something.

"Pardon my ignorance," Digby said. "But if you blow up the ship won't that be the end of us all?"

"No worries, Dilly," Jaxon said jovially. "It's only enough for the wheelhouse. The rest of us will be just fine, but those poor sods will be goners for sure."

Just as Jaxon and Digby made it back to the professors cabin, everyone else was moving back to the dining room.

"Are we finished already?" Digby said as Jeremiah, Darling, Professor Nettles and then Miracle streamed passed him.

"Not by a long shot," Miracle said. "Come along Digby."

Digby sighed.

"Why did she call you Digby?" Jaxon said.

"Because that's my name!" Digby said exasperated.

The group made their way back to the dining room. It was now empty of passengers and crew. Jaxon had already shuttered the first class passengers below deck with the coach passengers. It wasn't bad enough their ship had been taken over by terrorists, one man said at the time, "but now we're being downgraded to coach."

In the dining room the group gathered around a single table at the center of the room. It was one of only a few which wasn't broken in the fight. Chairs were collected from all corners, and everyone had a seat except Darling who was busying herself at what was left of the buffet, loading a platter with more fruits, bread and cheese – whatever she could find that wasn't too badly disturbed. When it was loaded Jeremiah came over to help and she tasked him with carrying it to the table while she went into the kitchen to fetch a pitcher of ice water and some glasses.

Digby looked around at the motley collection of people who were now inexorably caught up in whatever it was that he and Miracle had originally been caught up in: Darling, Miracle's friend and roommate; an old man who may or may not be able to shed some light on what this was all about; a dirty street kid and some strange man with a strange gun who might accidentally blow them all to kingdom come before they ever solved anything.

Digby was not filled with optimism at that precise moment.

Miracle Lowell, on the other hand was feeling just the opposite. She looked around the table and saw the potential inherent in everyone present. Although she had no idea who Jaxon Price was or what role he might play, she was quite happy at the way he had rescued them all and had taken control of the ship without further incident; Darling had not yet failed to amaze her or keep up with her, no matter how hard Miracle had pushed; Professor Nettles had resolved several outstanding issues, including her own father's involvement, and his young friend, Jeremiah, seemed quite able to handle himself; and Digby, well. Miracle looked over at her lifelong friend, saw the dejected look on his face and smiled.

Digby looked up and saw Miracle smiling at him and asked, "What?"

Miracle said nothing, but kept smiling. She was also thinking. Turning over in her mind all the bits and pieces of what she knew so far, planning what to do next, and perhaps most importantly, how to do it.

Darling returned to the table with a large pitcher of ice water and some glasses.

"Is that water?" Jaxon asked. "No beer?"

Yes, I wouldn't mind a nice glass of sherry if at all possible," Professor Nettles said.

"It's water for everyone," Darling said. "My father always told me it was important to keep your head in times of trouble."

"Your father was a fount of wisdom, I'm sure," Jaxon said. "But probably not much fun at parties."

"Indeed," Professor Nettles said.

Everyone took a glass of water and started eating, silently at first, but it wasn't long before the questioning began, with Digby.

"Well, this is all fine and dandy," he said. "Sitting here, enjoying a meal with new friends and old, as we drift lazily down the Delaware River on a stolen steamship, but I for one would really appreciate getting some answers. Sooner rather than later would be nice."

"Relax Digby," Darling said. "Can't you see Miracle is still thinking?"

"She better be thinking fast," Jaxon said. "We've got the ship for now, but we can't keep it forever. If we're planning on making a run for open water we'll need to get these passengers off-loaded; more supplies, fuel and more weapons would be nice."

"I don't quite understand what you are even doing here," Digby said. "That might be a good place to start. Yes, in fact, why not start with you telling us who you are, why you're here and why you're helping us. What's in it for you?"

Jaxon sat back in his chair, one hand stroking his unshaven chin. His eyes scanned the table as he rocked forward in his chair, grabbed a glass and the pitcher of ice water to fill it.

"My story is," he said, and paused. "Complicated."

"Complicated though it may be, we would still love to hear it," Miracle said. "Why not start by explaining how you came to be on this ship at this exact moment."

"Actually, that's a question for you, from me," Digby said. "How did we end up on this ship, the right ship, at just the right time?"

"What I want to know is how that tramp ended up on this ship with us," Darling said. "And why she felt the need to kiss Digby. Right in front of us, like he was a piece of meat. Or a kitten."

Digby blushed. Jaxon and Jeremiah laughed. Professor Nettles sat and ate his bread and cheese, gazing out the window.

Miracle just sat there smirking.

"One thing at a time, Darling," Miracle said, still smiling. "Now, Mr. Price, if you would indulge us with your tale, and how you came to be right where we needed you, right when we needed you."

Jaxon narrowed his eyes and rubbed his brow with his calloused fingers. He was unsure exactly how much to tell them. He was unsure how much he could trust them.

As he looked around the table at the motley crew assembled before him he was quite certain no one here posed any sort of threat to him. Still, their allegiance is what he valued most, and he wondered just how much he could risk that allegiance at this point in time.

Miracle had fixed him with a steely gaze and he was feeling her piercing stare quite acutely. He was sure that any lies he told her would not get much farther than his lips, so he immediately nixed the idea of telling too tall a tale.

Jaxon rocked back in his chair, carefully reviewing the facts that had brought him to this place at this time. He looked at Darling, then Digby, then the professor, his eyes finally coming to rest on the young boy sitting beside Darling, eagerly devouring everything he could get his hands on.

Jaxon smiled. Then he thought of Penelope. His heart ached at the thought of her, away from their farm – assuming Steersman and Paulson hadn't convinced the bank to foreclose – on her own at her parents house. He had been unable to contact her for days now. No doubt she was worried to pieces about him.

He had told her he would see her soon. He had promised her he would be careful. He had promised her a great many things in the past year, all of which he seemed now to be engaged in breaking. Where was it going to end, he wondered. How far would he have to go this time to make it home safely. And at what cost?

Jeremiah suddenly belched, laughingly and with gusto. Darling laughed too, Digby chuckled. Professor Nettles said "Oh my!" but Miracle just sat there, her eyes piercing into Jaxon's skull as if she knew the debate he was having within himself and wondering which way he would finally lean with the truth.

Jaxon made up his mind.

"I am the man who was hired to blow up Princeton University," he said, quite calmly and matter of factually. The table erupted in shouting. Digby jumped from his seat, pointing a finger Jaxon and swearing an oath to have him arrested. Darling was shouting at Digby to sit down and be calm. Professor Nettles, apparently unaware of what had happened at Princeton was uttering curious gasps and sputtering questions.

Jeremiah was still stuffing his face with food as if he hadn't eaten in days.

Miracle shouted, "Digby Ross!" Then more calmly, she said, "Sit down, if you please."

She fixed her eyes on Jaxon again.

"You say you were the man hired to blow up Princeton University," she said. "But are you the man who did?"

"No," he said. "I am not."

Miracle smiled. Digby settled back down into his chair. Darling leaned forward to hear more.

"Do explain," Miracle said.

Jaxon explained his involvement from the first. He left out key details about his background, of course, as these did not seem relevant to what they needed to know. He simply said that he had been hired by Paulson, through Steersman, from time to time, to do "odd jobs."

"Odd jobs?" Digby asked. "That seems like a tall order. My mum has me do odd jobs around the farm when I come and visit but it never involves blowing up buildings and killing people."

"I didn't blow up the university and I didn't kill anyone," Jaxon said angrily.

"I believe you," Miracle said. "We believe you." She looked at Digby with eyes that led him to believe he should accept what she said without further input. "Tell me what else you know. How you ended up here."

Jaxon explained how he had decided the job was no good, too many lives at risk, so he decided to simply rig a device which would make a great deal of smoke and noise; scare everyone a little but nothing else. He also explained how he had been told to follow Miracle if she fled the campus after the device went off. He told them about being on the campus at the time of the explosion, and how he had discovered two men lurking around, setting off sticks of dynamite, blowing up the buildings like they were made of playing cards.

"I recognized the men as belonging to the Calabricci crime family," he said. "I'll know them again if I see them, and I will see them."

"Plenty of time for vendetta's later," Miracle said.

"Well, this is enough right here," Digby said. "Let's go to the police, tell them what he just told us, and get this whole thing cleared up."

"Better not go to the coppers," Jeremiah said suddenly. Everyone turned to him. "It was one of 'em that kept me caged up like an animal for days, finally making me take me to you. I heard him talking to some of the guys he brought down to the dock about Mr. Calabricci, so he must be a part of this whole thing too."

"Jaxon, all of this is great," Miracle said. "But it still doesn't explain how you knew to be here, now. Have you been following us all this time?"

Jaxon smiled. "Not exactly," he said. "I followed you from the university to Trenton, where I got hold of some old friends of mine to secure some necessary equipment." He flashed the numb-gun on his hip.

"I wound up losing you after that fracas at The Jack," Jaxon said. "I hit up my contacts in the city for more information. Things that had been going on. I heard that the good professor here had 'died' in a mysterious explosion, but since everyone, including Calabricci, was looking for him, I assumed he was still alive. It was too much of a coincidence, his disappearance, what happened at the university, Paulson's interest in you. I knew it was all connected somehow. So, I called one of my old buddies at the newspaper for whatever he knew about the professor and learned that while he is an eminent scientist, physician and inventor, he also has a few, well, quirks. Those quirks led me here, where I just happened to bump into the three of you, and just in the nick of time, too, I might add."

"Seems great minds think alike," Miracle said. "Once we got into the city I also had my people do a little research into Professor Nettles – "

"People?" Digby said. "You have people? What people?"

Darling put her hand on his arm. "Shh!" she said. "We're finally getting some answers."

"-- and they discovered that although he possesses a great intellect, he also possesses a great fear of flight and a strong distaste for train travel," Miracle continued. "A check of all passenger travel out of Trenton in the last week showed this was the next scheduled steamer. Hence, if he was alive, this is where he would likely be. All we needed to do was cross the city unnoticed by police and sneak aboard. Which is what we did."

"You clearly had a much tougher time than I did," Jaxon said. "Nobody is looking for me. All I had to do was buy a ticket."

Miracle admired Jaxon for his honesty and his tenacity. She trusted him now so she felt comfortable explaining the conversation they had had with Paulson and what new information had come to light since finding Professor Nettles.

When she was finished everyone at the table was silent. Even Jeremiah had stopped eating. Professor Nettles squirmed in his seat, feeling the eyes of everyone upon him. Now it was his turn.

Chapter 18: Good Boy Rex

"Is this true?" Digby said. "What she said. Have you really done it?" Nettles looked up at him and ever so slightly nodded his head. "Yes, yes it is," he said. "And, I have."

"Amazing," Digby said. "Truly amazing."

Jaxon was rubbing his chin, taking in all that he had just been told.

"Is that what I saw under the sheet on the table?" Jeremiah asked.

"Yes, Jeremiah," Nettles said. "It was indeed."

"Can we see it?" Digby said.

"Just a minute," Jaxon said. "Are you trying to tell me that you created an artificial man and brought him aboard this ship with you this morning? Did you buy him a ticket?"

"The trunk!" Jeremiah said excitedly. "It's in the trunk."

"Indeed, my boy," Nettles said. "but he'd prefer to be called a 'he' rather than an 'it'."

"Wait-" Digby said. "You mean, it thinks? Independently? A clockwork autonomous human that thinks? This I have to see."

Digby rose from the table and when he did, everyone joined him, except Professor Nettles.

"Nobody needs to go anywhere," the professor said. He reached a hand into a vest pocket and retrieved a small metal tube on a silver chain. He put the tube to his lips and gave it a puff of air. It seemed to Digby to be some sort of whistle, but it made no sound when the professor blew into it.

Everyone just stood there silently, looking at each other questioningly. The professor remained seated.

Just as Digby was about to ask another question there was a strange clattering echo coming from outside the dining room doors. It sound like a metal pipe banging on the steel steps, but it was definitely getting closer.

All eyes were on the door as a brass man, a few inches shy of six feet tall rushed into the room. It had a simple body: head, torso, two arms, two legs. It had two eyes, or what appeared to be eyes, a nose, or what appeared to be a nose, and a sort of smiling mesh mouth. It had three lights on its chest. The one in the middle and the one on the right were not lit, but the one on the left—the creatures right--was green.

This was all amazing enough to everyone standing around the dining room table. But then it spoke, and the mouth of every person at the table, except for Professor Nettles, dropped open.

"Professor Nettles, I have come as you beckoned," came a voice. It sounded tinny, like the voice from a drawstring baby doll.

"Good boy," Professor Nettles said, motioning to his side. "Please sit, here."

The autonomous man walked to where Nettles had pointed and promptly dropped on the floor with a squeak and a clang, resting in a crouched position.

Digby rushed around the table in amazement. His mouth was still hanging open as he leaned down to put his hand on the creatures head.

The thing turned its head in Digby's direction and a tinny growl emanated from it.

Digby quickly withdrew his hand.

"It's quite protective, Mr. - er," Nettles said.

"Ross," Digby said. "It growled at me. Did you make it do that? Some sort of protection instruction?"

"Ross, yes," Nettles said. "Mr. Ross, it's slightly more complicated than that."

"Do try to explain, professor," Miracle said, also still standing.

Professor Nettles rose from his seat, and as he did the metal man seated near him followed his movements, turning his head slowly as the man walked around him.

"The autonomous nature of this mechanism is mostly miniature gears and pulleys," he said. "Steel cables and springs, powered by an internal power source, in this case, steam cartridges which are easily recharged or replaced, are what allow him to move about. Much like what we use in our steam cars, or home dynamos, only smaller. However, what gives him the ability to think, to perform actions independent of instructions is his brain."

Nettles put his hands on the metal head before him and rubbed it lovingly.

"There are no gears, or springs, or cables which could do as well as what nature has been doing for eons," he said.

"Are you saying this thing has a human brain?" Digby said.

"No, of course not," Nettles said. "Well, not a human brain at any rate."

Miracle stepped around the table to have a closer look. "What sort of a brain did you use, professor?" she asked.

"I looked to that most loyal and devoted of all creatures," he said. "A dog."

Jeremiah sprinted around the table. "A dog!" he said. "That's a dog? I ain't never had a dog before."

Before anyone could hold him back, Jeremiah had run straight up to the creature and wrapped his arms around it. No tinny growl emanated from its voice box. In fact, it just simply crouched there nonchalantly while Jeremiah squeezed it and rubbed its shiny metal head.

"Most unusual," Professor Nettles said.

Darling had moved around the table following Jeremiah, and now stood at his side as he crouched and hugged the brass man crouching beside him on the floor.

"Can I keep him?" Jeremiah said. "I promise to take good care of him, professor. I do promise, indeed I do."

Professor Nettles was suddenly lost in thought, muttering something about behavioral patterns and circuitry. He didn't answer Jeremiah at first, so the boy kept asking.

Finally the professor looked up and said, "Well, I suppose you could. Yes, certainly. It will give me time to study this obvious instinctual response."

"I'm not sure that's a good idea," Darling said.

Jeremiah looked up at her. "Why not?" he asked.

"It's not safe," she said. "We don't know anything about this – thing – or what it might do. What if it decides to bite you, or harm you?"

"Likely no risk of that as he has no teeth," Nettles said. "Quite safe, in fact, once he gets to know you. Or if he takes an immediate liking to you, which is what appears to be happening right here. I need more notebooks. Let me just go get my notebooks so I can record some of my initial thoughts. This is quite extraordinary..."

He trailed off, muttering something about his notebooks as he walked away from the table and out the doors of the dining room. Jaxon had stayed seated this entire time, watching the scene unfold before him. He had seen some very strange things in his days with the military. Clockwork tanks, and automated munitions; machined-guns which could spew bullets faster than a man could blink his eyes, mowing down men like bowling pins. But this, he thought. This was something totally new. Something he had never seen before.

Jeremiah was still crouching near the brass man, with Darling, Miracle and Digby standing over him, watching him talk to the creature, and listening for it to make its tinny panting noise back at him.

Digby suddenly took a step back. "Miracle, is this what the professor had written to your father about?" he asked.

"No," she said. "Apparently he was simply sending along a recipe for an intellect-enhancing stew, made from beets."

"Stew?" Digby said. "This whole thing was about stew?"

"No," Jaxon said. "It's about war."

All eyes turned toward him as he rocked back in his chair again.

"War?" Digby said. "How does the professor's marvelous invention, this incredible brass man, have anything to do with war?"

"I'm afraid he's right, Digby," Miracle said. "The professor created this brass man on contract to none other than Charles Paulson. Paulson said he wanted it for dangerous coal mining operations in Pennsylvania, New Transylvania and West Virginia where he has large swaths of productive property, but once it was finished the professor became suspicious that he had other intentions for the creature. Seeing it as I do now, here, I tend to agree with him. Anyway, he took his creation and fled – well, he tried to flee, anyway, though it seems he didn't get very far."

"So, this has nothing to do with your father," Darling asked.

"Apparently not," Miracle replied.

"So, what do we do now?" Digby asked.

Miracle looked down at Jeremiah.

"Rex!" Jeremiah said, to no one in particular. "I am going to call you Rex. It sounds a whole lot better than 'brass man' or 'machine' and it's easy to remember."

"The question is, what do we do with it now that we have it?" Jaxon said. "And how do we do whatever we intend to do with it --"

"Rex," Jeremiah said. "His name is Rex."

"-- with Rex, without getting ourselves killed in the process."

"And how does any of this exonerate us from charges of terrorism?" Digby said.

"The answer to your question, Digby, is, it doesn't," Miracle said. "Jaxon, the answers to your questions, well, I need some time to think this through, now that I have the missing pieces of information."

Jaxon rocked forward in his chair. "Well, whatever thinking you have to do, better be quick," he said. "We're just a couple hours from Cape May where river traffic will be much heavier, and those agents will be waking up just around that time. All it takes is a quick phone call once they get to shore. We better have a plan of action by then." Jaxon stood up from the table and stretched. "In the meantime, I better see how our wheelhouse crew is doing," he said. "Fairly likely somebody needs a bathroom break. Dilly, can you give me a hand with that?"

"It's Digby," Digby said. "And what do you need me for?"

"Somebody needs to stand guard," Jaxon said. "We don't want anybody jumping ship."

"What about the ship to shore telephone?" Darling said. "You have taken care of that, haven't you?"

Jaxon suddenly looked panic stricken. Then he smiled.

"Yes, boss," he said. "All taken care of. Now Dickie--"

"Digby!"

"Whatever. Can we go?"

Digby looked at Miracle who was moving to sit back down at the table, seemingly lost in thought. Then he looked at Darling. "You alright here for a bit?" he asked.

"Quite, Digby," she said without looking up. "And try not kiss too many sailors while you're gone."

Digby let out a heavy sigh.

"Come on Jaxon," he said. "I need some air anyway."

Chapter 19: A Day at the Beach

Cruising at the tip of the long shadow cast by the Cape May
Lighthouse, the Steamship Platypus chugged happily out to sea. At
the wheel the first mate made do with one shaking hand, wiping the
beads of sweat from his forehead with the other.
"Steady there, Mr. Parker," The captain intoned. "We'd best continue
to take it nice and slow until we're far out of sight of land. Just do as
the man said and we'll be back to shore, safe and sound, for
breakfast."
Around the wheelhouse the men stood more or less stock still,
almost at attention. They had no tasks at this juncture. Just monitor
the pressure gauges, keep a close eye out for rough weather
(although none was expected) and take a turn at the wheel if needed.
The passengers and stewards and any crew not essential to operating
the ship were still locked below decks so there were no distractions
for the men in the wheelhouse to deal with. All they had to do now
was steer the ship safely away from shore, at least a mile off shore in
fact. Or so Jaxon had advised them.
Meanwhile, a single lifeboat landed safely on a secluded section of
marshy sand, away from the eyes of anyone who might be enjoying
a day at the beach. The little steam motor chugged happily as all
eyes scanned the shoreline for safety.
Once ashore, Miracle, Darling, Jeremiah, Professor Nettles and Rex
strode through the mucky bottom to dry ground, while Jaxon and
Digby, wading waist deep, dragged the little boat into the heavy
grass and weeds, making certain it would be difficult if not
impossible for anyone to find even if they had been looking for it.
Then they rejoined the others.
It was late afternoon now and the sun was hot overhead. Everyone
gathered beneath a tree, seeking shelter in its shade. Digby sat down
and pulled off his shoes and socks; everyone was wringing water
from their clothes however they could, except Rex who merely

crouched silently between Jeremiah and Professor Nettles. The professor had also brought along the trunk for storing Rex. The group could hardly be expected to wander in public in the company of a steam powered, six foot tall brass man.

"Right, well, that went as planned," Miracle said. "Now that we are ashore everyone knows what they have to do, yes?"

Digby, shoes and socks off, was massaging his feet. "I suppose," he said. "I'm still not certain this is the best plan, all of us splitting up, heading in different directions."

"It's the only way," Miracle said tersely. "We've discussed this already, no point in discussing it again."

Digby looked sour, but said nothing.

Jaxon was already lacing up his boots. "Miss Lowell is right," he said. "We've wasted enough time already. If we're going to do this thing then now is the time. The sooner the better."

"Safety concerns are not a waste of time," Digby snapped. "Neither are issues of trust."

"What's your problem Dilly?" Jaxon said.

"For starters, you don't even know my name," he said. "Once we've established that, we can discuss the fact that none of us even know who you are, but for some reason we're supposed to trust you blindly to deliver us from all our troubles."

"I'm not a delivery boy," Jaxon said, standing up and walking over to where Digby was still sitting on the sandy ground. "Anything I do for you now is only to help myself. And if anyone doesn't pull his weight, I'll have no problem leaving them behind."

"This is the only option we have right now, Digby," Darling said. "If Mr. Price can help then we should trust him to help. He does have a vested interest in our success after all."

"Once again I would like to take just a moment to remind everyone that we have already discussed all of this, and decided on a course of action," Miracle said. "Changing our minds now would only lead to further delays, confusion, and a much more diminished chance of success."

"Quite right," Darling said.

"Indeed," said Professor Nettles.

"I'm hungry," said Jeremiah.

Everyone turned to the boy, crouched beside the large mechanical man, now named Rex, and Professor Nettles. Like all of them he was wet, tired, and now, hungry.

"Me too," said Digby, and smiled. He looked up at Miracle who had turned to him.

"Ok, Miracle, no more complaints from me," he said. She smiled at him. "If we're going to do this thing then let's get to it."

"Indeed," said Professor Nettles.

"That's the spirit, Danny," Jaxon said.

Digby rolled his eyes, but refrained from correcting him again. He just finished pulling on his shoes and lacing them up. Jaxon stretched out a hand, Digby took it and the other man hauled him to his feet. Miracle looked around at her friends, which now included Jaxon Price. She hardly knew the man, didn't really know him at all in fact, but she felt she could trust him. At this point she felt she had no choice but to trust him. Without him she calculated their chances were somewhere close to zero. If he could do as he promised he could they would at least have a fighting chance.

Watching Jaxon brushing the dust and sand off Digby while her friend struggled away from him, saying he was "fine, fine" she couldn't help but smile. He seemed a perfect fit for their odd little crew.

Darling was stroking Jeremiah's dirty blonde hair as the boy fidgeted with his new friend, Rex; poking at the creatures face, exploring every nook and cranny with his little fingers. Professor Nettles, was polishing his glasses, carefully watching how the boy at his side engaged with the creature and how it responded in turn.

"If we're decided then," she said. "Everyone knows where they are to be, what they are to do. Timing will be of the utmost importance. We must coordinate our efforts, everyone doing exactly what they need to do and then meeting at the appointed hour in the appointed place."

"I think we're all clear," Jaxon said.

"Especially you, Mr. Price," Miracle said. "If for some reason you cannot do as you say -"

"I am a man of my word if nothing else," he said.

"-then all we do preceding it will be lost. Am I understood?"

Everyone was looking to her now, and everyone nodded on cue.

"Good," Miracle said. "Darling will take Professor Nettles and Jeremiah--"

"and Rex!" Jeremiah said.

"Of course," Miracle said. "And Rex."

"Digby, you and Mr. Price will retrieve the needed equipment and bait the trap, then meet us later at the rendezvous point, and I will take care of my end."

"Alone," Digby said and frowned.

"Yes, Digby, alone," she said.

"Right then, come along Jeremiah," Darling said. "Professor, if you please."

As Jeremiah and the Professor stood, Rex stood as well. Miracle marveled at how much they reminded her of the foursome from The Wizard of Oz.

"Can we get something to eat please, Miss," Jeremiah said, rubbing his stomach for emphasis. "I'm awful hungry."

Darling smiled at him. "Of course," she said. "First, let's make it to the train station. There will be something to eat on the way."

With one hand around Jeremiah's shoulders, Darling waved goodbye to Digby and smiled, then turned toward the eastern wood. Professor Nettles fumbled along after her, still rubbing his glasses, with Rex, dragging the wooden trunk behind him bringing up the rear.

Miracle was watching them go when she felt Digby close beside her. "Once more, Miracle," he said. "Please consider taking me with you. It's just not safe."

"She sure looked safe enough to me, holding her own against those federal agents," Jaxon quipped.

"I am practiced in the art of KoongJoon MuSool," she said. "It is an ancient Korean martial art. I promise you Digby, I'll be quite safe." Digby frowned.

"Come on Dewey, we've got a job to do," Jaxon said, putting on hand on his shoulder.

"Digby," he said. "My name is Digby. Her name is Miracle, your name is Jaxon and my name is Digby. D-I-G-B-Y. Digby."

Miracle laughed.

"I know how to spell," Jaxon said. "It's the pronunciation I sometimes get a little mixed up. Regardless, we need to get going, and the sooner the better."

Miracle looked at her friend. He was looking at her. She saw the worry in his eyes, but she had little time for it. She reached one hand up and stroked his cheek.

"I'll be fine, Digby," she said. "You take care of yourself. Go with

Jaxon, assist him however he may need it, and we will see each other again very soon. In fact, I'm counting on it."

Miracle turned to Jaxon.

"As for you Mr. Price," she said. "I consider myself a very good judge of character. Please, don't prove me wrong."

Jaxon gave a slight bow, and smiled. Miracle returned the smile, then turned around and strode away, into the brush, a slightly different course from the direction Darling had led her group.

Jaxon looked at Digby, but before he could say anything, Digby held up his hand to silence him.

"Don't say anything," he said. "Let's just go. The sooner, the better."

Outside the Cape May Train Station, hidden behind a stand of trees, Darling brought her small company to a halt. She instructed Professor Nettles to put Rex in the trunk, then used a little spittle to help smooth down Jeremiah's hair. The boy squirmed uncomfortably.

"We can't have you looking like a street urchin," Darling said.

"But that's exactly what I am," Jeremiah said.

"Not any more you're not," she replied with a smile. Then she licked her fingers again and began rubbing some dirt marks from his face while he wriggled like a fish.

Once Rex was loaded into the trunk and Jeremiah sorted out, Darling led the way into the station to purchase tickets for the three of them to Trenton. Tickets in hand, she kept a close watch on everyone else on the platform, but nobody seemed to take any notice. When the train arrived the three of them found a porter to help them load the trunk aboard in the storage car, then took their seats together.

"Can we get something to eat now, Miss?" Jeremiah asked.

"Just as soon as the train gets underway," she said.

Within 30 minutes the train had left the station and the three friends were seated in the dining car, ordering a meal.

Jaxon and Digby slogged through the thickest part of the marsh, away from the direction of their friends, toward what Jaxon promised was a roadway where they could find a car. Gradually the marshland gave way to solid ground with trees towering above them.

Making their way through the trees, finally out of the wet and muck of the marsh, Digby felt his clothes finally beginning to dry. But now that they were deep into the trees the mosquitoes, gnats and stinging insects of all sorts suddenly appeared in swarms. Digby didn't know which was more exhausting, the walk through the forest or the constant swinging and waving to fend off the bugs.

Jaxon didn't seem the least bit bothered by the insects. He led the way steadily through the forest, his eyes scanning the woods ahead and around them, not saying a word.

"Don't you get tired?" Digby asked.

"Only after hard work," Jaxon said.

"What do you call this?"

"This? This is just a walk in the forest. The hard work starts later, so you better rest now."

"Rest? How can I get any rest with all this walking?"

Jaxon laughed. "Trick I learned in the militia," he said. "Learn to sleep with your eyes open, sometimes walking, sometimes sitting up on watch. You learn to rest whenever and wherever you get the chance."

"You were in the militia?" Digby asked, swatting at a large dragonfly buzzing his head.

"Yup."

"See any action?"

"Yup."

"Is that where you learned how to blow things up? Make wireless transmitters and such?"

"Yup."

"Guess you're not going to give me any details are you?"

"Nope."

"I thought as much."

They walked on further in silence until Jaxon suddenly came to an abrupt stop at the side of a large tree. Just ahead, through the trees, Digby could see a small road.

"That's the main road in and out of the town of Cape May," Jaxon said. "If we wait here a bit there should be a car or truck coming along shortly."

Digby started to say something but Jaxon held a hand.

"In fact," Jaxon said. "Here comes one now. Looks like this is our lucky day Dickie."

Before Digby could correct him once again, Jaxon slipped from behind the tree and started sprinting toward the road.

"C'mon kid, we've got a truck to catch," he said over his shoulder.

"By the time this is over," Digby said to himself. "I won't know my own name."

Within minutes Jaxon and Digby were seated in the back of a steam-powered pick-up truck loaded with crates of raspberries heading toward Trenton. The driver said he could take them most of the way to the city; close enough for them to walk if they had to. Fortunately the truck driver also told them they could eat some raspberries along the way.

As Digby and Jaxon settled into the back among the crates of berries, the truck driver slowly reached over and clicked open the glove compartment under his dashboard. He fished out a folded piece of paper and nodded to himself. On the paper were photos of Miracle, Darling and Digby, and the words: "Wanted, Reward."

Chapter 20: Captain Francis Harold

Miracle Lowell left just minutes behind Darling, Professor Nettles, Rex and Jeremiah, but their paths did not cross. She veered slightly to the east, taking what she hoped was the shortest distance to the Cape May Federal Naval Station. Along the way she practiced what she would say once she got there; how she would convince them – had to – convince them her story was true and that she could prove it, and do so quick enough that she would be able to make the morning rendezvous with her friends. This was an integral part of the plan, and the one she was least confident of. If for some reason she was taken into custody, or prevented from leaving the base in time to meet her friends, they would be on their own. Unfortunately, she was also not very confident in their ability to pull the entire operation off without her.

And that was hardly the end of her worries. If Jaxon was lying about his ability to secure weapons; if Darling was unable to safeguard Professor Nettles and take him directly to Governor Edwards at Trent House; if Rex should malfunction; if Jeremiah should not get something to eat soon; if Jaxon keeps calling Digby by the wrong name. Miracle knew anything unexpected might be enough to bring her precarious house of cards crashing down all around her; she and Digby and Darling would end up in prison on charges of treason, Jeremiah would end up back in the city jail, and Professor Nettles' wondrous machine would end up in the hands of people who knew exactly what it is best suited for which is definitely not mining coal. But Miracle also knew these were hardly the worst case scenarios. It was entirely possible that Digby could be killed tonight. Or Darling, or Jeremiah, or Professors Nettles, or even Jaxon. There was no guarantee that someone wouldn't be shot either intentionally or by accident by an overly eager law enforcement officer or two-bit gangster. The risks they were taking, at her request, made Miracle uneasy, but she knew this was the only way to resolve all the outstanding issues simultaneously. This was the only way she knew to do what needed to be done. And she was willing to risk her friends lives to do it.

Miracle emerged from the woods at the edge of the beach area where tourists were busying packing up after a day at the beach. She looked around and spied a group of young men, close to her own age, loading a picnic basket and sandy blanket into the back of a steam powered car.

"Excuse me," she called, walking briskly over to them. "I was hoping you gentlemen might be able to help me."

There were four young men in the group, dressed for a day at the beach in dark colored romper style bathing suits. The tallest among them, a dark haired young man with a pencil mustache stepped forward.

"For a pretty young lady such as yourself," he said, smiling over his shoulder at his friends. "Anything. What can we do for you?"

His three friends gathered behind him as he spoke. Miracle chuckled to herself how much like a school yard recess conversation this was. But she had no time to dawdle.

"I need a ride, if you please," she said. "Not very far, just to the Cape May Naval Station."

"I'm sure that could be arranged," the mustachioed young man said. "But what are you offering in exchange?" He snickered over his shoulder at his three friends and they chuckled in response.

Miracle had no time for school yard antics and she certainly had nothing she would be willing to trade for a short ride to the naval base.

"On second thought," she said. "I think I'll just ask someone else." She turned to move past them when one of the young men stepped in front of her blocking the way.

"If you'll please excuse me," she said, moving around him.

"Now just a minute girlie," said the mustachioed young man, grabbing her by the elbow. "If you need help why don't you just let us help you?"

The group of young men began closing in around her. She felt their piercing stares, smelled the mix of sweat and salty water they were exuding. The young man's grip on her elbow tightened and Miracle knew this was a situation which could quickly get out of control.

Miracle looked down at her elbow, then up into the eyes of the big young man who had stepped in front of her. She smiled at him and he smiled back. Without further notice she stomped on his bare foot with her boot, and he howled with pain. Before the mustachioed young man even realized what had happened Miracle wrested her elbow loose, then brought it crashing back into his rib cage. He crumpled over, grasping his side.

The two other young men stepped forward to grab her, but Miracle was too fast for them. In two quick moves she brought her right palm into the nose of the first young man, and kicked the other man square in the solar plexus, sending him sprawling backwards into the sand. Before any of the young men could do anything else, Miracle stepped quickly to the drivers side door of the steam powered car and slipped inside. She cranked the steam-choke, then jammed her foot down on the accelerator. The steam cartridge released a heavy dose of power into the motor and the car tires spun, spraying the four young men with sand and gravel as she sped out of the parking area onto the road.

Miracle looked into her rear view mirror and saw the young men trying to chase after her, swinging their fists in the air. She chuckled to herself.

"See you later boys," she said.

Miracle slowed to a safer speed as her vehicle rounded a curve in the dirt road. She felt the rear end of the steam car swing out, sliding in the gravel, and thought it best if she focused on arriving at the Navy base alive as opposed to the alternative.

The Navy base was only a short drive away, minutes really. She reached an intersection with a sign indicating the way, and took the turn. Just ahead she could clearly see the guard post and chain link fencing indicating the entrance to the base. She slowed the vehicle down and cruised to a stop at the guard post, one Naval Security Force officer blocking her way, with his hand raised.

Walking slowly around the vehicle clockwise, he completely circled her vehicle before he approached the driver's side where she was seated.

"Can we help you miss?" he asked, with a deep baritone.

"My name is Miracle Lowell and I've come to see a friend," she said.

"What friend might this be?" he asked.

"Captain Francis Howard, Base Commander," she said. "If you'd simply tell him Miracle Lowell is here to see him, I'm sure he'll let me through."

The guard's eyebrows rose slightly when he heard the base commanders name, but otherwise, he was expressionless.

"Is that right?" he said with a wry smile. "Well, you just wait here. I'll be right back."

Slowly he stepped back from her vehicle, never taking his eyes off her, and moved toward the guard post. There was another NSF officer in the guard post. The two men spoke briefly, and Miracle saw them laugh, shake their heads in disbelief.

The first man picked up a phone receiver inside the guard post. Miracle couldn't hear any of what was being said, but she saw his laughing countenance fade away, replaced by a much more serious look.

He hung up the phone, said something to the officer beside him, then walked back to her vehicle.

"Miss, do you know your way around the base?" he asked.

"Not really, no," she said.

The NSF officer nodded at her, turned back to the other guard and said something Miracle couldn't make out. Then he turned back to her.

"I'll ride along with you, show you the way," he said. "If that's alright with you, Miss."

"Of course," she said, and smiled.

The guard crossed in front of her steam car and entered the passenger side. The door thudded closed and he nodded at the other guard who raised the wooden barrier, and waved Miracle through. She eased the vehicle forward slowly, following the NSF officers instructions through the base. She saw sailors in various training activities. Over to her left she saw Naval airships being pulled into and out of large hangars. To her right, between the various sized buildings she caught glimpses of the Atlantic Ocean

The base itself was enormous, stretching for miles to the north and south. It had been built during the Revolution, one of many designed to repel an attack by the British Navy. These days it was part of the Federally Regulated Military Force, comprised of citizen soldiers and sailors from across the state of New Jersey.

As she drove, Miracle rehearsed to herself what she would say to

Captain Howard when she saw him. It had been years since she had last seen him. True he was once one of her father's closest and dearest friends, but what she had to say, and what she had to ask him for, was teetering on the brink of madness. Could she convince him at all? She wondered. And could she convince him to such a degree that he would be willing to take action immediately? Everything she had planned required immediate action on her part. If she failed in her mission, and everything else they had planned worked perfectly, still it would all be for nothing. Miracle's support, and at the right time, was absolutely crucial.

"If you don't mind me asking, Miss," said the NFS officer beside her. "What's your relationship to Captain Howard?"

Miracle was shaken from her thoughts.

"He's an old family friend," she said. "A dear friend of my father's and of mine whom I have not seen for many years."

"I see," he said. "Captain Howard doesn't normally get many personal visitors. It's all just a little peculiar, if you don't mind my saying so."

"That's quite alright," Miracle said, and laughed. "Lately everything in my life has been a little peculiar. Looks as if you boys are getting ready for something around here."

"You could say that," he said. "Word is that we might be called to service soon. In case you hadn't heard, two of the world's oldest and most powerful Empires just teamed up to hold off the new Germanic Union – or whatever they're calling themselves these days. I can't keep up with the politics over there any more. Too confusing. Besides, we've got some of our own troubles right here, what with some crazy anarchists trying to blow up our colleges -"

"Oh really? I hadn't heard about that."

"Yeah, right at Princeton. Blew the damn place to hell and back – pardon my language."

Miracle kept right on driving, slow and steady. Clearly this man had no idea who she was; had been too busy lately to read a newspaper.

"Pull up in front of that white building over there, please miss," he said.

Miracle did as instructed. When she stopped, the man got out of his side and rushed over to her side of the vehicle, opening her door for her.

"Thank you," she said, and smiled.

"Of course, miss," he said. "If you like to just walk on inside. The man at the desk will see you the rest of the way. I'll go ahead and park your car for you. When you're ready to go again he will let us know and we'll bring your car back around for you."

"Thank you again, Mr.- uh," she paused.

The man stood at attention and said, "Sergeant Ferrel, miss. Sergeant Percy Ferrel."

"Well, thank you again Sergeant Ferrel." The she turned and walked up the sidewalk toward the white building. Inside was a very small lobby, sparsely decorated, with doors heading off in different directions. A single small wooden desk was at the center. A young man sat at the desk. He looked up.

"Captain Howard said I should see you right through, miss," he said, standing. "This way, if you please."

He turned and motioned toward one of the doors. He stepped over and opened it, revealing a long hallway. Miracle stepped through and waited. There were several doors leading off this hallway, likely Captain Howard's office was one of them.

The young man stepped through silently, then led her down the hallway to the last door. He rapped his knuckles twice on the door. From inside came a muffled call, and the young man opened the door.

There was a very large, very cluttered wooden desk, behind which sat Captain Francis Howard, Base Commander. He had serious, deep set eyes, and graying hair swept back from his head in a short no-doubt, regulation cut. The lines in his faces told her it had been many years, many long, hard years, since she had last seen him. And indeed it had been.

"That'll be all, thank you," Captain Howard said.

"Yessir," the young man said, and closed the door behind him as he left.

"Miracle Lowell," he said. "I don't know whether to hug you or arrest you on sight for being a traitor to your nation."

He smiled when he said it, so Miracle relaxed.

"I hope that you will be willing to at least hear my side of the story first, Captain," she said.

Captain Howard looked at her, smiling gently.

"Your father saved my life, more than once, I might add," he said. "What sort of a gentleman would I be if I didn't at least hear what you had to say?"

"Indeed," she said. Howard motioned for her to take a seat at his desk, waited for her to get situated, then sat down himself.

"I imagine this is a long and complicated story?" he said. "Are you hungry? Shall I call for something?"

Miracle spied a pitcher of water and a tray of glasses nearby. "Just a drink of water would be fine," she said. He rose immediately and brought her a full glass.

She sipped first, then drained the glass when she realized how thirsty she was. Her palms were sweating and her feet had started a gentle rhythmic tapping. The water helped her relax a bit.

"I can only assume you have been reading the newspapers," she started.

"The newspapers?" he said, chuckling. "I received official notification from the Federal Service. My entire base was already on high alert because of the recent tribulations in Eastern Europe. Domestic terrorism was just another ball to juggle. However, you can imagine my utter shock when I saw your name associated with what happened at Princeton."

"You must believe me when I tell you that is all a lie," she said. "We have been framed by a man named Charles Paulson, and at least one other group of unsavory individuals, in order for us to either reveal what we know about a Professor Harold Nettles or deliver him to them. Although initially their request was for me to reveal the current location of my father, the claim was that he would lead them to Nettles, or at least point them in the right direction. When I refused, Princeton was attacked, we were blamed, and have been on the run ever since."

Captain Howard settled back into his chair. He held his hands in a praying position in front of his face, the tips of his middle fingers just touching the tip of his nose.

"I see," he said. "You know, Miracle, if it were anyone else sitting in my office, telling me this story, I'd have already put them in irons." Miracle squirmed uncomfortably.

"But as I said, your father saved my life more than once, and I've known you since you were a baby. I knew there was no way you could be mixed up in any of this. Now, all you have to do is help me prove it, and we can square everything with the local police, state police and the Federal Service, and get the right people in the brig where they belong."

Miracle beamed. "I am so glad to hear you say that," she said. "Allow me to relate the entire story to you, in detail, along with the evidence I have which bolsters everything I say, and then, if you're willing we should be able to catch at least a few of the actual perpetrators red-handed."

Captain Howard smiled. "I like the sound of that. Carry on, if you please."

Miracle told him everything that happened so far; about Digby and Darling, and their trip through the steam tunnels, and the fracas on the dock, and the situation with the steamship and the agents (at which point he immediately stopped her and made a call to the coast guard to find and secure the ship, and sent a crew out to retrieve the agents who may or may not still have been adrift in the river). Then she told him about their current plan, the one which involved her being here, talking to him, while her friends made other arrangements.

"And you say you have evidence which bolsters your story?" he said when she had finished.

"Indeed," she said. "If you will allow me to use your phone, I'll just make a quick call and you can hear for yourself.

"By all means," he said, swinging his telephone around, putting it within her reach.

She dialed. A gruff voice answered.

"Mr. McPherson?" she said. "I trust you have those recordings ready? Excellent. Would you be so kind as to play them for me? Yes, now, over the phone, if you please. Also, I am seated with Captain Francis Howard, Base Commander at Cape May Station. He is very interested in what you have uncovered on my behalf so if you would please introduce yourself and briefly explain the work I have engaged you with. I am handing him the phone now."

Miracle handed the phone to Captain Howard, who had an incredulous look on his face.

"This is Captain Francis Howard. To whom am I speaking? Angus McPherson. Mr. McPherson, please hold on for one moment."

Captain Howard fished a pad of paper and a pen from his desk drawer and placed them in front of him.

"Carry on," he said. Immediately he started writing.

After what seemed to Miracle to be an interminably long time, with

Captain Howard asking the man to stop, repeat himself; clarify some points; pause or rewind the recording, he thanked the man, instructed him to keep all of his information secure for retrieval soon. Then he got McPherson's contact information and address, bid him goodbye and hung up the phone.

Captain Howard was staring intently at his notepad. He didn't look up at Miracle when he said, "I remember once when you were 8-years-old. Your father and mother invited me to join the three of you at a show in Atlantic City. There was a magician there -"

"The Great Zandini!" Miracle chimed in.

"Yes, yes, that's the one," Captain Howard said, still keeping his gaze on the notepad. "Anyway, he did some really amazing things. Made a girl disappear and re-appear; levitated a chair, even escaped from a submerged trunk right there on stage in front of our eyes. And through it all, after every single trick, you turned to me and said, 'I know how he did that' and then you explained it to me. And everything you said made perfect sense."

He set the pad down on the desk before him and finally met her gaze.

"I only have one question for you now, Miracle Lowell," he said.

"Yes, Captain?"

"How can I help you?"

She smiled. "It truly is good to see you again, Captain. I wish it were under less dire circumstances, however, be that as it may, time is of the essence."

Then she explained exactly what would be required, when it was required, and where it would be required.

Chapter 21: Trouble On The Train

The train ride from Cape May Station to downtown Trenton was
scheduled to take 2 hours and 45 minutes. By the time Darling,
Jeremiah and Professor Nettles finished their meal an hour had
already passed. They returned to their seats in the Coach car and
settled down, relaxed. Jeremiah almost immediately began to nap.
Professor Nettles was furiously writing in his notebooks. Darling
was like a hawk, watching everything and everyone coming and
going in the car.
It had been a quiet ride so far. They had boarded without incident,
eaten without incident. It appeared everyone thought they were
simply a family traveling home to Trenton after a day at the shore,
and Darling's group had given no one any reason to think otherwise.
A half hour after returning to their seats Darling finally felt she could
relax. Jeremiah had fallen sound asleep, and Professor Nettles,
letting his notebook fall to his chest but still clutching his pen, had
quickly followed. Looking across at Jeremiah and Professor Nettles,
nestled up against each other like a grandfather and his grandson,
warmed her heart. She smiled.
The train rolled quietly into the thickening darkness. It was night
now, and the day had been long. Darling had not slept in some time
and she felt weary beyond words. She glanced around the train car
once more. Everything was quiet. What other travelers there were in
this car seemed content to engage with each other in whispered
conversation, or had long since closed their own eyes, succumbing to
the gentle rocking of the train.
Darling felt safe here. For the first time in days she felt she could
relax. She settled a little deeper into her bench seat, adjusted her
blouse, her hair. Professor Nettles snored a great rasping snore and
shuffled himself to get more comfortable, eyes still closed. His pen
slowly slipped from his fingers and dropped to the floor. Darling
bent to retrieve it and as she did she heard the train car doors open
and close. Slowly she rose enough to peek one blue eye between the

shoulders of her sleeping companions.

It was the Federal Special Agent, Violet Putnam, shadowed by two of her men, standing in the doorway of their car. All three were casting steely eyed stares at everyone seated within.

Darling froze. From her position Violet could not see her, but with so many passengers seated with their backs to the train car door Violet would have to start walking down the aisle to get a clear look at everyone's face.

They were seated nearly at the exact middle of the train car. Darling made some quick mental calculations as to how many seconds it would take Violet to be within view of her, bent over as she was between the seats. She shifted her feet slightly beneath her, to make it easier to spring up and forward. As Violet approached Darling tensed herself.

Suddenly she heard the door at the rear of the train car open.

"You there – Federal Agents, don't move!" Violet suddenly shouted. But she wasn't talking to Darling. She was pointing at the rear of the car. Darling couldn't look in that direction from where she was, so she popped her head up and turned. When she did, she heard Violet say, "You—don't you move either!"

At the rear of the train were three men, dressed in matching tweed suits. They looked strangely out of place, each with a carefully waxed, bushy mustache. They had matching watch chains hanging from vest pockets and each had a round bowler covering the top of their head.

The moment Darling cast her eyes on them they spotted something behind her. One pointed directly at Professor Nettles and the three together rushed forward.

In the meantime Violet and her men also rushed forward, only to be met by the cracking of a pistol shot. One of Violet's men collapsed and Violet herself and the other man jumped between seats, just one seat in front of Darling.

Jeremiah and Professor Nettles awoke with a start and Darling dragged them both to the floor with her. The train car erupted in panicked screams from other passengers as the three men continued firing wildly around the car.

Darling and her friends were trapped. Violet and the remaining Federal Agent in front of them, three armed men behind them. There was no place for them to go.

Violet Putnam peered at Darling from between the seats. "Don't you move!" she said.

"And where could we go even if we had a mind to?" Darling shouted back.

"I sure wish we had some firearms!" said the agent crouching behind Violet. "Do you have any firearms?" he shouted over her shoulder to Darling.

"Shut up, Casey," Violet said to him.

"Well, do you have any firearms?" Violet whispered to her.

"Of course not!" Darling said.

The shooting subsided. Darling guessed the men would be cautiously approaching now.

Violet popped up from behind the seat back and launched a boot at one of the men. Darling heard an "Ooof!" and more shots were fired, slamming into the seats just above where the three friends were crouching.

From between the seats, Darling could see Violet pulling her other boot loose from her foot.

Jeremiah and Professor Nettles huddled together, low to the floor. Darling was afraid, and confused. Obviously the men behind her were more dangerous than the Federal Agents in front of her, but either way, this was a losing situation.

Suddenly she had an idea.

"Professor, give me your whistle!" The professor looked at her confused, and pointed a boney finger at Jeremiah. The boy reached beneath his shirt and drew out the tiny silver whistle. He looked at Darling, who nodded silently and quickly.

Jeremiah put the whistle to his lips and blew. Bullets were still flying into the seats around them. When the shooting stopped, Darling assumed the men were reloading their pistols. Suddenly Violet and the agent with her stood up and hurled shoes at the men.

Darling heard the pounding feet of the men behind her come charging up the aisle. She crouched, tensing her muscles, wrapping Professor Nettles and Jeremiah in her arms. She glanced quickly at Violet and the two women exchanged a nod. Suddenly Violet and the agent sprang up out of their position behind the seats to meet the men in the aisle.

Violet kicked the first man in the chest. He flew backwards against his two friends, who pushed him forward again. The second Federal

Agent swung a heavy fist at the second man from over Violet's shoulder, but missed, instead taking a punch from the man he intended to hit himself. The two men grasped each other and rolled against the seats on the opposite side of the train from Darling. Two female passengers seated there squealed in horror as the fighting men tumbled onto their laps.

Violet was shoved backwards by the shoulders, grasping the arms of the man who shoved her and pulling him down on top of her, rolling him completely over her head. But he refused to let go of her blouse, dragging her, tumbling down the aisle together.

The third man reached Darling, grabbed her by the collar and dragged her up to her feet. She spun in his grasp and brought her hand crashing into the side of his face. He smiled at her, but said nothing, didn't flinch. He brought his right hand back and used it like a club to slap her across the face, first one side then the other. His hands were big, and tough, covered in calloused skin. Her face stung and she couldn't prevent the tears which streamed from her eyes. She tried again to strike him, but he tossed her aside, into the seats across from where they had been seated.

He glared down at Professor Nettles and Jeremiah, crouched and huddled together on the floor of the car.

"Professor Nettles, I presume," he said menacingly. "I believe you have something which belongs to us. We have come to claim it."

Professor Nettles sighed. "Indeed I do," he said.

Suddenly the door to the train car crashed open. Pieces of splintered wood and glass sprayed across the front of the car. More passengers screamed. Darling dragged herself up to look and saw Rex come charging down the aisle, leaping over where Violet and the man were still struggling, straight to the man hovering over Jeremiah and Professor Nettles.

"Ah, here it is now," Professor Nettles said as Rex crashed into the man, pushing him forcefully backwards all the way down the aisle and straight through the doors at the rear of the car.

Taking advantage of the lull, Darling brought herself up from between the seats. She used the heel of her palms to push the tears from her eyes, then quickly crossed to Jeremiah and Professor Nettles, dragging them to their feet. Some passengers were still screaming, the air was whistling and howling through the train car now that the doors were smashed open.

Violet had turned the tables on the man she was wrestling and now sat atop him, pounding her fists into his chest. The other agent was on the floor, as the man atop him, pressed down with his heel on his neck.

Darling ran to where the agent was being crushed. She grabbed a purse from a nearby woman and brought it crashing against the face of the man standing over him. Once, twice, and he was flung against the seat. This gave the agent enough time to wriggle off the floor, catch his breath, and pound his fist against the head of the man.

The agent turned to Darling.

"I'm much obliged, miss," he said. "I'd tip my hat if I still had one."

"Never mind that," called Violet from down the aisle. "We need to go. Now."

Darling hesitated.

"Obviously those men weren't alone," she said. "There were only three of us on this train-now's there's just two. The rest of my men are scattered around the countryside looking for you and your friends. I suggest we take advantage of this moment and escape."

"What about Rex?" Jeremiah said.

"Who's Rex?" Violet said.

Suddenly the brass man appeared at the door he had crashed through. He came clunking down the aisle and stood beside Jeremiah and Professor Nettles. His throat emitted a tinny growl at Violet, but otherwise, he was motionless.

"Good God Almighty," said the agent. "What is that?"

Violet was silent, studying the machine-man before her.

"This?" she said. "Is this what this has been all about?"

Darling nodded. Jeremiah was holding Rex's metal fingers in his own. Professor Nettles was smoothing out his jacket and then, rubbing his glasses.

"This is my invention," Professor Nettles said. "At the behest of one Charles Paulson, and some other foreign investors I built this machine and then – I took it away from them. Everything which has happened as a result of that decision has been my fault, my responsibility, alone. These young people have had nothing to do with any of it."

"That's not what I've heard," Violet said. "And while I almost always appreciate a confession, this is neither the time nor the place for it. The proper authorities will decide who did what to whom and what the consequences will be. My job is to find who they tell me to find, and today, that's you." She pointed a finger at Darling's bosom.

"Well they told you wrong," Darling said, pushing the woman's finger away. "Our whole purpose these past few days has been to find Professor Nettles and prove our innocence. We're halfway there already."

"Look," Jeremiah said, pointing toward the rear of the car. Three more men, all dressed the same as the first three men, burst through the opening left behind when Rex crashed through.

Rex growled, but Jeremiah held fast to his hand.

The three men stopped and stared at the small group and the metal man, then slowly started reaching into their jackets. Nobody doubted these men would be armed as their friends had been, but before they could draw their weapons, Violet grabbed Darling and Jeremiah and started dragging them toward the front of the train.

"Come on!" she said. "Now!"

Darling, Jeremiah, and Professor Nettles followed Violet. The agent was close behind, and behind him, between the group and the three armed men, was Rex. Pistol shots rang out, followed by the clang of brass as the bullets bounced harmlessly off his back.

Through the pass-way between cars, into the next car, the group fled. Darling was anxiously looking behind her, hearing sporadic gunshots, and harmless clangs of metal, pushing Jeremiah and Professor Nettles ahead, following closely behind Violet. The other agent was right behind her, urging her forward. Every now and then she heard him cursing Federal firearm laws and praying out loud that God would deliver him a Colt .45 or even a .38 Special.

As they fled through the car the passengers shrieked and huddled together. A man stood up suddenly to shout something, but a bullet cut him down. His blood sprayed across Darling who kept running. Into the second pass-way between cars, this time opening the doors and shuffling through, they all fled into the next car, Rex trailing behind.

"We're going to run out of train sooner or later," Darling called to Violet.

"And they're going to run out of bullets," Violet called back.

As they shuffled into the third pass-way Violet stopped short. Darling peered through the glass past Violet's shoulder into the car beyond. Three more men, dressed as their friends, were hurrying down the aisle in their direction.

"Back!" Violet called, but there was no place to go. The two agents behind them were positioned halfway down the car, ducking behind seat backs. They must have known their friends were in the car ahead as they didn't push further forward. The small group of friends, and the two agents were now trapped in the pass-way.

Darling looked from side to side. Through the window she saw the countryside streaming past and wondered briefly how fast the train was moving.

Before she could make a move, Violet pulled open the door to the outside.

"Alright, you three, or four, whatever," she said. "Now's your chance. Make this thing right—prove me wrong. Now go."

Darling looked at the darkened scenery rushing by. Heard the wind roaring. Looked again at the men hustling down the aisle.

"Young lady," Professor Nettles said. "I can't possibly jump off a moving train!"

Violet looked at him to say something, but in a flash he was gone. Darling had pushed him off the train.

"Tuck and roll Professor," Darling shouted after him. "You're next Jeremiah. Now, get along."

"What about Rex?" he asked.

"You have your whistle?" Darling asked. Jeremiah pulled it from his shirt. "Keep a good hold of that and give it a good blow when you stop tumbling. Now, tuck and roll." Jeremiah jumped from the train. The three men behind them now saw the three men in front of them, and wordlessly seemed to have agreed that they should converge on the pass-way between the cars.

"Jerry," Violet said to the other agent. "Bar that door and don't let them through. I'll take this side." She turned away from Darling.

"Bar the door?" the agent said. "With what?"

"With your dead stinking corpse if you have to. I don't care. Just keep them out of here."

Darling put her hand on Violet's shoulder. "Your trust in us is not misplaced," she said.

"This won't be the first mistake I've ever made," Violet said over her shoulder. "But it might be my last."

Darling turned away from Violet toward the open door. She didn't hesitate and stepped right through into the rushing air. As she did, she felt a nudge from behind, and cold metal arms wrapping around her. Rex had been summoned so he brought her safely to the ground with him.

Looking up at the train Darling saw flashes of gunfire. The train kept moving, faster it seemed from the ground now that she wasn't moving. It disappeared around a bend in the tracks ahead.

Jeremiah rushed up beside her.

"Are you alright, miss," he asked, brushing the dust from her blouse.

"Yes, quite," she said. "And you? All in one piece I see."

"Not so sure about the professor, miss," Jeremiah said. "He seems stuck on something."

"Show me," she said.

They walked back along the tracks and found Professor Nettles quite secure on a low hanging branch. His belt had caught, leaving him at least two feet off the ground.

"The good news is, I don't seem to have broken anything," he said.

Darling giggled. "Let's get you down from there."

Together, with Rex hauling down the branch, they released the professor.

"I have a bit of a tightness in the seat of my trousers," he said, reaching back to loosen his britches.

"Well," Darling said, looking around in the darkness. "A good walk should help you work things out."

Darling looked up at the star filled night to get her bearings then said, "This way gentlemen."

"Surely you don't intend for us to walk the rest of the way to Trenton?" Professor Nettles said.

"No," she said. "Only to the town of Cherry Hill, which, if my calculations for longitude and latitude are correct, judging by the stars, should be just over there." She pointed into the darkness.

Jeremiah and Professor Nettles had no idea where they were, but they followed along behind her because she was leading the way. Sure enough, after about 15 minutes of walking, twinkling lights could be seen in the distance and the town of Cherry Hill rose up to great them.

"Wow, miss," Jeremiah said. "That's a pretty good sense of directions you got."

"My father insisted I learn how to navigate by starlight," she said. "He said every young lady should be prepared for anything at all times."

"Indeed you seem to be," Professor Nettles said, huffing to keep up with them.

"Now, all we need is a car," Darling said.

"Don't tell me you know how to drive, too?" Jeremiah said.

"Of course I do, Jeremiah," she said. "Father insisted on that as well."

Chapter 22: Into the Woods

The steam powered pick-up truck belched and kicked, bouncing
along the rutted road north as daylight faded away. Digby and Jaxon,
squeezed between crates of raspberries rested silently, each staring
out behind the truck into the column of dust which trailed them.
Suddenly the truck darted off the main road.
"This doesn't seem right," Jaxon said to Digby before leaning his
head over the side of the truck to shout up at the driver.
Digby had no idea where they were or what road they were on, so he
wasn't sure what to think. He started looking over his side of the
truck, trying to get a glimpse of the road ahead. It was nearly dark so
there was little he could see. He heard Jaxon shouting something to
the truck driver, but the vehicle continued on its way. If the truck
driver had any response for Jaxon, Digby couldn't hear it.
"Hang on," Jaxon said. "We're speeding up."
The truck bounced more vigorously now as indeed, Digby felt it
gaining speed. Suddenly it swung to one side, crates crashing down
around and on top of them both. Jaxon and Digby were helpless in
the back amid the debris. The truck slid to a stop and the truck driver
jumped out of his side of the vehicle, shouting.
"I got 'em! I got the anarchists! Right here in the back of my truck!"
Jaxon was the first one up from beneath the crates. Grabbing Digby
forcefully by one arm, he made to jump off the back of the truck.
There was a crash like thunder, and raspberries exploded around
them.
"Don't you move!" came a shout.
"Not my truck Larry! Don't shoot my truck!"
"You there," came the shout again. "This is Cumberland County
Deputy Marshall Lawrence Allen. You just put your hands up nice
and slow and nobody needs to get hurt."
Jaxon and Digby were frozen in place. Digby looked at Jaxon for
their next play, but Jaxon just shrugged. He slowly raised his hands
above his head and Digby did the same.

"I'm coming around there," came the voice. "Don't move. Let me get a good look at you."

"Don't shoot my truck no more, Larry."

"Daryl, shut up or I'm gonna shoot you in a minute."

Cumberland County Deputy Marshall Lawrence Allen moved cautiously around to the rear of the truck, both hands holding tight to a double-barreled shotgun. Digby and Jaxon had not moved. Just sitting in the bed of the truck, covered in splattered raspberries, with both hands raised above their heads.

"That's him, right?" Daryl, the truck driver, said.

"Shut up, Daryl."

"You," Deputy Allen said, pointing his shotgun straight at Digby's face. "What's your name?"

Digby gulped, sweat beads bursting from his forehead like a summer shower.

"No use asking him," Jaxon said suddenly. "He's foreign. Don't speak no English."

"That right?" Deputy Allen said. Digby just smiled at him stupidly and said, "Oui."

"We what?" Deputy Allen said.

"That's French," Jaxon said.

"Right," Deputy Allen said, lowering his shotgun just a bit.

"Don't let them fool you," Daryl said. "I got the flyer right in my glove box." He ran to the front of the truck and grabbed the piece of paper with Digby's picture on it. Then ran back to Deputy Allen. "Here, see for yourself," he said, thrusting the flyer in Deputy Allen's face.

That was all the opportunity Jaxon needed. Without saying a word or alerting Digby in any way, Jaxon went from sitting in the truck bed to flying through the air at Deputy Allen in a flash. He crashed down on him, his arms powering the shotgun down and to the side. It blasted a fountain of rocks and dirt into the air around them.

Daryl sprang unexpectedly into action, trying to grab Jaxon from behind.

Digby sprang from where he was, plowing into Daryl's side and knocking him off his feet. Then he turned to Deputy Allen. Jaxon was still struggling to wrest the shotgun away from him when Digby brought his fist down on the man's shoulder, temporarily loosening his grip, causing him to drop the weapon.

Jaxon grabbed the shotgun and fired a blast in the air. Daryl and Deputy Allen froze in place.

"Now, settle down a bit," the deputy said. "Nobody here needs to get hurt."

"Big words coming from the man who just tried to kill us!" Digby spat at him.

Jaxon smiled. "I'll tell you what we we're going to do, deputy. And you there, laughing boy," he said, waving the shotgun at Daryl who was still sprawled on the ground. "Both of you, handcuff yourselves together and get in the back of that patrol car."

Daryl was still sprawled on the ground, his hands raised above him, sweat pouring from the sides of his face.

"Now look here, son, you don't know what you're doing," Deputy Allen said.

"Oh, sure he does," Digby said, moving behind the deputy and pulling the steel handcuffs from his belt. He snapped one on the deputy's wrist, then tugged him closer to Daryl, snapping the other on his wrist while he was still more or less in a sitting position. Hauling Daryl to his feet he hustled both men over to the patrol car, opened the back door and shoved them both inside, slamming the door shut behind them.

Then he turned to Jaxon. "You do know what you're doing, right?"

"Sure I do, David," Jaxon said. "Just bear with me a minute while I consider a few things.

Jaxon went over to the rear of the patrol car and opened the door. "I forgot something," he said. "Gimme your keys."

With keys in hand he turned back to Digby.

"Ok," he said. "Let's go."

"Go? Go where? And with them? That's practically suicide. Definitely criminal – even more criminal than most of the other things I've done today."

"Simmer down a bit Danny boy," Jaxon said. "We need them. Well, we need one of them. The other one is useful just to keep the important one from getting away. He wouldn't make it far if he had to drag a corpse with him. Now, get in and let's hit the road. There is no time to lose."

Jaxon was slipping behind the wheel as Digby was still standing there, mulling over what Jaxon had said, and wondering if it was not too late to choose a different partner. Finally, as Jaxon was actually starting to roll the car away Digby made a last minute decision to get in the front seat behind him and hold on for dear life.

"Glad you finally decided to join me," Jaxon said. "Here. Hold this." Digby took the shotgun.

"What's all this about?" Deputy Allen said.

"You guys can't just leave my truck there!" Daryl said. "Somebody might steal it."

Jaxon laughed. "Can't think of a much safer place than the Marshall's office, can you deputy?"

Night had completely fallen by the time Deputy Lawrence Allen's patrol car rolled past the Trenton City Limits sign with Jaxon Price behind the wheel and Digby Ross riding shotgun, their two prisoners handcuffed and quiet in the backseat.

On the ride to the city Jaxon and Digby had explained as best they could what was really going on, and what they intended to do. If Deputy Allen truly believed them, neither knew for sure. But regardless, he would bear witness to what was about to happen and could then judge for himself. Assuming they all survived. Daryl, for one, was most certain they were all going to die and that his truck and berries would likely be stolen even if he did somehow manage to live through the night, which would mean his wife was likely to kill him when he got home.

"Shut up, Daryl," Deputy Allen said. "Can't you see we've got a real situation here?"

"All I care about is my truck, Larry!"

"Blast your truck, Daryl! This is serious business. Now look boys, why don't you just let me get on that wireless radio to my friends at the state police. We can get this whole thing sorted out in a jiffy."

Jaxon sighed. "You haven't been listening, Larry. No police. The Trenton City Police are likely involved, which means we can't really trust anyone. I had half a mind to dump you and your buddy in the closest ditch, but fortunately for you my friend Davey here had a good enough heart to convince me otherwise."

Digby sat silently, still holding the shotgun, both eyes on Deputy Allen and Daryl in the backseat. He did manage a slight menacing look when the men turned their eyes to him, and they shrank back in their seats accordingly.

"All we're asking you to do is witness what's about to happen, that's all," Jaxon continued. "When it's all over, you can decide for yourself what's right."

Deputy Allen sighed and settled into his seat.

Jaxon knew Deputy Allen's type: grew up in the Pine Barrens; married his high school sweetheart; took a job at the Marshalls office like his daddy; never had no need for city life, so was likely not a part of whatever corruption was currently working against them. That didn't mean they could trust him, however. He was still a danger to them, to their plan, ultimately to Miracle's grander plan. Trusting him now, bringing him with them was a gamble, but Jaxon was hoping the odds were in their favor.

The steam powered patrol car slipped silently through the dirty streets and back alleys of Trenton, parking across the street and down the block from the garage where Jaxon had said they'd find who they were looking for.

He pulled the car into the lot and shut it down.

"Is this the place?" Digby asked.

"No, it's my mother's house," Jaxon said. "I thought we'd grab a bite to eat, maybe listen to a radio program before we head out."

He smirked at Digby who just shook his head and rolled his eyes.

"Do you know how to use that thing, son?" Deputy Allen asked from the backseat.

Digby checked the shotgun in his hands and nodded. "Yes sir. I am a champion skeet shooter with several trophies at home to prove it."

"Skeet, huh?" Deputy Allen said. "Skeet ain't a man, son. Skeet don't squirt blood all over you when you hit it. Skeet don't scream and beg for mercy when you blast a hole in it."

"That's enough of that," Jaxon said, turning in his seat. Digby was starting to look a little whiter than usual. "Don't worry, Danny. If we're lucky, nobody is going to be squirting blood on anybody. Now, you boys just sit here and wait. If we're coming back, we'll be back in about 20 minutes. If we're not coming back, then I suppose someone will come along and find you in the morning."

Jaxon reached his hand under the dashboard and ripped out a handful of wires leading to the wireless radio.

Chapter 22: The Road to Trenton

Miss Darling Kinder was tired. Exhausted was a more apt description. She was also hungry again and her body ached in ways she had never known it to ache before. But this was not a deterrent. In fact, just the opposite. Glancing once in her mirror to check the vehicle lights far behind them she mashed her foot down on the accelerator, jumping the car forward with a lurch of speed.

Professor Nettles in the backseat held onto his hat in the stiff breeze. Rex sat motionless beside him. Jeremiah, sitting next to Darling in the front seat, whooped with joy as the car sped through the darkness.

"Give it the juice Miss Kinder!" he shouted.

"That is all she has, young man," Darling said. "Now sit back and hold on tight. We have company."

Jeremiah whipped his head around and looked behind them.

"Are they following us?" he asked.

"Yes."

"How do you know?" Professor Nettles had turned to look behind them as well.

"Well, despite my best efforts, they continue to gain on us," Darling said. "And judging by those flickers of light, it appears they are also shooting at us."

Jeremiah sank back down is his seat, eyes forward. Professor Nettles continued to hold onto his hat but he too sank a little further down in his seat.

Darling, both hands on the steering wheel, kept her right foot hard on the pedal. The steam engine roared as the landscape sped by on either side. She was trying to determine how soon before the cars behind them caught up, glancing every now and then into the mirrors. She had no idea what she would do when they did, but she at least wanted to know before they were side by side, running her off the road.

The road to Trenton was freshly paved with asphalt so the ride was smooth, but it was also unfamiliar to her. Every curve presented a new adventure. Trees grew at either side, and the occasional idle driver presented dangerous obstacles for them to avoid as they hurtled down the road at high speeds.

As she watched, the lights in the mirror grew bigger and brighter. Every now and then a bullet clanged off the body of the car. She tried pushing the pedal down further but it was already hard against the metal floorboards.

"Jeremiah, sweetie," she said. Jeremiah was pinned to the lower half of the seat, one hand on the door one on the dashboard for balance. The novelty of riding in a speeding car had quickly wore off. Now the reality of his situation had fully sunk in.

"Y-yes, Miss?" he said.

"There's a little box there in front of you – built right into the car. Would you please open it and see what's inside."

Jeremiah fumbled with the little knob before pulling it open.

"Just some papers, and a pair of gloves; a little oil can --"

"Oil can," Professor Nettles said. "Please be so good as to pass that to me, Jeremiah."

Professor Nettles used the oil to lubricate Rex's limbs. Carefully applying the oil to wrists, elbows, shoulders and hips, then leaned down to lubricate Rex's legs, all the way down to his ankles.

"Better now," Professor Nettles said, handing back the now mostly empty oil can. Jeremiah took it, shrugged and went back to searching the glove box.

"Nothing else, Miss," he said.

Darling checked the mirror again. She could see four lights closing in behind them; two cars were chasing them down the dark road to Trenton. She knew she had to shake them off, to lose them somewhere, somehow, but she wasn't sure how.

Watching the cars close the distance between them Darling felt her hands begin to sweat. She gripped the steering wheel tighter for fear the sweat would make them slip. The shooting had stopped making her hope they had run out of bullets. She checked her mirror once more.

"Jeremiah, stay very low, if you please," she said. "And don't let go. Both hands, hold tight!"

As the nearest car suddenly sped up beside them Darling looked over. There were three men sitting inside. Three well dressed men who looked as if they could be brothers of the men on the train. All three were brandishing weapons, one was frantically motioning her to pull to the side. Darling smiled at him, and his face relaxed. He smiled back. She waved. He waved back. Then without warning, and still smiling, she suddenly jerked the steering wheel to the left, smashing their car into the nearby trees.

"Way to drive, Miss!" Jeremiah shouted. Bullets rang out again as the second car, no doubt inspired by the abrupt end their friends met, began to close the distance, but staying directly behind them.

"I'm afraid we are not of the woods yet," Darling said. "Stay down, please."

The following car crashed into their bumper, bouncing the three friends. All three kept their heads down as bullets ricocheted off the metal around them. One bullet went right through the windshield in front of Darling. She cursed, then glanced aside at Jeremiah.

"Don't you dare repeat that," she shouted.

"Never, Miss," he said, smiling despite the fear he felt.

"Hold on everybody," she said, then suddenly pulled her foot off the accelerator and mashed down the brakes bringing the car to a sudden, screaming stop. The driver behind them swerved to avoid their car, clipped the passenger side quarter panel, and went off the road into the woods. It crashed like thunder in the darkness.

Darling didn't wait to see what happened next. She jammed the accelerator down again and the car jumped forward with a screech.

"Yeah!" Jeremiah shouted.

"My sentiments exactly, Miss Kinder," Professor Nettles said, dabbing his forehead with his handkerchief. "Very well done."

Once their followers were safely out of the picture Darling slowed to a safer speed, taking the twists and turns in the road with much more care. The lights of Trenton began to twinkle in the distance about an hour later and soon after that they were safely within the city limits. Darling cruised the streets slowly. The wind was calm, leaving the smoke from the coal fired steam plants to lay across the city like a blanket.

At this point she needed Jeremiah to guide her through the maze of Trenton streets. He told her when to turn, adding in bits of trivia about the places they passed.

"That's where I buy my bread," he'd say. "Right there is where I made a dollar just watching some guy's car for an evening while he visited a lady friend." Darling turned to him at this and he blushed, but he kept on talking, describing his hometown as best he could. They cruised through downtown to the site of the old dockside warehouse laboratory. It was a jumble of rubble now. The street leading past it was open again, but since it was late there were no other cars. What few people they passed here seemed just as disinterested in being seen by them as they were in being seen themselves. Darling found an alley near the warehouse site and pulled in. She looked around before cutting the engine and the car released a soft hiss of steam.

"Ok gentleman, this is our stop," she said.

Professor Nettles struggled to pry himself out of the car while Rex remained seated. Jeremiah reached to help haul the professor out, none to gracefully. Darling stepped out of the car on the driver's side, still glancing nervously around. She was in unfamiliar territory here with an elderly man, a young boy and some sort of mechanical beast she nothing about. Her heart fluttered at the thought of it all.

"Now is not the time Darling," she said to herself, taking a deep breath of coal dust filled air. It scratched her throat and made her cough just a little.

"What was that, Miss,?" Jeremiah asked.

"Nothing," she said. "Just a little difficult to breathe this evening."

"Yeah," he said. "That'll be the smokey fog we get around here when the steam plants are fired up and the wind does down. It'll clear up once the air starts moving again. Don't you worry."

She smiled at him. He was just a boy, true, but without his help now all the adults would be hopelessly lost. She believed they could count on him. At least she hoped they could.

"Well, now we place ourselves into your capable hands, young Jeremiah," she said with a smile, waving the air from in front of her face.

He stood up straight. "I know just where we are and just where we need to be," he said. "Follow me."

Jeremiah led the way down the alley and onto the street, along the side where the remains of the warehouse laboratory sat in a massive pile of broken bricks. There was reflected moonlight, dispersed by the clouds hovering over the Delaware causing the pile of bricks to cast an ominously large gray shadow over them as they walked. Out on the river a large steam driven barge dredge was working to keep the channel clear for ships. Without the regular dredging the Delaware would be useless for shipping and all the goods made in Trenton would sit idle, waiting to be crammed onto steam trains or taken by trucks to the closest port in New Amsterdam. A long and wasteful trip that would greatly reduce profits for the factory owners in the city. Without the Delaware, Trenton would just be a sideshow for the places where the real work got done.

Darling couldn't help gazing around at the docks and the buildings, but Jeremiah kept on walking, head down, feet moving. Professor Nettles shuffled along behind them both, and Rex obediently clanging along with every step bringing up the rear.

Down the street, turning at the edge of the docks, keeping to the shadows, Jeremiah kept them just out of the moonlight. He walked them around what would have been the front of the old warehouse, facing the river, to a small patch of concrete at the corner of the lot. "This is the old water cistern," he said, grabbing the iron handle. He strained at it, lifting it just high enough for him to wedge his leg under it, then pushed his entire weight against it to open it all the way. Darling wanted to help but thought better of it. Jeremiah had no doubt done it before, and this was his moment. She decided to let him enjoy it.

Below the lid it was pitch black, not a sliver of light. What moonlight there was did little for the depths below. Jeremiah fished into his pocket and drew out a small brass lighter. He flicked it a few times, coaxing a small flame to life.

Darling frowned into the hole, while Professor Nettles fiddled with something on the Rex's back. "Don't worry, Miss," Jeremiah said. "It's perfectly safe. There's a ladder down and everything. And a light. I'll go down first and get the lamp going and then you can follow me down."

Without missing a beat Jeremiah swung one foot into the hole and descended into the darkness, his feet making muffled metal bangs on the ladder with every step. To Darling it seemed a long climb down, but when the lamp below illuminated the darkness she saw it wasn't quite so far as it had seemed.

"Come on down, Miss," he said. "it's alright. All dry and everything."

Darling motioned for Professor Nettles and Rex to go before her, then glanced around once more before following. Just before closing the lid behind her she took one final look around. There was nobody in sight. The night was dark and quiet. Darling closed the lid and went below.

At the bottom of the ladder were a couple old wooden chairs and a small cot. A wooden cupboard sat to one side of the brick room. There was an assortment of dry goods there and some tin cans with the labels removed. A small lamp dangled from the ceiling. There was also a small cast iron stove in one corner with a chimney that connected to an old iron pipe leading up into a corner of the bricks. The room was spacious but spartan. On the walls were movie news bills with pictures of women in evening gowns. One was dressed only in a knee high one piece swimming suit. Darling tried not to notice as Jeremiah hurriedly ripped it from the wall and stuffed it behind the cupboard. Professor Nettles was seated on the cot with Rex standing motionless before him, back turned. Nettles was still fiddling with something and was clearly lost in his own thoughts. Jeremiah, all smiles and pride, pulled out one of the small wooden chairs and brushed it off with a small hanky he pulled from his back pocket.

"Please, Miss, have a seat, won't you," he said. Darling took the seat graciously. As she sat she felt the aches in her body return, but she smiled daintily, as a young lady should when offered a chair. She touched her hair, tossed and battered by the wind and elements. It had been more than a full day since she had taken a brush to it and she could only imagine just what a state it must be in. Even on the drive she had only used the mirrors for escape, not personal grooming.

Jeremiah smiled at her. He looked at her hair. "Your hair looks just fine, Miss," he said. "Are you hungry? I have some beans and – no wait, a lady such as yourself won't want beans. Peaches! I have cans of peaches. Just a minute, let me look around here."

"It's ok Jeremiah, " she said. "Really, I'm fine for the moment. Aren't you tired? How long since you slept?"

"Oh I'm fine, Miss, truly I am. I could eat though. You wouldn't mind if I ate some beans or something would you?"

"Not at all."

Jeremiah found the can he was looking for, then grabbed a church key from the cupboard to open it. Then he brought it over to the cast iron stove. He opened the door to the stove, poked the coals a few times and added a few small pieces of paper he kept nearby in a stack. Fishing the brass lighter from his pocket again he lit the paper and closed the door of the stove, adjusting the flue to feed the fire. He set the can on top of the stove and wandered back over to Darling.

"Are you thirsty, Miss? I've got some jugs of water or apple cider in the cupboard."

Darling was thirsty. "Cider would be wonderful, Jeremiah," she said. "Thank you."

He grabbed her a mug from the cupboard and poured her some cider from a jug. Then he walked over to check his can of beans, came back and sat at the small table across from her.

"So what do we do now?" he asked.

Darling looked at him and smiled. She checked her watch.

"We wait, Jeremiah," she said. "We wait until dawn."

Jeremiah just looked at her, obviously anxious to do something but knowing that the plan was for them to remain here until the appointed time.

Eventually the beans were hot and Jeremiah finished them with a flourish. Professor Nettles shifted away from the cot to the table allowing Darling to stretch out and rest her eyes. The last thing she remembered was watching Professor Nettles call Jeremiah over to explain something about what he had been fiddling with on Rex's back. Then she closed her eyes again and fell asleep.

Chapter 23: Chasing Chickens

Jaxon Price was nothing if not punctual. A mere twenty minutes after leaving the Deputy and his friend in the backseat they returned to the car. And they weren't alone. Jaxon was pushing a scrawny looking guy with a plaster across the bridge of his nose ahead of him while Digby kept the shotgun leveled at the man's middle. They opened the backdoor and stuffed him into the backseat. All the while the man was strangely silent. Digby kept the shotgun in the man's face as Jaxon went around and got behind the wheel. Digby got in the other side in one quick motion, only taking the shotgun off the man for a second, then whipped around his seat and put the shotgun back in the mans face.

"Careful where you're pointing that thing," Daryl cried.

"Shut up Daryl," Deputy Allen said. "Now who's this fella?"

Jaxon turned around in his seat. "This, my friends, is Simple Simon. Say hello, Simon."

The man said nothing. Jaxon continued.

"Simple Simon here is going to tell you all about why he decided to blow the hell out of Princeton and kill a whole bunch of people, and it has nothing to do with me, my friend Donnie here or his friends. And nothing to do with any anarchist plot. Right Simon?"

"I ain't saying nothing," he said. "You took me from my job by force. Never seen you before in my life. I don't know nothing about nothing and damn sure ain't gonna say nothing."

Jaxon smiled. He slipped his hand inside his coat pocket and pulled out a small pistol.

Simon didn't flinch.

Jaxon opened the chamber of the pistol and reached back inside his coat pocket, talking all the time.

"Now look, Simon. I know you didn't plan this. Just like you didn't plan on me breaking your nose in the alley. You're not smart enough for that. You're just a soldier, a dog boy, and you do as instructed, provided you get paid. I understand that. I was a soldier once myself.

That's all fine and dandy. But you see, right now you need to provide me with the name of the people, or person, who hired you, or else you're gonna take the blame for the whole damn thing."

Simon looked at the two men next to him, then back at Digby who still had his shotgun leveled at the man's chest.

"I see we have company," Simon said, inclining his head toward Deputy Allen. "Anything I might have to say about anything you just said wouldn't even be whispered around this particular type of company."

Deputy Allen sat motionless, just looking at Simon who was seated immediately to his right.

"Awww man, I just want to get back to my truck," Daryl said. "And my wife. She's gonna kill me. If ya'll don't kill me first."

"Shut up, Daryl," Allen said. "Now look here young fella. In case you hadn't noticed we're sitting here trussed up like a couple hogs headed to the county fair. I don't know what it is you have to say, or what it is you think I'm gonna do about whatever it is that you might say, but clearly, I'm no threat to you or anyone. If you got something to say to this man here, I suggest you say it so we can all go about our business."

Jaxon was still toying with his pistol, smiling, but saying nothing. When Deputy Allen finished there silence in the backseat of the patrol car. That made the solid click of him closing the chamber on his pistol even louder.

Jaxon leveled the pistol at Simon and smiled.

"Do you know what this is?"

Simon looked at him. "Yeah, it's a pistol. So? You can shoot me all you like, but it ain't gonna make me say anything about anything that I don't know anything about."

"Well, you're half right," Jaxon said. He pulled the trigger and there was a muffled "pop!" Simon grabbed his belly and doubled over. Daryl screamed and Deputy Allen squirmed a little farther away from Simon.

"It's actually a little toy I picked up from a friend of mine. Doesn't actually shoot bullets at all. It shoots darts. You can load those darts with anything really, poison say, or even truth serum. I wonder which one I just put in it? I think it was truth serum, maybe it was poison, it's too dark in here for me to tell. Either way I'll bet it still hurts like hell, right?"

Simon sat bolt upright, teeth clenched and arms rigid at his sides. Deputy Allen nearly jumped into Daryl's lap.

"Well, that answers that," Jaxon said. "Poison. Damn, wrong dart."

Simon crumpled over again, gasping for air and grabbing his belly. Daryl was panicking, begging to be let go to his wife, Deputy Allen wasn't too happy about being right next to a poisoned man but he didn't say anything.

Simon convulsed again, rigid back, teeth clenched, fists at his sides; his eyes seemed ready to burst from their sockets.

"Wow, Simon, that really looks painful," Jaxon said, slipping his hand back inside his coat pocket and fumbling around. Digby said nothing, but kept the shotgun steady. "That's Tritocin Anti-Coagulation Maripresis in your veins right now. As the seconds tick by that stuff is going to slowly turn your insides into black goo. Soon that stuff will start leaking out of your eyes, your nose, your mouth – every hole you got is gonna start leaking real soon."

Daryl had shifted into a near panic, clutching at the closed and locked door with his bound hands, begging to be set free. Deputy Allen started begging Jaxon to reconsider murder.

"This is just a vile way to go," he said. "Ain't right to turn a man to goop like this. I'm an officer of the law by golly and I say this man has rights!"

"The only right he has is to die a slow and painful death," Jaxon said. "Now you shut up cause I've got plenty more darts. So what do you say Simon? Starting to remember anything relevant to our earlier conversation?"

Simon convulsed again and this time a tiny trickle of something dark began to ooze from his nose. Gasping for breath, but free from his convulsion he wiped at it, then stared at his hand.

"Oh, here it is," Jaxon said holding up a tiny dart. "The antidote. I knew I had it somewhere."

"Give it to me!" Simon shouted before being racked with another convulsion.

"Not so fast," Digby said. "Tell us what you know."

Simon collapsed again, sobbing. "It was just a job, I got paid, just like usual only this time for a whole lot more money than breaking a leg. This time it was real money. Real money!"

"Who hired you?"

"Mr. C! It was Mr. C wanted that place burned up and right good, but he was only doing it for someone else because he sure as hell doesn't care anything about a bunch of snot nosed college boys."

"Watch what you say," Digby said. "I'm a snot nosed college boy and I don't like your tone."

"Easy now, Donnie. Let the man have his say. Go ahead."

Simon convulsed again, this time losing more liquid from his nose and each eye. Free from the convulsion his grabbed his stomach again and doubled over "Oh, my guts are on fire!"

"It only gets worse from here, I promise you," Jaxon said. "So you did the job on the university? You and nobody else, right?"

"Right, right, yes, well, no, Little Bobby helped he. It was the two us, got hold of some dynamite and went around blowing rooftops. Easy as apple pie on Sunday morning. We didn't know it would set off the gas lines, though. That was an accident. The fire. Not my fault. I was just doing a job. It was just a job, I needed to get paid. I got kids to feed. Oh god, oh god, oh god..."

He convulsed again, teeth clenched, fists like claws, black liquid now covering his face.

"Please, dear god, have mercy. I don't want to die like this."

Digby felt the sweat running down the side of his face. He watched as Simon convulsed and collapsed. Saw the look of panic in his eyes. He felt relief at hearing someone else claim responsibility for the horror Digby himself had been accused of, but he took no joy in watching a man die. Especially not like this.

"Jaxon," he said. "Give him the antidote now. He confessed. It's over."

Jaxon smiled. "I'm afraid it isn't over Dexter. It's just beginning." Jaxon pressed the button to channel the steam drive. "And there is no antidote."

"What! Oh god, oh god, I'm gonna die."

Daryl was still clawing at the door handle, Deputy Allen squirmed a little further away from Simon and Digby blanched.

"No antidote?" Deputy Dan said.

"Nope," Jaxon said. Simon convulsed again, rigid as an oak door this time, then he collapsed into his own lap, doubled over and soaked with sweat. "Of course, there's no poison either. He's gonna feel real bad in the morning though. Real bad."

Jaxon put the car into gear and drove out of the alley.

"So who is this 'Mr. C' fella he was talking about?" Deputy Allen asked from the backseat as Jaxon turned the corner.

"Mr. Calabricci, runs the entire dockside operation for the Trenton gangs, real bad news."

"I take it that is our next stop?" Digby asked.

"Nope. First we have to drop these fellas off someplace safe."

"Oh, thank god," Daryl said.

"Now just a minute fellas," Deputy Allen said. "I'm pretty sure you're up to your eyeballs in something that you only half understand. And I'm guessing you could use a little extra firepower on your side. This Calabricci, I heard of him of course. Read the stories in the newspapers, heard the rumors. He's untouchable. Lives in that building on the Westside like some sort of armored fortress. There ain't no way you two fellas are gonna get anywhere near him without a little help."

"And just what do you propose, Deputy Marshall?" Jaxon said.

"Well, why don't we come to some sort of agreement, like. I help you, you get your names cleared and I get to arrest one of the biggest threats to the Great State of New Jersey."

"How do we know we can trust you," Digby said.

"Yeah, Dixie is right. How do we know we can trust you?"

"Well, I give you my word of honor," Deputy Allen said.

"Oh geez," Daryl said. "What is wrong with you? They just killed that man and you're ready to make a deal?"

"Shut up Daryl. He ain't dead. I can feel him breathing. Besides, you heard what he said, about 'Mr. C' and all that. This is a big deal. A big deal for me if I was involved. No more 'deputy' any more. I'd get a big fat promotion. I need a big fat promotion. I deserve a big fat promotion. And seems to me if these boys wanted to kill us they've had plenty of time to do it and wouldn't need to be taking all these risks in dragging us all over creation. They could just park on some lonely road and put a bullet in us."

"Don't give them any ideas!"

"Shut up, Daryl" Digby said.

"Alright Deputy Allen," Jaxon said. "If you want to help, we could sure as hell use it. But you understand the risks right? We've got nothing to lose. And you understand we need Mr. C alive, right? We can't just go in there guns blazing and killing everybody. That's not what we're doing, understand?"

"Son, I am an officer of the law. I understand the difference between right and wrong, alive and dead, and I know exactly what you boys need. In fact, I probably understand it even better than you do as I have actually been inside a courtroom, taken part in trials, and done all that legal business that we have to do to get bad guys off the street and protect the innocent."

"Larry you ain't never done any of that stuff," Daryl said. "You can't even round up Mary Catherine's cows when they bust out of the fence. You have to call in for re-enforcements for god's sake."

"These ain't cows, Daryl, and I am a damn good Deputy Marshall, I know I am. I just need a shot, a chance to show people I can do my job. Not herding cows, but fighting evil and protecting the innocent."

"Protecting the innocent? All you're gonna do is get yourself killed and me too, probably."

"Alright deputy, you're in. Daryl, what about you? Got any "fight for the innocent" running through your veins?"

"Hell no! Ya'll can just drop me off someplace where I can get a ride back to my truck, if you'd be so kind."

"Ok, consider it done, although I can't trust that you won't do something stupid if we just turn you loose on your own, so we're gonna have to take a few precautions. Besides, we need someone to sit with Simon until we get back."

It took them about 30 minutes to find an empty building with a private parking lot out back. They uncuffed Deputy Allen, though Digby still watched him closely. They left Daryl cuffed and tied to the still unconscious Simon inside the building, both securely gagged. Then they sorted out their weapons, made a quick plan and climbed back inside the patrol car, this time with Deputy Allen driving.

Digby sat in the front seat beside the deputy with Jaxon in back. "Do we have time for this,?" Digby asked.

Jaxon checked his watch. "I think so, and if we don't we'll have to make some time. Rendezvous is still about four hours away. We need to be quick, but effective. And if we show up with Mr. Calabricci in handcuffs, compliments of Deputy Allen here, we'll be that much more effective."

Digby nodded. His heart was pounding in his chest. He was hungry, thirsty and exhausted, but the adrenaline coursing through his veins kept it all in check. His life, Miracle's, Darling's depended on him now; and all the people they knew that died or were hurt at Princeton, deserved justice. It was a mixed bag of emotions he felt, but he was focusing it on their mission.

From the backseat Jaxon explained what he thought was the best idea for gaining entrance to Calabricci's apartment building and making their way to see the man himself. After that it would have to be an impromptu operation.

"What's that mean, 'impromptu'? Deputy Allen asked.

"Off-the-cuff, make it up as we go along kinda thing," Digby said.

"I take it this whole thing has been a bit impromptu, then."

"Yes, I supposed it has. I should be studying for my finals this week. Instead I'm fighting for my life; stealing cars, kidnapping strangers, shooting at people, stowing away on steamships, having knife fights, fist fights, gunfights...."

"Yeah, but you can't get this kind of experience at school, Dizzy," Jaxon said.

"Dizzy? I thought your name was Donnie?"

"It's actually Digby."

"Digby, right. Ok."

"Turn into this next alley and stop in the shadows, Larry," Jaxon said. "Dimbly and I are gonna get out and wait, find a way in through the back while you make your way in through the front. It's gonna be a whole lot like chasing chickens, but if everything goes according to plan we should meet somewhere in the middle. Oh, and try not to shoot us."

Everyone nodded in agreement. Digby felt his heart continuing to pound in his chest. From the backseat Jaxon leaned forward and turned to him.

"You ready for this, Don?"

"As ready as I'm ever going to be."

Chapter 24: A Long Way Down

"Careful miss, it's a long way down."

Miracle had been lost in thought, staring over the railing down at the passing ground. It was sunrise in the air where they were and the darkness below had already faded to a dull gray with slips of orange here and there where the sunshine had begun to spread. Thinking back to the past few days; her friends, their futures (if they were to have any) and wondering where Digby and Darling were now; how closely they had stuck to her plan and how effective her plan would turn out to be for each of them.

"Thank you," she said to the passing sailor and smiled.

Space aboard the airship was cramped. It wasn't made for personal transport after all, or comfort. She was riding aboard the *Bunker Hill*, a part of the New Jersey Navy, being commanded by a family friend, Captain Francis Howard. At her insistence, maybe request is a better word, he had scrambled a team and lifted the ship almost immediately, but time continued to slip forward at a rapid pace. He estimated they would arrive at her planned rendezvous point right on time. Whether or not her friends would be able to meet her there as planned she had no way of knowing. Either they would or they wouldn't. If they were there, then everyone would be under the protection of the Federal Militia and this heavily armored airship. If they weren't, or if some were and some were not, then she would need to decide the next step. Assuming of course she would be allowed to make suggestions to Captain Howard after that. It was very possible he would assume full control of the situation once Professor Nettles and Rex were aboard as a matter of national security. So far he had been very willing to listen to what she had to say and offer his support. But Miracle was no fool. She knew the ramifications of what a fully autonomous metal man would mean for the Federal Militia – or whatever country controlled it. No doubt Captain Howard understood just as well as she did, if not better.

The air was calm and cool and from her place at the railing she could see a long way across the Pine Barrens below and to the surrounding fields and farms. The sun had finally fully popped above the horizon. The airship was surprisingly quiet, just a steady whirring of blades and hum of the engines. The observation deck ran around the outside of the command module fixed to the bottom of the envelope. Inside the envelope was a cargo area, crew quarters and of course the lifting bags filled with hydrogen. A single biplane dangled from the bottom of the command module for reconnaissance. Although the airship had the advantage of height it moved slowly through the skies. Having a biplane available meant captains could get a better idea of their surroundings, or even have information from two places at once. The *Bunker Hill* had been built for observation only. It carried no heavy weapons, just an armed crew of about a dozen sailors, plus Captain Howard and Miracle.

"That's Trenton, just over there," said a nearby sailor.
Miracle could see the dark edges of the city now. The billowing smoke stacks, pumping smoke into the sky which drifted lazily to the east.
She hurried inside the cabin to Captain Howard.
"We should be there within the next 30 minutes," he said. "Are you sure your friends will be there?"
"I can't be sure of anything at this point. I can only tell you what we planned. What happened between our plans yesterday and this morning is anyones guess."
He stared out the window ahead of them. "Fair enough."
She thought a moment. "Captain Howard, if my friends are not there, what will be your next move?"
"Well, truth is, as much as I appreciate your situation, I'll have to report exactly what has been going on to my superiors and let them guide my actions from there. I know that won't be the best for you – or your friends – but it's the only option I'll have available. Right now, I am following a lead, which is within military guidelines, but I can't let this situation spiral completely out of my control."
I see," she said. "Fair enough."
Together they both stared off into the distance, awaiting the city which gradually drew closer, and the coming day, which would bring answers and resolutions, one way or another.

Trenton passed beneath them, the city slowly coming to life with the new day. Factory workers changing shifts, electric taxis and trollies buzzing back and forth, crowds slowly moving along sidewalks as people made their way to work. Miracle noted this peripherally, her eyes straining toward the dockside warehouses, and their destination. As the warehouses loomed into view below her, Miracle scanned the area she was looking for. Like an enormous mouth with a single missing tooth, Professor Nettles now destroyed laboratory lay before them. It was little more than a pile of rubble now, with bricks everywhere; glinting glass pieces and metal sparkled in amongst the rubble. And there, at the edges of the pile, moving backward and forward frantically, Miracle saw a form.

Before she could notify Captain Howard she felt the front of the dirigible tilt down and saw the figure coming closer.

"Is that someone you know?" Captain Howard asked.

"I think so -yes! It's Darling. Miss Kinder." she said. "I don't understand. I don't see the professor or Jeremiah. Can we land this thing?"

"Not exactly, I'm afraid. But we can get low enough to drop a ladder, put some sailors on the ground."

"Forget the sailors. I need to speak with her first."

Because the building which once stood in the area was nothing more than flattened rubble, the dirigible was able to get within 30 feet of the ground. A hemp ladder was lowered down, and Miracle stood ready to descend.

"Hold tight, Miss!" the sailor said, opening the floor door to allow her to access the ladder. "It's bound to swing a bit, but just hold on like you would your favorite dollie, and just put one foot in front of the other."

Miracle looked at him steadily. "Only little girls play with dollies." Then she slipped through the floor door and started down the ladder. Darling had noticed the dirigible approaching, stopped her pacing and stood waiting. A small crowd of dock workers had also gathered to watch what was happening. Miracle was down the swaying ladder in no time, with a few sailors right behind her, just in case.

"Darling, what's going on?" she asked. "Where is the professor and Jeremiah?"

Darling was red faced and winded. Her eyes darted about, still searching.

"Miracle, it's all my fault. I fell asleep – I know I shouldn't have fallen asleep, but I was so tired, I just had to close my eyes. And when I opened them, they were gone."

Miracle looked around at the gathering crowd and the sailors.

"Any idea where they might have gone or how long ago they left?"

Darling shook her head, he eyes welling up with tears.

"Right, well there's only one thing for us to do then," she said.

Darling looked at her, eyes ready.

"Run!"

Miracle grabbed Darling by the wrist and together they sprinted into the nearby crowd. The men gathered there parted easily and Miracle shouted over her shoulder, "Stop those men!"

She heard shouting behind her, but they were down the block without a sign that any sailors had been able to make it through the dockworkers. Down the block, around a tight corner and into a narrow alley. She still had Darling by the wrist, and pulled the near frantic girl close to her.

"Darling, you must remember something, anything, that might give us some idea as to where they went, and why."

Tears were streaming down the girls cheeks and she shook her head.

"No, nothing. We made it to the safe place Jeremiah had told us about. We ate a little. Professor Nettles was tinkering with his – thing – and then I fell asleep. That's it. When I woke up they were both gone."

Miracle was staring intently into her eyes, trying to gauge some measure of the girl before her. She needed something more to go on. Some hint or clue. Were they taken? No, couldn't be, or Darling would have awakened, or been taken as well. So, they left of their own accord. Snuck out, apparently. But to where?

In the distance she heard the bellow of a steamship horn, and suddenly something registered in her brain.

"All this time," she said.

"What?"

"All this time," she said again. "Professor Nettles. He orchestrated the initial explosion at his laboratory. That must have been the signal that brought them. Brought them all."

"I don't understand," Darling said, dragging her palms across her tear stained cheeks.

"Of course you don't," Miracle said. "And I really don't have time to explain. Suffice to say we need to get to that ship. Now."

"Ship?" Darling said, sniffing up the last of her tears. "What ship?"

"The last ship to leave for Philadelphia."

Miracle grabbed her by the wrist again and dragged her out of the alley.

"Come along, Darling!"

"Where?"

"Back to the airship," Miracle said. "We need speed and accessibility if we're going to stop professor Nettles before he makes it to his rendezvous point and escapes."

"I am so confused!"

"Indeed. Just follow me. Don't fall behind or I'll have to leave without you."

Miracle exited the alley and started back the way they had come. There was now a full blown brawl between dock workers and sailors amidst the pile of rubble which was once Professor Nettles laboratory.

Miracle and Darling approached the fringes of the throng and tried to muscle through. But the backs of the men waiting their turn to throw some punches were an immovable object.

"Oh, c'mon! Make way! Make way!" Miracle shouted.

Suddenly Darling pulled her wrist free of Miracles grasp, put fingers from each hand in her mouth and whistled so loud, everyone in the melee just froze, mid-punch.

Miracle turned toward her. "Let me guess, your father teach you that?"

"Well, how else could I call back the hunting dogs?"

The crowd, now aware of their presence, moved apart to let them through.

"Sorry—wrong sailors," Miracle said as she passed. "So sorry, these men are actually our friends. Thank you all so much, however."

The sailor who had opened the door on the dirigible for her was standing nearest the swinging hemp ladder, with a trickle of blood running from his lower lip and a torn uniform shirt.

"Bloody hell! What was that all about," he said.

"Just a miscommunication," Miracle said, and started up the ladder. Darling was right behind her.

Miracle called down that all the sailors should follow along quickly, but they needed no encouragement.

Standing in the crowded cockpit of the *Bunker Hill* Captain Howard looked cross. Miracle stood firm.

"It's been his plan all along," she said. "Or at least started with his plan."

Captain Howard put his hand on his chin, as if trying to rub his anger away.

"So, you're saying, the professor blew up his factory as a signal to his conspirators that his work was finished, then was attempting to make his way to Philadelphia for a rendezvous when you and your friends accidentally stumbled upon him, diverted him from his mission to here. And then he snuck away in the middle of the night, back to his original planned rendezvous in Philadelphia?"

"Indeed," Miracle said.

"Ridiculous."

Darling could stand idly by no longer.

"It makes perfect sense to me," she said. "How else to explain how suddenly everyone – well, those bad men – knew where to find him, unless they had been waiting for his signal. Or known about his signal. And why else would he sneak away from me in the middle of the night knowing full well Miracle would arrive this morning with a rescue party?"

Captain Howard stood thinking. He turned to the radio operator.

"Notify headquarters that we are returning to base."

"Captain Howard, no!" Miracle said

"With all due respect to you and your father, I give the orders on this ship young lady," he said tersely. "We tried it your way, I indulged you and your plan as far as I dare, but further risking my career in the Navy is simply not going to happen."

Miracle considered. The hemp ladder having been withdrawn the ship had slowly drifted over the river, turning gently south at the captain's command.

"Fine," she said. "But consider this. By the time you return to Cape May base, Professor Nettles, and his miraculous machine man will have safely debarked at Philadelphia, and likely departed the Federation, for some unknown destination. It is your patriotic duty to attempt any and all options for apprehending him and securing his infernal machine."

Captain Howard was unmoved, reviewing charts handed to him by a nearby sailor.

Suddenly Darling, gazing out the window at the river below, spoke up. "It seems to me, Captain Howard, that our course, right now, is moving in the general direction of Cape May, and also the general direction of Philadelphia. Couldn't we do both things at the same time?"

Captain Howard looked up from his chart, leaned in close and whispered. "That's exactly what we are doing, albeit in a more discreet manner."

Miracle smiled, and he winked at her.

The next hour or so was tense as the dirigible poured on the steam, cruising low and fast over the Delaware River, south toward Philadelphia. They passed several ships, some coming toward Trenton, some moving away, all loaded with materials and trade goods. Captain Howard had made the decisions that it would likely be a passenger ship they sought, as that had been the first type of ship Professor Nettles had attempted to escape in. It was a risk, but a quick radio check with the dockyard at Trenton assured him that regular passenger steamship service stopped at midnight, and the first steamship in the morning had left about an hour before they arrived. He was betting the professor – if Miracle was correct about him orchestrating this entire ordeal – would be on that ship. If he wasn't on the ship, if this was another wild goose chase, they would still be back at Cape May in a timely fashion.

Suddenly the lookout ahead called back: a passenger ship had been spotted.

Miracle and Darling, hurried to the front railing, peering into the distance. There it was, blowing white steam into the air and chugging peacefully down the river.

Captain Howard ordered more power to the airship and a slight descent. He wanted to reduce the likelihood they would be spotted from a distance, and close that distance as quickly as possible.

Miracle grabbed a pair of binoculars from a nearby sailor and sighted the ship.

"Yes!" she cried.

"What? What do you see?" Darling asked, nudging against her side, almost giddy with excitement.

"Look for yourself." Miracle handed over the binoculars and made her way inside the cockpit to speak with Captain Howard.

Darling grasped the binoculars and focused them in on the tiny ship in the distance. Almost immediately she saw a small form on the top, standing at the rail, looking in their direction, but not at them. She knew that shape almost immediately.

"Jeremiah," she said.

Chapter 24: Trent House

Digby Ross, Jaxon Price and Deputy Marshall Lawrence Allen arrived at the governor's mansion in style. They had commandeered an ice truck which was now packed not with blocks of frozen water, but several unsavory characters none too happy about being trussed up and left to roll around the floor of a cold, dirty trailer for the last few hours.

Pulling up to the governors mansion, Deputy Allen driving, they honked the horn exuberantly. The deputy and Digby jumped out immediately, while Jaxon lingered back. Miracle and Darling ran down the front steps to greet Digby, both wrapping their arms around him and kissing his cheek – one on each side. Digby felt a rush of blood to his face and sheepishly bowed back at their affection.

"That's a right proper fella you ladies got there," Deputy Allen shouted.

Uniformed guards rushed out of the mansion behind Miracle and Darling, surrounding the truck.

"Easy there boys," Deputy Allen said, displaying his badge. "I'm a Deputized Marshal with the Federal Service. My name is Lawrence Allen and I think you're gonna like what I've got in the back of this truck."

He jostled with some keys, walking toward the back of the truck. Just then Captain Howard and New Jersey State Governor Edward Edwards came through the doors.

"Are these the men we've been waiting for?" The governor asked.

"It would appear so," Captain Howard said, watching the girls embrace their friend.

"You there," Governor Edwards called to Digby.

"Sir," Digby stammered. "Yes sir."

"What's the meaning of this – er, truck?"

"That's the beauty of it, governor," Deputy Allen called from the back of the truck, keys jangling as he fumbled with the lock. "We put these fellas on ice, for you."

When he opened the door, Nicolas Calabricci came tumbling out of the back, hands tied behind his back, shouting about his "lawyers" and how he would "sue the city!" and the marshals service and "the whole damn state!"

Deputy Allen gave him a kick in the side, and he quieted down. "There's a few more fellas in here for you, and some of them are much more eager to talk to us like gentleman. Also, I will gladly provide sworn testimony to the amount of illegal weaponry this one here has stored at his place, and the amount of illegal alcohol he has on his premises. Also, it seems, from some ledgers I obtained, that he's been doing some illegal, possibly murderous, business with some fella named Charles Paulson. Possibly even bombings and such."

Deputy Allen was in his element, and anyone looking at the big wide grin on his face knew it right away.

The governor stopped in his tracks when he saw Nicolas Calabricci on the ground at the back of the truck.

"Officers," he called to his security team. "Secure the prisoners. Especially that one."

Miracle was brushing the hair out of Digby's eyes and Darling was searching him for bullet holes. Neither of them seemed to care much that Miracle's plan was coming together as she had promised it would.

Captain Howard approached them, extending his hand to Digby. "You sir, must be Dylan -"

"Digby, Digby Ross!" Came a voice from inside the truck. "That's the man who captured Nicolas Calabricci – Digby Ross!"

Captain Howard clapped Digby on the shoulder. "Digby Ross! Well done, young man. Well done."

"Well, I helped!" Deputy Allen said. But it was of little use, drowned out by the cries of congratulations being heaped on Digby. Digby knew it was Jaxon who had called his name, but he didn't turn around. Jaxon had said he'd prefer to remain anonymous and Deputy Allen and Digby had respected that. It was nice that he finally got my name right though, Digby thought.

After several hours of explaining all that had transpired, when, to whom, by whom, and the evidence they had collected to back up their story, Miracle, Darling and Jeremiah were sitting down in an empty banquet hall, voraciously stuffing themselves with food. Between gulps Jeremiah explained how professor Nettles had convinced him it was in Darling's best interest if they just left her behind and went to meet some "friends" of his. That was why he had agreed to go with the man in the middle of the night while she slept. "But I promise I won't ever do that again, Miss" he said.

"You are quite right about that young man," she said, flipping the end of his nose with her finger.

"And you, Digby Ross," Miracle said, sipping from her tea cup. "Big hero, as I understand it from Deputy Marshall Lawrence Allen." Digby blushed.

"Well, once I realized that the shotgun was going to be almost as hard on me as it was on whatever I had pointed it at, I was a little more sturdy on my feet."

Everyone laughed.

"Really, it was all – um, well, someone else really deserves the credit for it," he said, raising his glass. Nobody said Jaxon's name, but everyone understood, and everyone raised a glass to him. For his part Jaxon had waited until security dragged away the prisoners and everyone had gone inside the mansion before slipping away. No one had seen him since. They assumed he was alright, wherever he was. They all knew the part he had played, and they wished him well.

"And what about Professor Nettles?" Digby asked, breaking the silent reverie for their absent friend.

"Well, once we apprehended him on the steamship, he became strangely silent. Didn't say a single word to me, of course – knowing that I had seen through his machinations at last – and they have since taken him away, somewhere. Him and his machine -"

"Rex," Jeremiah said. "His name was Rex."

"Abomination, is a better name for it," Digby said.

"Hey now, that ain't right," Jeremiah said. "he was a good boy, dog, whatever. He was good."

"Well, we'll see about that young man," Digby said, frowning. "Time will truly tell whether he is 'good' or 'bad' and I imagine that depends a great deal on who his master is."

"Indeed," Miracle said, sipping her tea.

Suddenly the doors opened and Captain Howard came strutting in, with grins for everyone.

"Well, it seems you have all ended your fast," he said.

"Yes, thank you," Digby said. "I was famished."

"So was I!" Jeremiah said, trying to hide a belch, and dodging a gentle swipe from Darling who frowned at his ill-manners.

"You will be happy to know that with the information we have obtained from former associates of Nicolas Calabricci, and his ledgers, and the evidence collected from Professor Nettles, your names are now cleared of all pending charges.

A quiet cheer and great sighs of relief went up from the table.

"And -" Captain Howard continued. "It seems likely there will be more arrests coming soon as other parties to this sordid affair are apprehended."

"Paulson?" Miracle asked quietly. Captain Howard said nothing, but gave her a quick nod.

"Now, if you will excuse me, I have a mountain of paperwork I must complete," he said, Turning to go.

"Captain Howard," Miracle called to him. He turned. "Thank you. Thank you very, very much."

A few weeks later Miracle Lowell is sitting with the same group of friends she dined with at Trent House nearly a month earlier. At that time they were all tired, dirty and in a state of near-shock at what had transpired in the days before. Now their names have been cleared of all charges and responsibilities for the terrorist attack at Princeton University. Professor Harold Nettles has been whisked away to a Federal prison somewhere, his invention ostensibly being fully examined by Federal scientists at some secure location, and their lives allowed to continue at the gentle pace they had all become accustomed to.

"So, I said to the man, can you lift his trousers a bit more – here and here," Darling said, tugging at Jeremiahs cuffs as he twitched uncomfortably. "What do you think, Miracle, too much?"

"I ain't a little doll baby, you know," Jeremiah complained. "And I don't need no schooling neither."

"I'd say from the poor state of your grammar that is exactly what you need young man," Digby called his place at the head of the table. Darling smiled at him. Miracle smiled at him. Each caught the other smiling at the gorgeous friend they shared and quickly looked away. "Well, regardless of how you feel, those are the terms you agreed to, Jeremiah," Miracle said abruptly, in an effort to carry on as if no smiles had been shared. "So you may as well get used to it. Besides, you look absolutely smashing in those new trousers."

Jeremiah twitched and groaned, but secretly adored his new situation: a home, with a warm bed and friends, no – family, such as they were. He might complain but he really wouldn't change a thing.

"So, Digby, any word on when we might expect classes to resume?" Miracle asked.

"Not as yet. Although I was there just the other day and work is progressing nicely. Looks good as new, although the old ivy will take years to re-grow as it once was."

"And our friends who shall never return at all," Darling added.

They all nodded, and raised their glasses. Except Jeremiah who was too busy fidgeting in his itchy new trousers.

The servants brought the dinner and they ate, conversing lightly about the current news: war spreading across the Asian continent.

"I heard they call themselves 'Mongolians'," Darling said. "And they offer no quarter except full and complete surrender by their enemies when offered. And they offer it only once."

"Seems strange," Miracle said. "Mongolia had its heyday a thousand years ago or more. I wonder what is really going on over there and how bad it will get."

"Well, I for one could really care less," Digby said. "It's not our fight. We have enough trouble right here. I heard the Cherokee Nation may secede from the Federation, try to join up with the Republic of Texas to start a new union, or some such nonsense."

"I want to fight a war!" Jeremiah said between mouthfuls.

"You hush right now," Darling said sternly. "You will do no such thing. At least not until you graduate university."

"Aww—you're no fun," he slouched back into his dinner, unperturbed really.

Miracle laughed, Digby chuckled and even Darling smiled at his exuberance.

Suddenly the doorbell chimed. Miracle looked up, waiting for the servants to announce the disturbance.

The doorman shuffled into the room. "Excuse the interruption Madam. There are two people who would like to speak with. If you would like, I will send them away."

"Not at all, Benjamin. Please, show them in."

The servant disappeared. From the outer room, which would be the foyer of the apartment, there were some raised voices heard, a muffled thump, and then steady, heavy footsteps drawing closer. All eyes were on the dining room doorway as a vision in white slowly drifted in.

A beautiful young woman, hair long and dark, with soft brown eyes appeared. She smiled, gently and without the slightest bit of threat. Her feet made no sound on the floor as she moved closer, directly to where Miracle sat. No one at the table said a word. She was dressed in a flowing white dress, with a small golden headband across her temple. In the center of the headband was the mark of the Atlantean Council.

"Miracle Lowell," the woman said. "I am Vigil."

The owner of the heavy footsteps entered the room. He was a young man with shaggy red hair; a towering man, with a dagger strapped to his hip; his eyes everywhere at once as he searched the room for threats. On his chest he wore the insignia of the Atlantean Military.

"This," the woman said, indicating the young man with red hair. "Is the Schaefer."

"Aye," he said, nodding at Miracle, but keeping one eye on Digby who sat partially frozen in his chair.

Jeremiah leapt from his seat and approached the man. He reached out to touch his shining dagger but the man made a quick motion in the negative, and Jeremiah drew back.

Digby looked at Darling who was staring intently at the shaggy-haired man. Miracle looked into the eyes of the woman beside her and rose from her seat. The shaggy haired man put his hand to his dagger, but Vigil waved him to motionlessness.

"I am Miracle Lowell."

Vigil smiled. "Good, I have been searching for you for some time. It is important we talk."

Miracle shifted uncomfortably. Digby couldn't decide who he needed to watch more, the woman standing with Miracle or the shaggy-haired man who seemed bound and determined to stab something in this room. Darling had eyes only for the shaggy haired man. Jeremiah also only had eyes for the shaggy haired man, but frankly, just the pointy dagger which hung at his waist.

"Well, it seems you have found me at last," Miracle smiled. "how may I be of assistance?"

"First," Vigil said. "Do you have any idea how I might find your father?"

Digby groaned aloud. "Oh no," he said. "Here we go again."

Epilogue

Charles Paulson sat at his grand oak dining table, a plethora of newspapers around him, all denouncing his name and calling for a state enquiry into his company, his life, his heretofore good name. He was strumming his fingers on the table top with one hand. His other hand was holding an empty wine glass as his frustration rose to new levels. His face was bright red with anger and frustration.

"Callis!" he called. "Callis, come here this instant!"

The old man shuffled slowly into the room. "Apologies sir, I was attending to the door."

"I don't care about your damn apologies, man," he cried. "More wine. Now!"

"Very good, sir," Callis said and made for the wine cabinet

"Never mind that, Callis," came a voice from the hall outside the dining room. In walked a middle aged man, with dark hair showing wisps of grey at the temples. Distinguished. Debonair. He was Charles Paulson's son, George. And he had no doubt brought more bad news.

"I have what the old man needs right here," he said, brandishing a bottle of wine.

"Old man," Charles Paulson said with a huff. "How dare you?"

"It's just a figure of speech, father. Pay it no mind."

George Paulson approached the table just as Callis returned, producing a corkscrew.

"Very good, Callis. Thank you, that will be all for now. Father and I have some delicate items to discuss."

"Sir," Callis said, and shuffled away.

George pulled the cork on the wine with a pop! And let the bottle breathe for a moment, while his father shifted uncomfortably in his chair.

"Well, don't take all night with it," he growled. "Pour me a glass then tell me what they said."

George smiled, and poured a little wine from the bottle into the waiting glass.

"Not enough, blast you. Fill the damn glass. God knows I need it. I've earned it, after all."

"Indeed you have, father." George said, filling the glass to just below the rim.

His father pulled the glass to his lips, and drank deeply.

"Well," he said, after draining the glass. He held it out for more. "What did they say?"

George re-filled his father's glass, then set the bottle down.

"I do have some good news for you," he said with a smile.

"Really? How good?"

"Especially good. It seems the Paulson name shall stay in good standing--"

"That is some good news!"

"- so long as it comes under new management."

Charles Paulson felt his blood pressure increase at the words. Felt sweat begin to trickle from his scalp.

"New management," he sputtered. "What do you mean 'new management'? I founded this company. It was me that laid the pipes that deliver the steam that turn the dynamos in just about every home up and down the East Coast of the Federated States. How dare they dismiss my contributions!"

"Oh, no one is dismissing your contributions," George said. "Yours is a name that shall go down in history. When the new Empire rises, and new coins are minted it shall be your face emblazoned there. Of course, you won't be around to see it."

"What do you mean I won't be around to see it?"

Suddenly, without warning, Charles Paulson's head came crashing down on the oak table. He was dead.

"Dearest father, it shall indeed be your face on our new coins, however it shall be placed there by your son," George said, leaning close to his lifeless father.

"Callis!" he called.

After a second call, the old man shuffled back into the room. He saw Charles Paulson lying at the end of the table perfectly still.

"My father is dead," George said. "Please alert the media. Oh, and give them this." he produced a letter from his inside jacket pocket which was a confession for all his father's misdeeds.

"Very good, sir."

"Oh, and after that please contact my attorney, tell him my father has passed and that I will need to move forward with the takeover of his corporation immediately. Not a moment to lose, you know."

"Indeed, sir."

George Paulson studied his father's lifeless body for a long moment, then turned on his heel and left. Outside on the street he had left an electric car waiting. He told the driver to take him to the nearby hospital.

Once inside the hospital he rode the elevator to the bottom floor. Made his way as quietly as he could down the hall. This was the Special Care ward, full of patients who were nearly or fully incapacitated. He approached a gray door, partially open, and went inside.

Former Trenton Police Department Patrolman Mark Crosby was lying in a supine position, arms elevated, in full casts. His body was beneath a starched cotton sheet, but it was obvious his legs were missing.

"Patrolman Mark Crosby?"

Crosby didn't turn his head, or look in George's direction.

"Patrolman Crosby, my name is George Paulson and I have an offer you might like to hear about."

Crosby turned slightly to look at him. His eyes blazed with fury.

"Unless your offer involves me walking out of here on my own two feet, I'm not interested," he said. "Besides, I've already told the investigators everything I knew about your father's involvement in the conspiracy, which wasn't much, but was enough for me to escape prison."

"I see," George said, smiling. "Well, you'll be happy to know my father is now dead. By my own hand, no less. What do you think of that?"

Crosby turned fully to face him. "I'd say that was a good start. What else do you have to say to me?"

George smiled more broadly.

"Well, about my offer," he leaned close. "They wouldn't exactly be your old feet you walked out of here on, but they would be yours."

Made in the USA
Middletown, DE
16 September 2022

73439118R00132